"Come," Neil said, drawing her toward the outside door. "Let's have that walk in the garden you promised me."

"Oh, yes, yes."

He threw open the door and they bounded together down the path between the flowers, guided on their way by a thin flame of moonlight. The fragrance of honeysuckle hung heavy on the cool night air.

With her hand held tightly in Neil's, Sarah led him to the edge of the furthest path near the banks of the river. The soft lapping of the water seemed to add a touch of music.

"Happy?" Neil whispered.

"So happy."

He tipped her chin up to let the light fall on her lovely face. Then their arms closed around each other, and they were lost in absolute delight. . . .

Another Fawcett Gold Medal
by Maryhelen Clague:

MOMENT OF THE ROSE

COLE'S LANDING

Maryhelen Clague

FAWCETT GOLD MEDAL • NEW YORK

A Fawcett Gold Medal Book
Published by Ballantine Books

Library of Congress Catalog Card Number: 84-90950

ISBN 0-449-12642-0

Manufactured in the United States of America

First Edition: February 1985

One

꩜

BY EARLY morning word spread through the village of Cole's Landing that Ferris Blunt had struck again during the night. Swooping across the river like a scavenger in the dark, Ferris and his henchmen had fallen on Andries Stoakes's isolated farm, herded the family outside in the chill night air, and tied them together where they could watch, frightened and shivering, while their furniture was broken up, their stores and cattle carried off, and their house and barn burned to the ground.

As soon as he heard about the raid the following morning, Lieutenant Neil Partherton ordered his horse to be saddled at once. With mixed emotions he rode down the steep path to the flatboat at the river's edge, dreading having to face Andries Stoakes—an unpleasant experience in the best of times—but delighted with the opportunity it gave him to seek out Sarah Reed. His thoughts kept returning to her as he stood on the boat, watching the ferry house drawing nearer on the flat shore ahead. The sun was already strong

1

even at this early hour, and the day promised to be one of those brilliant summer delicacies when even the air seems washed and hung out to dry. It felt good to be young and alive on such a day.

Half an hour later he was seated at one of the scrubbed plank tables in the dining room of the Green Man while Deborah Miller, the tavern keeper's young wife, served him a breakfast of fish, eggs, cheese, and corncakes.

Deborah fussed around the young lieutenant, delighted to have so handsome an officer appear first thing in the morning.

"I suppose you'll be heading up to the Stoakes's farm?"

"That's one of my errands," Neil answered, digging his knife into a crusty cheese wheel. "I've also come over to call on Nat Reed. You don't happen to know if he is home, do you?"

With one free hand Deborah tucked a wisp of hair under the ruffle of her cap. "I don't believe he is. He's been away these last few days, and I haven't heard when he's due to return. But Sarah is coming by later this morning to help me with my netting. We're making fringes for the coverlets and testers in the upstairs rooms. I'll ask her then."

The suggestion of a smile played around Neil's lips at this welcome information, but Deborah, busy pouring him a brimming glass of cider, failed to notice.

"Oh, well then. Perhaps I shall see her on my way back," he said very matter-of-factly. "I'll ask her myself."

"Yes. Do that," Deborah answered and turned back to the caged bar to set down the cider pitcher and begin rearranging Noah Miller's collection of wooden tankards and trenchers.

The lieutenant bent over his plate, while from across the room Deborah quietly studied him: his blond hair waving gently back and queued with a black grosgrain ribbon; his lean profile; his curving lips; his lashes, so long and thick for a man; and those eyes, gray-blue like the Hudson on a blustery day. Even his hands looked elegant, with their long fingers and those tiny blond hairs just visible below the ruffle of his sleeve.

"If I weren't a happily married woman . . ." she sighed.

Word of the raid reached the Reed household by way of Cato, the outdoors servant, who told Jurie, the housemaid, who passed it along to Sarah and her sister, Darcy, as they sat at the mahogany table in the dining room finishing their breakfast.

"And they frightened poor Mistress Stoakes half to death," Jurie went on with excitement, full of importance to be the bearer of bad news. "Why, those ruffians—no telling what they might have done to that poor defenseless woman!"

"I don't think Anetje Stoakes had anything to fear," Darcy said dryly. "She's better able to defend herself than Andries, if it comes to that."

Sarah attempted to supress a smile. "Perhaps so, but nevertheless, it must have been a terrible shock. Imagine losing your house, your belongings, your cattle—all in the space of a few dreadful minutes. Poor thing. We must find some way to help her."

"*You* find some way to help her. Personally, I cannot abide Andries or any other member of his family. He probably brought it on himself."

Sarah drained the last of her chocolate and gently set the china cup down beside her plate.

"I wonder if Lieutenant Partherton will be over to see the damage."

Darcy brightened at once. "Do you think he might?"

Pushing back her chair, Sarah picked up her plate. "Since it was Ferris Blunt who led the raid, I suppose the army must get involved. Someone will have to come over to inspect the damage, and it is usually Lieutenant Partherton.

But then, actually Colonel Greene could send any number of other officers, couldn't he?'' She walked toward the kitchen door, her plate in hand.

"Here, Miss Sarah, let me do that," Jurie cried, trying to head her off.

"No, no, Jurie. I don't mind. You get the rest of the dishes.''

"Here, Jurie," Darcy said, extending her plate. "You can take mine.'' She sat leaning her chin on her hand thoughtfully as Jurie fussed with the dishes until Sarah came back in from the kitchen.

"I've been thinking, Sarah. Perhaps you're right. We should do something to help the Stoakeses. I'll go through the clothes press and put together a few old things we can spare. Then I'll take them down to the Millers'.''

"That's very thoughtful of you, Darcy. I'm going down later this morning to help Deborah with some netting. Why don't you wait and come with me?''

"Why, that will be perfect," Darcy said, jumping up from the table. "Just give me an hour.''

She was out the door in a moment. Sarah watched her go, smiling at the mercurial way her sister had of changing her mind. Across the room she caught sight of her image reflected wavily in a large gilt mirror above the lowboy. For once, thinking of Neil, she was pleased with what she saw: a full figure swelling above the ruffled blouse of her waist; a slim white neck; a perfect oval of a face, with large, shadowed eyes and a gentle mouth; and her glorious hair, waved back from her brow and caught at the nape of her neck, with one long curl cascading over her shoulder and down the swell of her breast.

Enough! Enough dwelling on herself.

Sarah looked briskly around the room with its gleaming mahogany furniture, glowing Staffordshireware plates and silver candlesticks polished to a brilliant perfection. But it needed something more.

Flowers. Yes, that was it. This was a day for flowers everywhere, inside and out.

Collecting her scissors and a low basket from the corner cupboard, she went through the hall and out the front door to where rows of roses, asters, pinks, and gillyflowers lined the house and the path to the road. Humming to herself, she cut and piled the fragrant blooms in her basket, all the while dreaming images of Neil Partherton striding up the path to the doorway of the Green Man while she waited, all her heart in her smile, to welcome him.

By the time Neil Partherton arrived to stand staring at the charred ruins of Stoakes's house, Andries's fright had long since turned to blind, incoherent rage: at Ferris, at Congress, at General Washington and his ineffectual army, at Magistrate van Tassel and his Committee on Conspiracies, at Tories and Whigs and the whole world in general.

"It was Thomas Collins that done it," he said to Neil, swinging one long finger back and forth as if to include the whole sorry mess in his accusation. "They told me as much. 'You called out Thomas Collins,' they said. 'A good Tory.' That's what they said. If'n I had minded my own business like I wanted to do in the first place, this never would of happened. Now what am I goin' to do? Answer me that. How am I goin' to get my young 'uns through next winter with no stock and no seed? Just you tell me that. And who cares? Not your almighty generals nor any of the rest of them so-called patriots!"

Neil shook his head and kicked at a charred piece of bedstead with the toe of his boot. It was difficult to know how to answer Stoakes. This kind of thing was happening so often lately that it was almost too easy to shrug it off when you weren't directly affected by it.

" 'Twasn't enough that they burned everything," Stoakes went on bitterly, "but they trampled their horses right through my fields. Drove my own cattle and hogs right along with them. And the corn near ready, too! Goddamn that Ferris Blunt. May his black soul rot in hell! And all because of one of them Shakin' Quakers. It ain't right. It just ain't right.''

"We'll get Ferris eventually," Neil said levelly. "He's crafty and smart, but he'll make a mistake, and when he does he'll be hanging from the nearest tree so quickly he won't know how it happened."

"Humph. And a lot of good that'll do me and the rest of us what's been burned out by that devil. You should have catched him long ago. What's an army for? This war's been goin' on too long and for too many years while that evil villain has wrecked folks' lives on both sides of the North River. It's long past time he was swinging from a tree. Long past.''

At the edge of the yard near an ancient sling well, Stoakes's eldest son and two men from nearby farms poked long-handled peels at the charred pile of rubbish that was all that remained of Andries's furniture. Turning away from them, Neil and Andries began to walk slowly around the perimeters of the ruined house.

"At least your chimney still looks sound," Neil said to Stoakes, who was shuffling along beside him. "And the walls of your cellar. If you can salvage some of the timbers that aren't burned through, surely some of your neighbors will help you put up some kind of shelter in the next week or two. And I imagine you should be able to save something from the fields. They are not totally destroyed.''

"That's easy enough for you to say. You aren't the one to have to start over from nothin'.''

"Perhaps I can detail a few men from West Point to help you when you're ready to set up something."

"That's the least you should do, seeing as how it was my patriotic efforts that got me into this in the first place. I should've left Thomas Collins to his Tory pleasures.''

Neil stopped, looking directly into Stoakes's pinched face and narrow, suspicious eyes. He looked almost ludicrous in a pair of borrowed pantaloons, bunched over his nightshirt under a wide leather belt. His lank, uncombed hair and stubble of beard did nothing to soften the habitual scowling and quarrelsome expression that had been on his face so long it had frozen to his features. Because he had always been a difficult man, Neil was finding it hard to sympathize with him even in such extreme adversity.

"Come now, Mr. Stoakes. We both know that you hauled Thomas Collins in front of the Committee on Conspiracies because otherwise you yourself would have been brought up before them. It was a case of using another man to get the Committee off your back, and if it brought Ferris Blunt down on you, well, that's too bad, but no more than you might have expected."

Andries's sallow complexion flamed red. "Are you sayin' this . . . this calamity is no more than a man should have to bear for doin' his duty?" he spluttered.

"No, of course not. Ferris Blunt is an outlaw, and he will eventually end up where he deserves to be. But you are not innocent either."

"Well, it's a pretty pass when a man has to see his family ruined no matter where he takes a stand. Accuse me of being a Tory and I have to pay one hundred dollars or rot in jail. Let me do my duty as a Whig and I get burned out. I say to the Devil with all of you!"

Neil glanced around at the people across the yard, thankful that there was no one within earshot. "I don't blame you for feeling bitter, but the facts are what they are, and there is little we can do right now to change them. Once this war is won and over with—"

"Humph! And God knows when that'll ever be!"

"—this kind of thing can be set aside and life can go on peacefully as it should."

Andries's dark eyes turned cold as granite under his scowl. "I'll never put it aside. If the army don't hang Ferris Blunt, I swear by Almighty God that I'll kill him myself, with my bare hands if I have to."

Neil took one last look around. He knew all he needed to make his report, and there was little else he could do now. Andries's rage, however justified, was wearying, and there were other matters that needed his attention. Matters far more pleasant. He veered off toward a scrawny tulip tree near the road, where his horse, Sampson, was tied.

"Look, come up to Fort Clinton at the Point tomorrow and we'll see what we can do to help you. Meanwhile, try to rally your neighbors to save what you can. Where is your family staying?"

"At the Tates'. Reverend and his wife were good enough to say they could put us up there until we can find a better place. And Barnet Sindon says he'll supply us with flour from his mill, at least for a time."

"What about Mr. van Tassel and Nathanial Reed? They'll help you out, won't they? Hendrick is the chairman of the committee and Nat has been up before it often enough. They both should understand what you are going through."

Andries shrugged. "Maybe. But I wouldn't call Hendrick van Tassel an understanding man. Nor Nat Reed neither."

Pulling loose the reins, Neil swung his horse around and vaulted into the saddle.

"I expect to see Nat today. I'll put in a word for you. Meantime, come up to the fort tomorrow."

"I'll be there," Stoakes muttered, "for whatever good it will do me."

Neil gave Sampson a kick and cantered off, leaving Andries still staring at the shell of his house. He knew that after some of Stoakes's shock and rage had eased, he had his neighbors would throw themselves into the business of putting up a new cabin and, later, a barn. Yet his anger would stay with him long after his farm was rebuilt. Unfortunately, Stoakes was only one of a growing number of embittered men scarred by this long, unresolved rebellion. And Neil knew too well that even a swift end to the war was not going to resolve the hatred it had engendered.

Neil's depressing thoughts were in stark contrast to the beauty of the country through which he rode. The summer harvest was nearing its peak, and already those small fields that had been cultivated on this hilly terrain were alive with field hands, children, and young people gathering in the hay and corn. Berry bushes and apple trees were thick with unripened fruit. Verdant woods grew dense on either side of the narrow dirt path. Now and then a stone fence lined an open field. As the road bent down toward the river and the marsh grass that bordered it, Neil urged his horse to move a little faster. Soon he spotted the meeting-house belfry and the low rooftops of the village over the rim of the trees. With a small shiver of anticipation he gave Sampson another kick. The horse shook out his long mane at this unaccustomed severity but picked up his hooves at a brisker pace. Neil smiled to himself. The morning was lovely, the time of day was right, and with any luck he would come across Sarah Reed somewhere near the Millers' tavern. Just the thought of seeing her was enough to do away with the unpleasant memory of Andries Stoakes and his ruined farm.

As he came around a curve he was forced to stop in the narrow road, which was blocked by a peddler's wagon. The thick woods grew so near the path that it was impossible for Sampson to ease his bulk around the rattling wagon, with its clattering tin pans and wooden bowls. At Neil's impatient yell a bent, scruffily bearded driver, with long hair straggling from under a round black hat, peered around the side. He gave Neil a languid wave and, without hurrying, rattled his vehicle on until he reached a patch of weeds where he pulled his mule over to one side, allowing Neil to canter past. Usually Neil would have given the old tramp a curse or two, but with his happy anticipation of seeing Sarah Reed, he contented himself with a dark glare as he rode by.

Another mile and the road veered sharply onto a small bridge spanning the inlet that separated the Landing from the mainland. As Sampson clattered across the loose planking, Neil looked up at Maude Sackett's strange little house lying at the very end of the village street. For years it had been rumored in the village that Maude was a witch. The practical-minded men of the village scoffed at the idea, yet they had never dared to face her with the accusation—because, Neil suspected, they secretly feared it might be true.

As Neil cantered off the bridge and turned down the main street of the village, he spotted Maude herself, her tawdry figure bending over a clump of herbs in her overgrown garden. She straightened and looked directly into his eyes. Neil kept her gaze with difficulty. Even from a distance it was uncanny the way she could fasten on you with that look of hers. Bending in the saddle, he politely touched a finger to his hat. She turned back to her hoe without acknowledging him in any way, and yet he fancied he noticed a smug satisfaction in her manner, as though she knew some secret concerning him.

But that was nonsense. He was letting silly rumors about the old woman cloud his usually clear judgment. And at a time when there were far more important matters to attend to.

Although the highlands across the river formed a border of steep, precipitous bluffs, the eastern side, by contrast, was comprised of a long, flat stretch of low ground, marshy in places, that gave way to modest, sloping hills and lush woodlands. This ledge of flat land was considerable enough to have allowed for several small villages

along its length, of which Cole's Landing was one of the
oldest and smallest. It was actually little more than a
cluster of cottages, a meetinghouse, and a tavern, scattered
haphazardly along one main street, with a rickety wharf at
one end and the bridge to the mainland at the other. Most
of the villagers lived near the south end of the street,
where the wharf jutted out into the water. Over the years
several enterprising businesses had grown up that catered
to the fishermen who frequented the dock. They included
the tavern, a carpenter who specialized in boat repairs, a
blacksmith, and a sailmaker, the widow Earing, whose
small cottage lay near the center of the village, opposite
the meetinghouse. Her husband had been a sailmaker before his death, and since then she had supported herself
and her weak-minded son, Jamie, by becoming as proficient at repairing sails as her husband had been.

Reverend Tate and his wife, Elizabeth, lived in a small
stone cottage near the meetinghouse on the west side of the
road. Behind them, stretched along the riverbank, were
several ramshackle huts belonging mostly to fishermen.
Behind the limits of the Tates' considerable gardens one
could always see nets drying on wheels and fish drying on
wooden planks.

At the other end of the main street, separated from
Maude Sackett's by a length of willow trees, sat the finest
house in the village—Nathanial Reed's. Nat's father had
been one of the first settlers along these banks and had
known Jeremiah Cole, the town's founding father.

It was in the last days of the transition from Dutch to
English rule that Jeremiah Cole built himself a shack near
the marshy banks of the Hudson, strung out his nets, and
put up a small dock from which he could set out every
morning to haul in the fish that teemed so abundantly in
the river. No one actually knew how he had managed to
get a grant for the land, but it was rumored that he was
owed a favor related to unseating the Dutch from the rich

prize of New Amsterdam. Although Jeremiah himself was never certain of what year he was born, it was pretty well accepted that he was nearing eighty when he died. By then an assortment of dwellings had grown up around his fishing shack, and the dock that he had originally built was known up and down the river as Cole's Landing.

Joseph Reed had come to the Landing as a young man to make his fortune mining iron ore from the rock-faced hills behind the flats. Soon he had prospered enough to build himself a fine house, a stable, and outbuildings. Though the iron ore had run out by the time Nathanial, his son, took over, the boy was enterprising enough to make money even into the present, difficult, war-ridden times. Neil felt sure that if it had not been for Nat's Tory sympathies, he would have been one of the leading citizens of the area.

Cole's Landing had been a sleepy place for most of its life, until now, when the struggle between the Americans and the British brought it an unwelcome prominence. With an important Continental fort guarding the North River just above it, the village had become strategically important to the American army. Of all the people who walked and rode along its sandy thoroughfare that fine morning, none knew better than Neil Partherton just how much more important it was soon to become.

Neil had barely turned his mount down the village street before he began to encounter the residents of the town. Elizabeth Tate waved at him from her kitchen doorway, where two small children sat on the stone stoop stripping ears of corn. Jamie Earing, Helena's feebleminded son, ran after his horse, babbling good-naturedly. Hendrick van Tassel, whose large farm lay nearly a mile outside the village, but whose position as a long-standing member of the Committee on Conspiracies brought him here often, doffed his round hat at Neil with pompous dignity. As Neil passed the smithy, the resounding clink of a hammer echoed like a familiar canticle, and Coenradt Johannes, the blacksmith, broke the rhythm on his anvil long enough to wave in Neil's direction.

Just past the smithy the street bent in a wide curve toward the river. Tucked neatly in this curve lay the town tavern, the Green Man, more commonly known as "the Millers' ordinary" after Noah and Deborah Miller, who ran it. A walkway of crushed oyster shells, beneath a trellis of thick wisteria, led from the open doorway to the road, where a gate gave out to a grassy edge around an ancient oak tree. A half-circle bench built around the tree trunk was a favorite loitering spot for men and women alike. Neil's heart gave a leap as he spotted a familiar figure sitting on the bench, leaning forward to support a wobbly tow-headed two-year-old whom he recognized as the Millers' small child. Sarah Reed sat with her skirts spread about her and her wide hat lying in her lap, laughing delightedly at the antics of the young boy. Her long hair fell forward like a golden nimbus around her face, and though Neil was not close enough to see, he knew that her eyes would be sparkling with that vivacious *joie de vivre* that he found so enchanting.

Next to her on the bench, Sarah's sister, Darcy, sat leaning forward, her chin on her hand. Her straw hat was held in place by a wide green ribbon that pulled the sides down around her face and fastened under her chin. Several other people were standing near the girls under the tree or lounging at a long stone water trough across the street. Among them Neil recognized Deborah Miller, the mother of the child Sarah was holding, and Christian Weiss, the village carpenter, who had left his work on an overturned dory lying near the dock to enjoy the conversation.

Riding casually up to the group, Neil swung easily out of the saddle and tied his horse to a hitching post. He was almost certain that Sarah colored slightly when she looked up and saw him, and yet it was so slight as to make him wonder if he was not hoping for too much.

"Good morrow, Lieutenant," Deborah said cheerfully. "And how did you find Andries Stoakes?"

"Good morning, ladies," Neil answered, sweeping off his hat. Sarah Reed smiled serenely up at him, while next to her, her sister sat straight up with a small startled cry.

"Andries is in a poor way, Mrs. Miller. This has been a grievous blow."

"How did it look?" Christian Weiss asked, moving up closer to Neil. "Was he able to salvage anything?"

"Nothing much, I'm afraid. A few sections of the cornfield, perhaps. Everything in the house and barn was burned. And unless he can retrieve some of his stock wandering in the woods, his cattle are gone as well."

" 'Twas not much of a farm, I ever thought," Christian said, shaking his head. "But when it's all a man's got, it's a heavy loss."

Deborah Miller reached out for her two-year-old, who had managed to toddle over to her. "That terrible Ferris Blunt! How many men has he ruined in just these last two years alone? At least three or four. Something ought to be done about him. Why doesn't the army catch him and hang him?"

"We are trying to, mistress, but he is a very cunning man who has many friends on both sides of the North River who help to hide him. Then too, he knows those mountains and woods like no one else."

Sarah said in her gentle voice, "I'm sure the army wants to catch him, Deborah, just as much as we want him caught. It does not help them to criticize."

Neil smiled his thanks at the girl. "You are kind to defend us, Miss Reed, but the truth is we feel as badly about things like this as everyone else. We should have hanged Ferris Blunt long ago. It's a humiliation that we have not been able to."

"Well, I'm sure I didn't mean to criticize you, Lieutenant," Deborah added.

"Lieutenant Partherton," Darcy cried out suddenly, jumping up to stand beside Neil, "I do wonder that you've left your horse standing there after your long ride. Would you like me to water him? He looks as though he needs a good drink."

"Why, that would be very kind of you, Miss Darcy, but I wouldn't want to cause you any trouble."

"Oh, it's no trouble at all. I would be very happy to do it for you."

Bouncing jauntily, Darcy tipped her dark head at Neil, then went skipping over to where Sampson was tied, her skirts swaying provocatively. She had no more than left the bench when Neil took her place beside Sarah. Darcy glanced back, and when she saw what she had inadvertently caused, a shadow fell across her cheerful smile and some of the bounce went out of her step. The time allowed for Sampson to enjoy a drink was abruptly shortened.

Neil turned his full attention to Sarah. "I am happy to have this opportunity to speak with you, Miss Reed," he said, lowering his voice, and grateful that both Deborah and Christian Weiss seemed engrossed in discussing the best way to catch Ferris Blunt. "In fact, I was hoping I would meet you in the village today."

Sarah's porcelain cheeks deepened to a dusky rose. "It is a pleasure for me also, Lieutenant," she answered shyly. Immediately she regretted her words, wondering if they sounded too bold.

"Aside from the pleasure of talking with you," Neil went on, diplomatically, "I was hoping to ask if you thought your father would be at home this evening. I am anxious to have a word with him about some business relating to the fort."

"Papa? Why, yes. I believe he will be at home by this evening. He has been up to Fishkill these past two days, but we expect him back early this afternoon. And he is often so weary after one of these trips that he is not likely to go out again."

"Then it would be agreeable for me to stop by?"

"Most agreeable."

Her shy smile and congenial reply were so encouraging that Neil plunged on.

"Perhaps if I conclude my business with your father before dark you might walk with me to the river. On such a fine day the sunset should be quite beautiful."

"I should like that very much," Sarah replied, feeling certain that her happy anticipation was written all over her face. It would have been more proper, she felt, to pretend indifference, to be alluring by seeming aloof. Yet she could not. Everything about her was so obvious that she sometimes despaired of ever acquiring the flirtatious demeanor ladies were supposed to have.

"La, Lieutenant," Darcy cried as she came bouncing back up to the bench where they sat. "Your old horse was not thirsty at all. And here I thought he looked parched. I suppose it is my imagination playing tricks on me again. I have such a strong imagination—don't I, Sarah?"

Neil quickly jumped up to offer Darcy her seat again, but she continued to stand, peering up into his face.

"Sarah is always telling me that I should be more practical and not fly off on tangents—aren't you, Sarah? But I just cannot help myself. It is my nature to be impulsive, I suppose."

"Ahem, yes," Neil answered, stepping back out of her close scrutiny.

"Don't you think so?" Darcy went on, almost leaning against him.

"Think what?"

"That people who have impulsive, passionate natures simply must give way to them."

Neil was beginning to feel uncomfortable. "Why, I

don't suppose I would know, Miss Darcy, since my character tends to be so very opposite to that."

"Come then, Darcy," Sarah said briskly, rising and
tying her hat under her chin. "I think it's time we got
home. We've dawdled enough for one morning. Come and
see us soon, Deborah. We are planning a quilting frolic for
next month, and there's lots to do beforehand."

"I'll come some afternoon when I can leave this little
one at home," Deborah said, stroking the blond curls of
the child clinging to her skirts. "Otherwise we'll accomplish nothing."

"I would be honored to escort you ladies to your house,"
Neil said, obviously speaking to Sarah, though he included
Darcy in his invitation.

"Oh, that would be lovely," Darcy exclaimed, taking his
arm. "Here, Sarah, you take the lieutenant's other arm,
then we'll each have a handsome beau."

"But your horse," Sarah said, trying to hide her embarrassment at her sister's obvious flirtatiousness.

"I'll come back for him. It's such a fine day that a walk
would be most pleasant. Especially with such charming
company."

"Oh, Lieutenant," Darcy sighed, "you are too gallant."
To her delight he offered Sarah his other arm, and they
set off down the narrow path toward the bridge. They had
only gone a few steps when they came across Reverend
Tate walking toward the tavern with Hendrick van Tassel
at his side. Both men stopped, bowing and lifting their
hats to the Reed sisters.

"Lieutenant Partherton," van Tassel said as he replaced
his hat on his long, expertly combed wig. "You come
from Andries Stoakes's farm, I've no doubt. A terrible
thing."

"So terrible," Tate echoed. "Poor Andries will have to
begin again from the very bottom. He saved nothing. Not
even a few scraps with which to clothe his children."

"It was kind of you to take them in, Reverend," Neil said. "Andries told me his family was staying with you temporarily."

"It was the least we could do," Harmon Tate replied. "The very least."

"But see here, Lieutenant," van Tassel went on. "Something has got to be done about this Ferris Blunt. Stoakes was only doing his duty, and for that he gets burned out and loses everything. It's not fair, and it makes it deuced difficult to get others to cooperate with the Committee. How many men are going to come before us willingly if they know reprisals of this kind are going to fall upon their heads? Why can't you fellows catch this rogue and hang him? He's the scourge of good patriots!"

"Perhaps if the Committee were a little less inclined to see conspiracies everywhere, or were slightly more lenient in handling them . . ."

"Why, sir, I am shocked to hear you say such a thing. There *are* conspiracies everywhere, as you well know. If we are to bring a successful conclusion to this war and restore liberty to this great land, we must be diligent about destroying our enemies."

Reverend Tate, a small man with a flat, round face, bobbed around the austere dignified bulk that was Hendrick van Tassel. "The Bible says, 'Watch and be ready, for the Devil comes like a thief in the night.' "

Unruffled, Neil looked down on him patiently. "Yes, but that is exactly what Ferris would say too. Where loyalties are so divided and feelings run so strong, we ought to be circumspect in our judgments."

"Forgive me, Reverend Tate," Sarah spoke up, "but does not the Bible also say that we should forgive our enemies?"

"Unto seventy times seven," Darcy added, not wishing to be left out.

Reverend Tate bristled. "Well, miss, I don't think I need you to remind me of what is to be found in Scripture."

But van Tassel had scented a possible dissenter and was not to be sidetracked by theology.

"Really, Lieutenant. I wonder what your general thinks of such liberal sentiments. He might not be cheered to hear such charity proffered to the very people who are making this war so long and so difficult. Statements like yours only lead the British to be more determined in their hopes of subduing us."

"General Washington knows my views well enough," Neil answered, giving Hendrick one of his coldest looks. "But now I really must escort these ladies to their home. You did say you were expected back momentarily, didn't you, Miss Reed?"

"Oh, yes, I did. Indeed, I should have been there long ago."

With a curtsy from each of the sisters and a nod from Neil, the soldier and the two pretty young girls moved away down the dusty street toward the bridge.

"I suppose old Hendrick will be having me hauled up before the Committee next," Neil muttered. "He'd love that. A traitor in the Third New York Continental. Benedict Arnold all over again."

"Why, he'd never!" Darcy spluttered. "He wouldn't dare. You are too . . . too important."

Neil's smile was more indulgent than convincing. "That would make it all the more fun for him."

Sarah glanced back to see van Tassel and Reverend Tate still standing at the tavern gate watching after them. "Sometimes I do think Mr. van Tassel takes an uncommon enjoyment in accusing men and sending them to jail. It cannot help our cause any."

"In fact, I think it hurts it very much," Neil answered. "You'd think he would realize that. But as I said, feelings run strong. I've seen families bitterly divided over this struggle, some adament about remaining loyal to King George and the mother country, and others just as committed to Congress and liberty. That is the nature of a civil strife.''

"Oh, Lieutenant Partherton, you have such a lovely way of putting things," Darcy sighed. "So, so . . . wise."

Sarah dipped her head, glad that the wide brim of her hat hid her embarrassment at her sister's antics. What must he think of Darcy? And of her, Darcy's sister? She might be too reserved and self-conscious to be alluring, but surely that was preferable to Darcy's sighs and false compliments. Poor Lieutenant Partherton would no doubt be glad to be rid of them both.

More than halfway to the path that jutted off the main road toward the Reed house they came across the same peddler's wagon Neil had passed on his way into the village. The three pedestrians stood aside to let it pass, nodding to the driver on the seat. He raised his greasy, battered hat to them, smiling what was probably meant as a congenial smile, but with his bad teeth, bent body, thin scraggly beard, and long hair, he gave anything but the appearance of congeniality. The wagon wove by, with its tin pans and wooden bowls clanking to the rhythm of its passage. After it was gone a strong stench was left hovering on the air, a miasma of unwashed man and mule compounded by a foul wagon that had probably not seen a thorough cleaning since the first day it was stocked.

Yet it was soon gone, replaced by the fragrant grass and clean, salt smell of the estuary, which gained in strength as they reached the end of the street and turned west along the path to the Reed house.

This imposing building stood near the water's edge, a corner of its rear portion embedded in the steep rock hill just behind it. It had been built many years before and had stood on this spot long enough for the trellis surrounding the front door to be thickly interlaced with climbing roses.

The front side of the house faced the path from the street. On the river side its windows looked out over the willows that edged the water, while the opposite side overlooked a substantial barn, several outbuildings, and two or three small fields. The kitchen at the back opened onto a large garden that stretched behind the house, between the river on one side and the steep face of the hill on the other. Across the river and to the north lay the steep precipices of West Point. The tiny flutter of color amid all the green marked the flags at Fort Clinton and, farther away, Fort Putnam, both carved from the mountainside to guard this strategic section of the North River—which is what the local people alternately called the Hudson. Both were comparatively new forts, built only a few years before to replace the two smaller ones to the south, which had fallen to the British in '77 with such ease that they were afterward abandoned. Above these newer forts the river made a sharp bend and was narrow enough to be under the control of several strategically placed six-pounders

As long as they held these bluffs, the Americans controlled the all-important Hudson River, which was why the chilling closeness of Benedict Arnold's treachery just the year before still gave several gentlemen of the Continental High Command cause for palpitations.

Neil relinquished his two attractive charges near one of the huge old black willow trees that lined the path in front of the house and grew in profusion along the river's edge.

"Won't you come in and have a glass of cider, Lieutenant Partherton?" Darcy said, still clinging to his arm.

Sarah glared at her sister but added lamely, "If you would like to wait for Papa . . ."

"No, thank you," Neil said hurriedly. "I've much to do, and I must get back to the fort. I'd rather take a chance of catching him home tonight. But thank you for the kind invitation."

"I quite understand," Sarah replied.

"If you would like to come for supper . . . ow!"

Darcy glared daggers at her sister, who had just pinched her arm not as unobtrusively as she had hoped.

"We are taking up far too much of the lieutenant's time, Darcy," Sarah said sweetly. "We will look forward to seeing you tonight, Lieutenant Partherton."

"It will be my pleasure," Neil answered, wishing that Sarah had extended the supper invitation. It would be heavenly to share a meal with her—or it would be if Darcy didn't take up most of his time.

The two girls were already down the path, nearing the door.

"What did you do that for?" Darcy whispered angrily. "He was ready to say yes!"

Two

BY THE time Neil returned to the Reed house that evening, the candles in the windows flickered like tiny jewels against the deepening dusk. He had been delayed first at the fort and then trying to find a boat across the river, and so had missed the spectacular sunset that he had hoped to share with Sarah. Yet the house, with its glimmering lights, seemed so cozy and friendly the loss did not seem to matter too much.

To his surprise and delight it was Sarah who answered the door. She had changed her dress to one of soft yellow chintz that reflected the bronze shimmer of the candlelight, and there were fresh daisies tucked into the sweeping coils of her long hair. The wide scooped neckline of her dress was lined with narrow ruching, cut low enough to expose the swelling cleavage between her breasts. Neil was so enchanted that he nearly forgot that his reason for coming was to see her father. Then he heard Nat's booming voice.

"Lieutenant Partherton. Come in, my boy. Come in."

Nathanial Reed entered the hall not from the parlor, as Neil had expected, but from the kitchen. He was in his shirtsleeves and old-fashioned long waistcoat, with coarse ribbed stockings and soft leather slippers on his feet. He wore a gray grizzled bagwig, and in his hand he held a long clay pipe. In one expansive gesture he took Neil's hat, threw it on the table, and ushered him through the dining room toward the kitchen.

"You don't mind if we sit in here, do you, my boy? I find it much more comfortable than the stuffy parlor my daughters have foisted on me. The kitchen was good enough for me when I was young, and I don't see why I should be made to sit on brocade chairs with spindly legs, surrounded by fancy little china ornaments, when my poor old bones need comfort more than ever."

"I don't mind at all," Neil said, taking the settle opposite Nat's broad wooden chair. Because of the August heat there was no fire burning in the wide hearth, though the pile of embers there and the fragrant odors still strong in the room attested to the cooking done earlier that day. The top half of the back door stood yawning wide, and through it he glimpsed the silver thread of the river and the dusky splashes of color in the garden.

"Will you have a pipe?"

"No, thank you, sir."

"Why, then, a glass of ale. Sarah, where are your manners? Get the lieutenant a glass now, and hurry about it."

Before Sarah could move there was a loud clatter on the back stairs, which opened onto the kitchen, and a swirl of lace-edged skirts flew down them.

"I'll get it for him," Darcy cried, rushing to a painted *kas* that covered nearly all of one wall. She also had changed her dress—to a flattering dark blue with an overskirt of flowered lutestring. Neil watched her, thinking how the one year's difference in the girls' ages had given Sarah so much advantage in maturity and roundness of figure. It showed most obviously in the way they each wore their clothes. Where Sarah presented just enough of the right touches to allure and tempt a man, Darcy seemed thrown together only to emphasize a figure too small to create the attraction her sister gave off unconsciously. She too wore flowers in her hair, but there was nothing fresh or pretty about them. Somehow they seemed incongruous with the rest of her.

Neil accepted the tankard Darcy held out to him and smiled at her pleasantly in spite of his unkind thoughts. Perhaps what it really came down to was that he loved her sister and did not love Darcy. Her complete lack of attraction for him no doubt stemmed from that.

He realized all at once that Nat had been speaking to him, and he hastily brought his thoughts back to the business at hand.

"I said, would you prefer some Madeira or claret? Ale's good enough, and this, being made by Cato himself, is not bad. But wine is often more preferable."

"No, no. This is fine, thank you. Just right."

"Good," Nat said, sitting back, satisfied. "Now then, you two young ladies, go back to your tatting or whatever it is young ladies do in the evening and leave the gentlemen to their pipes and their ale. We'll call you when we need you."

"Oh, but Papa," Darcy cried, "couldn't we stay? I love to hear all about the fort and the army and the generals."

"Go along, you saucy girl. What you really want is to hang on to the lieutenant's coattails, driving him wild with your flirting and your smile. Get! Get!"

"That Darcy," Nat went on to Neil as his daughters left the room, closing the door behind them. "She cannot even think straight when an eligible man comes in sight. Sometimes I wonder what's going to become of her."

"Your daughters are both very lovely," Neil said guardedly.

"Aye, they are. Like their mother. Sarah, now, she's the quiet, sensible one. She keeps a pretty tight rein on her sister. However, I must say, much as I love Sarah, I can sympathize with Darcy and her wild spirit. Had a bit of it myself when I was young. Well, now, young sir, what is it you wanted to see me about? Sarah told me you had some business or other to discuss."

Neil took a sip of the ale. Nat's black servant, Cato, had a reputation for making delicious brews, and this was one of his best.

"There is something. However, I must caution you that I speak in confidence. I must ask you not to repeat anything I shall say here tonight."

"Come now, Neil. You know that since I was before the Committee two years ago and spent those ghastly months in Newgate I've been as loyal a patriot as can be found in the province. I admit I did not start out that way, but a man can see the error of his ways. Loyalties can be altered, as you well know. And a good thing, too. No one has worked harder for the cause than I since those early days."

"That's true, sir. And I am not the only one who thinks so. I would not be here talking to you tonight without the blessings of my superiors."

"I suspected as much. They know they can trust me. Why, just today I've come from Fishkill after procuring beef for the garrison at Newburgh. You too should be receiving three hundred hogsheads of pickled beef by the first of next month."

"It will be most welcome. I don't suppose I have to tell you about the terrible unrest rampant in the army over the lack of food and clothing—not to mention pay."

Nat knocked the bowl of his pipe gently against the hearth and then sat back to refill it.

"I know, of course, about the mutinies last winter, but I had suspected that matters had improved."

"They have, considerably. But they remain very grave, sometimes desperate. If the war is not brought to some kind of a conclusion soon, no one knows what will happen. It takes an uncommon lot of money to run an army proficiently."

"Well, I shan't pretend I don't have an ear to the ground. Let me help you with this 'very private' matter you wish to discuss with me tonight." Leaning forward with his elbows resting on his knees, Nat made an effort to keep his normally booming voice very low. "There are rumors around that something big may be just before happening. Might it involve the Frenchies?"

"It might," Neil answered, also leaning forward and speaking quietly. "Let's say the French were involved. Whatever happens will require some careful coordination between the armies in the field here in the north and emissaries from Congress in Philadelphia. Decisions, plans, material support—all would have to be worked out in great detail, in some place of absolute secrecy. We can barely make a move these days without the British in New York knowing of it."

"But there is only a garrison force holding New York right now. The main British army is off down south somewhere. Surely they cannot be any danger to the Hudson or the northern colonies."

"It all depends. It is possible that the events in the south could make a deciding difference to the course of the war. But it would take some coordination between our forces and the French to bring it off. Of course, at this point we don't even know if the French are willing."

Nat turned the bowl of his pipe in his big hand and stuck the stem in his mouth. Of course the French were willing. Rochambeau was positively avid to head south if he could only dissuade Washington from his pet project of attacking

New York. Did Neil not know this? No. More likely, he hoped Nat didn't know it. Like most army men he was not too keen on the local civilians recognizing what was going on. And although the lieutenant obviously was not going to mention money, he felt certain it was involved. And it would be no small amount, either. Any secret meetings, wherever they were set up, would be bound to include an exchange of hard specie. That much was obvious. Otherwise why all this talking around the point?

"Well, supposing they are willing. What can I do to help? I cannot see how it could affect me one way or the other."

"You have a fine house here, Mr. Reed, conveniently close to the water"—Neil's voice was almost a whisper— "with a passageway between the river and your root cellar."

Nat's level gaze did not waver, but Neil saw the surprise deep in their dark depths.

"How did you learn of that?"

"One hears these things."

"One hears wrong. That 'passageway,' as you call it, has been blocked for years. My father built it back in the days when he thought to mine the hill in back of the house. I played in it myself as a very young lad. But landslides and rockslides closed it up years ago. No one could get through it now."

"Where does it come out?"

"Oh, I don't remember. Somewhere upriver. I doubt I could even find the entrance anymore; it is all so overgrown."

"Suppose we wanted to open it up again. Would it be so difficult?"

"By the Almighty, yes. And you'd never be able to do it in secret. Why, every village within ten miles up and down the Hudson would know of it."

Abruptly Neil sat back in his chair, resuming an almost normal tone of voice.

"It was only a thought. Your house, however, might still be useful to us as a rendezvous point. Would you be willing to allow us to use it?"

Nat's fingers ran down the length of his pipe. With a quick snap he broke off the end.

"Of course. Just let me know when and I'll help you all I can. Even to seeing that the servants, my girls, and I are out of the way the entire time."

"Excellent," Neil said, picking up his glass. "When arrangements are coordinated I will be in touch with you."

"Too bad about Andries Stoakes, isn't it? I hope to God you fellows find that Ferris Blunt soon. It is criminal the way he plagues people. Why, he must have hit farms within twenty miles on either side of the North River. I cannot understand how he can get away with it."

"He holes up in the highlands. He knows every inch of these mountains and can disappear into the most impossible terrain as though it were a park. But we'll get him sooner or later."

Nat chuckled as he slumped back in his chair. "Too bad he can't spend a few months in Newgate prison. Perhaps he'd come out on our side too!"

Although it was comfortable sitting in the kitchen, Neil soon found himself growing restless. Ordinarily Nat was good company, but tonight he found it difficult to keep his mind on his companion's rambling conversation. Once their business was concluded, images of the girls sitting in the parlor at the other end of the house kept intruding. He imagined Sarah bending over her tapestry frame with the candlelight playing on her hair. When she suddenly appeared at the door he felt sure that his thoughts must have drawn her there.

"Excuse me, Papa," she said, glancing shyly at Neil. "I don't mean to intrude, but Johnnie Tate is at the door. He says you promised Reverend Tate that they might use some of our extra bedding while the Stoakes family is staying with them.''

"Bless my soul, so I did. I clean forgot that I met that gentleman this afternoon. Tell Darcy to light a lantern and go with Johnnie to the attic and get him what he needs. Then she can help him carry it to the rectory.''

Sarah's eyes fastened on the floor. "Are you sure you don't want me to go? You know Darcy is not so familiar with the household affairs as I am.''

"No, no. Darcy is fond of the young man, and I'm sure she is familiar enough to find what he has come for. Besides, she'll be delighted to have the opportunity to flirt with him a little. Go along, now.''

Sarah hesitated. Although her sister pretended a contemptuous indifference to John Tate ordinarily, she seldom missed the chance to be around him when the opportunity arose. But with Neil Partherton sitting in the Reed kitchen, Sarah suspected Darcy's delight was not going to be as enthusiastic as it might have been.

After she left, Nat rose from his chair and laid his pipe on the mantel.

"Well now, young man. Although you are as polite as can be, I know that you would prefer the company of my daughters to my own. I was young once too, strange as it may seem now.''

Neil started to protest, but Nat stopped him with a wave of his hand. "The truth is I am excessively weary from my trip, and I long for my bed. You stay awhile and talk with the girls.''

Neil rose to shake Nat's hand. "That would be my pleasure, sir. And thank you again for your willingness to help us.''

"I'm happy to be of service to the cause. You know that. Just let me know when you need my house.''

"I shall inform you the minute the details are worked out.''

The door closed behind Nat and Neil resumed his seat, listening to the far-off voices in the front of the house, wondering if Sarah would come back into the kitchen. He had almost decided to go in search of her when he heard a soft step and the door swung softly open. She was standing in the doorway, her fingers still on the handle, looking at him. Neil stood up by his chair, drinking in the soft beauty of her shadowed face, the silvery light on her shining hair.

It was the first time they had ever been alone in a room together, and for the first moments the strangeness of it kept them both rooted to the spot. Then Sarah let the door swing behind her and she leaned against it, her eyes held fast by Neil's only a few feet away. The profound quiet of the room enveloped them, closing out the world. The air was charged with the feelings that flowed between them, and for the first time neither tried to hide what they felt. It was no surprise to either when Neil finally moved swiftly to her, enclosing her in his arms and bending to kiss her lips, lightly, as if a feather briefly touched their softness.

Sarah's arms eased slowly up around his neck. Her eyes were shining with shock and delight all at once.

"My dear," Neil whispered. "My dearest Sarah." He kissed her again, harder this time, more full of the longing he felt.

Sarah hesitated a moment before giving way to his kiss, then she felt she was melting in his arms, carried along on such a wave of emotion and joy as she had never known before. She nestled her head in the curve of his neck, reveling in the wonderful feel of his body. Then, as reason returned, she broke away, standing back while he held fast to her arms.

"Darcy! She'll be back soon. We shouldn't."

Neil drew her close against him again. "Oh, Sarah. You don't know how long I've wanted to do this."

Caution was lost in the happiness that enveloped her. "And I've wanted you to for so long."

"Ever since the first day I saw you sitting under that black willow tree, your hair blowing around your lovely face, I've loved you. All this time I've loved you, and now I must speak. I must tell you so."

"Neil, Neil. I felt the same way, but I was so afraid you didn't like me. Couldn't like me."

"How could I not?" Neil answered, kissing her throat, her cheeks, her hair, and finally again, her lips.

Giving a little gasp, Sarah pulled away from him once more.

"Darcy might come back at any moment."

"To the Devil with Darcy."

Placing a firm hand on his chest, she pushed him gently away.

"No, Neil. I would die if Darcy walked in on us and found us this way. This is too precious to me. Too sweet to be ruined by someone interrupting."

Neil stopped and lifted her hand, delicately kissing her palm.

"All right, my love, I understand. My happiness is getting in the way of my judgment. My beautiful Sarah!"

Sarah smiled deeply in spite of her cautious words. " 'Beautiful'! Oh, Neil. I love to hear you speak that way."

"There is so much more I long to say to you. How you've bewitched me, blinded me. Almost kept me from doing my duty by filling my thoughts with your sweet face, your voice, your body . . ."

He reached for her again and willingly she went, unable not to. Yet they both realized that should her sister come bounding into the kitchen, a treasured private moment would be flawed.

"Come," Neil said, drawing her toward the outside door. "Let's have that walk in the garden you promised me. In the dark we won't have to worry about being seen."

"Oh, yes, yes."

He threw open the door, and they bounded together down the path between the flowers, guided on their way by a fine sheen of moonlight. Sarah knew all the paths in the garden so well that the moonlight was not even needed, but only added to the magic of the night.

The fragrance of honeysuckle hung heavy on the cool night air. With her hand held tightly in Neil's, Sarah led him to the edge of the farthest path near the banks of the river. The soft lapping of the water seemed to add a touch of music.

"Happy?" Neil whispered.

"So happy."

He tipped up her chin to let the light fall on her lovely face. Then their arms closed around each other, and they were lost in absolute delight as their bodies pressed against each other.

Darcy Reed ran down the path off the village street that led to her front door, holding up her bobbing skirts and feeling smug and annoyed at the same time. Annoyed that her father had insisted she accompany John Tate back to the rectory, and smug that she had left him in the street looking after her with such blatant desire in his eyes. Any other night she might have been happy to spend more time with John, letting his hands stray on her neck until his juvenile desperation was painful to behold. She would laugh to herself about it later in her bed—laugh at his youthfulness, his silly desires, the foolishness of men.

But not tonight. Tonight Neil Partherton sat in her father's kitchen, and she had no time for children like John Tate. Neil was a man. A virile, mature, masculine man. What delights she could find in his embrace! What fun to tantalize him until he begged for her favors. With a man like Neil she might even be persuaded to give them. He was not simply another man to entrap, but someone for whom she felt a genuine longing. She had never before wanted any man so much, and she was determined to get him. She would do it too, if only she could get her straitlaced sister out of the way long enough to get him to notice her.

Running up the path, she threw open the front door, calling for Sarah. The parlor was empty, so she hurried to the kitchen, certain they would be there still talking to her father.

"Papa? Sarah?"

The names died on her lips as she saw that the kitchen too was empty. Her eyes were drawn as by a magnet to the open door. She crossed the room to stand in the doorway, scanning the garden.

She opened her mouth to call Sarah again but then stopped. Perhaps it would be better not to call, not to let anyone know she was there. Walking cautiously, trying not to let her soft slippers crunch on the graveled path, she glided along, walking on the grass where it was possible. She was nearly to the river when she saw them, silhouetted against the lighter shade of the water, their dark forms pressed together so as to seem almost one person.

He was kissing her! Murmuring nonsense words into her ears! His voice, even from where she stood, was thick with longing. Her sister! His arms were encircling her, his hands roving across her back.

Quickly Darcy threw her hands up against her face, stiffling the cry that nearly escaped her lips. Hot tears burned in her eyes. How could Sarah do this to her? How hateful! How typical!

Her only sister had flagrantly led on the only man she truly loved, deliberately taking him away from her, probably for no other reason except that she knew how dear he was to her.

Through her tears she saw the two merged figures sway together in the intensity of their embrace. Choking back a cry, Darcy turned and ran soundlessly back to the house, through the kitchen, and into the dining room, where she slammed the door and leaned against it, the tears searing her face. I hate her! I hate her! she cried deep within herself. She won't get away with it. I won't let her do this to me. I'll find some way to win him, even if I have to kill her to do it!

Three

~

THERE WAS a mist off the river early the next morning. Its thickness hid the shapeless mass of the mountains on the other side and enveloped the huge old black willows in a gray shroud like massive ghosts. Their huge branches reached through it like splayed fingers searching for the absent sun.

The mist was damp on Darcy's hair as she wound her woolen shawl tightly around her head, drawing the edges high enough to obscure her face from inquisitive servants going about their early-morning tasks. Even so, by the time she reached the road to the village and turned toward the bridge she could feel the droplets on her skin. Near the bridge the gray mass of the woods made the fog seem even more mysterious. A cow bellowed from the barn near her house, and from far down in the village she heard a cock crow dispiritedly. In spite of the weather the birds were already about, cawing at each other, the seagulls loudest of all. She could just catch the distant soft splash of fish jumping in the river below.

In spite of the early-morning noises there was a disturbing stillness in the air. Darcy looked up and down the empty road, almost wishing she could see another human form and yet knowing it was better that she be alone. Satisfied there was no one to see her, she moved through the emptiness toward the small, ghostly cottage that stood at the end of the bridge.

Even when the sun was shining and the world felt normal, Maude Sackett's house had a look of mystery about it. In the half-mist of this gray morning, with its stillness and quiet it looked positively foreboding. Darcy pulled her cloak tightly around her face and forced her feet up the overgrown path to the door. The shaggy weeds and briars that old Maude cultivated to discourage company clutched at and tangled her skirt. Snatching her way through them, she stood at the small window beside the door and peered inside. The glass was filthy and partly covered with the tattered remains of a checkered curtain, but Darcy could just make out a dim pinpoint of amber light that told her Maude was up and about. For an instant she almost turned and ran, but then the image of her sister silhouetted with Neil Partherton against the night sky steeled her resolve and she stepped up to knock softly on the door.

A long pause was followed by the scratching sounds of footsteps inside the house.

"Who's there?" The voice that came from the other side crackled with age and animosity.

"It's . . . it's Darcy Reed. I want to talk to you, Maude. Please let me in."

The door stood silent and immobile. Darcy had decided her soft response had not been heard when the old woman's cackle came again.

"Darcy Reed. I've naught to do with you. Go away."

"Please, Maude. I must see you. I . . . I need your help. Let me in, please."

Creaking on its hinges, the door opened a slit. In the

darkness Darcy caught the glint of an eye staring out at her.

"Does your father know you've come to see old Maude?" said the rasping voice. "I'll wager not. Go home, young missy. Leave me be."

"I can't. I must talk to you. Papa will never know, I promise. Look. I've brought money."

Pulling her hand from beneath her shawl, Darcy opened her palm to reveal a silver coin. "It's yours if you will only help me. Please let me in."

The sight of the bright coin did what all her pleading had failed to accomplish. The door creaked open wide enough for the girl to squeeze inside, then swiftly closed behind her. Darcy glanced around uncertainly, a little appalled that she was actually standing inside Maude Sackett's little house. It was a place that she and her friends had wondered about, joked about, and sneaked glimpses at all her life. Now that she was really here, curiosity was overcome by fear, and she was almost too timid to look around. To be this close to Maude herself was an experience that at other times she would have crowed about. Now she could not tell a single soul that she had come.

In a movement so swift it caught Darcy by surprise, Maude reached out and grabbed the coin from her palm, holding it up to the light, then gnawing it between what was left of her teeth.

"Aye," she said, nodding in approval. "You must want advice badly. Did you bring more of these? Old Maude's advice comes dear."

Darcy hesitated. But if Maude really was a witch there would be no point in lying to her.

"I've one more. You can have it afterward."

The old woman chuckled, with a dry shaking of her thin shoulders that had nothing of humor in it. In fact, it was almost obscene, Darcy thought, allowing her eyes to drift a short distance into the room. Evil, like Maude herself. Like this room.

"All right, then. Come and sit down. I'll give you a moment, no more."

Maude hobbled over to the plank table that stood in the center of the room near an empty hearth. It was a matter of speculation in the village as to how ancient Maude Sackett actually was, but seeing her close like this, Darcy thought she must be ninety if a day. Her skin was wrinkled like a basket of old laundry; her clothes hung on her like a shroud. Her hair was thin and white and straggled from under a limp old-fashioned mobcap. Everything about her was sinister: fingers perpetually curved into claws; fingernails long and yellow; teeth mostly missing, and those that were left elongated and discolored. She hobbled, bent over in a perpetual stoop, her slippers sliding through the sand on the floor in narrow tracks. At the chair nearest the table she shuffled a scrawny gray and white striped cat off the seat and lowered her gaunt body carefully down, motioning Darcy to take the seat opposite. Darcy was barely seated before Maude reached out in a second swift gesture and pulled the shawl away from the girl's face. Gasping, Darcy sat back, her hands at her throat. Perhaps Maude was not as old as she seemed. A ninety-year-old could certainly never move that fast.

"Darcy Reed," Maude muttered, pushing the single candle closer to the girl to scrutinize her face. "I thought ye'd come to see me someday. I'm not surprised to find ye here."

As her courage returned, Darcy began to grow a trifle annoyed. "If you know so much about me why didn't you let me in right away?"

"Oh, and ye're a snippy little miss, aren't you? Well, ye'd better watch your tongue with me." Leaning across the table, she peered into Darcy's eyes. "They say I'm a witch, you know. Maybe I am. You'd better be careful what you say to me, then."

Darcy tossed her head and let her shawl slip farther down around her shoulders. She might be a little nervous, but she was never going to let this old harridan know it.

"Maybe you are a witch. I'm not afraid of you, even if you are."

Maude gave another of her low, evil chuckles, implying she was impressed.

"A saucy girl. I thought as much. I've watched you since you were a young 'un, you and your sister. She'd never come to see old Maude, but I always suspected someday you would. We're cut from the same cloth, you and I. I could always tell."

"Really, now!"

Darcy fought down an urge to flounce out the door. This was too much! Even if this old crone had no special powers, she certainly could never have anything in common with a respectable young girl like her. It must be another of her tricks.

"Look here, Maude. I've come to see you because I want your help, and I'm prepared to pay you for it. Do you want to give it to me or not? If not, I may as well go. There are chores waiting for me at home."

"All right. All right. No need to get on your high horse. I'll help you if it is in my power. And I fancy it is. You want something to do with love, don't you? There is some gentleman whose interest you want to win, and you need old Maude to help you. That's what this is all about, isn't it?"

Darcy attempted to hide her surprise. "How did you know that?"

Maude swept her bony hand across the planks of her table as though she was spreading unseen cards. "I could say I had the gift of 'sight,' but there's no need. Even an idiot with no more sense than Jamie Earing could guess that was the reason you'd seek me out. What else do young girls care about?''

This little gesture of honesty where tricks would have been so easy won Maude a slight touch of respect from the young girl sitting at her table. Darcy looked more closely at the old woman, noticing for the first time that the ancient eyes held a glint that was perhaps more intelligent than evil.

"Well, if you don't have sight, then how can you help me? I'm wasting my time.''

"I never said I couldn't help you. Maybe I have something better than sight. Knowledge." She tapped the table with her claw of a finger. "Sight is only tricks and guesses and suppositions. Knowledge is much more—experience, truth, science.''

"You? A scientist?" Darcy scoffed.

Anger flared in the rheumy eyes. "There's all different kinds of science, young woman. I don't need sight to see that you are going to have a difficult time accumulating knowledge. But enough. I'm not accustomed to visitors, and you've interrupted my breakfast. State your business and be off.''

At Maude's little outburst of annoyance, shades of supernatural vengeance rose before Darcy's superstitious eyes. She hurriedly assumed a slight stance of humility and respect.

"I mean no disrespect. All I want from you is some kind of a potion or a charm. Something that will make a young gentleman love me and not my—not someone else. Can you give me one?''

"A love potion? Of course. I can't guarantee it will work for you, but it is as old as time, and it has worked for many others—Cleopatra, Helen of Troy, Madame Pompadour—they all knew and used it. It is a secret recipe passed down from generations of conjurers, gypsies . . .'' She leaned closer into Darcy's face and grinned. "Witches!''

"Is it dangerous? Darcy asked fearfully, straining away from the woman's sardonic grin. "How do I use it?"

"Oh, a little mixed into his drink will do it. I'll give you a charm, too, to say at night just before you go to bed. Guaranteed to keep him tossing in his bed, dreaming of you."

"What is the potion made of? It's not poison, is it?"

"Now, why would I give you poison? It's made of herbs and the pollen of flowers and a powerful root from Cathay, ground very fine. An aphrodisiac that drives men wild with desire."

Darcy stared at the old woman, wondering if this old hag was having some kind of joke at her expense. Yet she seemed serious enough. She had heard of ginseng and pollen and powerful herbs—they all sounded so plausible. She reached in her apron and took out the second coin, laying it on the table.

"Here. It sounds like just what I want."

After leaping at the first coin Maude now looked contemptuously down at the second. "You can give me that when you come to get it. I'll have it ready for you by tomorrow morning."

"You mean you want me to come back here again?"

"No. I'll leave the jar in the grass outside my door. You can leave the coin under a loose stone in the doorstep."

"But . . . you'll trust me to do that?"

Maude gave the nearest thing to a genuine laugh. "If you don't, I'll change the spell, and when you use the powder you'll get a result that you'll wish you hadn't."

The woman and the girl looked into each other's eyes, each measuring the other.

"You don't know whether to believe me or not, do you, young miss? But I think you'll want to leave the money just in case. No need to provoke the witch now, is there? She just might be able to do all she says she can."

Dropping her eyes, Darcy shrugged. "Well, I should hope so. After all, that is why I came to you."

Rising, she pulled her shawl up around her face once more. Maude gave no sign of showing her out, so she turned and walked to the door with as much dignity as she could summon. Her hand was on the handle when she heard the woman speak her name again. She turned to see her studying her quizzically.

"What's the matter?" she asked.

"What does a girl like you need with potions?" Maude said. There was no artifice in her manner now, and no trickery. "You could get a man with a snap of your fingers and a toss of those curls. You'll have a long line of them mooning after you before you're as old as I am. What do you want with herbs and aphrodisiacs?"

Darcy could not meet her gaze. The bitterness she felt last night at seeing her sister in the arms of the only man she loved was too searing. Too painful.

"The only one I want doesn't want me," she muttered. "But I'm going to make him want me somehow. Some way."

Maude studied the way the young eyes narrowed with hate and the lovely face grew hard.

"Posh! What's one when you can have forty? Perhaps he already has his mind set elsewhere. Leave him be and look further. There's plenty more to console you."

"You don't know what you're talking about, old woman!" Darcy said angrily. "I'll thank you to leave that potion where you said you would. You'll have your money. And you can keep your advice to yourself."

Throwing open the door, she ran out, hearing the cackle of Maude's laughter behind her.

Sarah had gone around the house all morning buoyed by happiness, feeling as though her feet were barely touching the floor. She longed to throw open the window and call out to the world that she and Neil were in love and were going to be married, yet she knew it was wiser to keep that delicious secret to herself for the time being. She would have liked to confide in Darcy at least, but on the two occasions when she came across her sister that morning, she found her sullen and uncommunicative, "in one of her moods," Sarah decided. When she could finally stand the solitude no longer, she put together a few more articles that the Stoakes family might find useful, tied her hat under her chin, and set out for the Tates' house.

As it turned out, sitting in the Tates' pleasant front parlor listening to a distraught Mrs. Stoakes was not the answer for a girl whose inner joy threatened to overwhelm her when she remembered the night before.

"I declare," Anetje Stoakes said for the fourth time, "I simply don't know how we're going to manage. Everything! Everything gone! All the effort of years, destroyed in an hour. What would you do?"

"I'm sure I don't know, Mrs. Stoakes," Sarah said sympathetically. "But you know that your friends will help you all they can."

"Oh, yes, I know that. But it's little enough they can do when so much is lost. They might have left us *something*. Why, they stole everything of value before burning the house, so between the two, we've nothing but the clothes on our backs. Nightclothes, at that!"

"Now, don't you fret, Anetje," Elizabeth Tate said, patting her hand. "We've extra clothing enough for you to get through these last days of summer, and by the time winter comes, I'll wager that among all the folks in this village you'll have woolens to see you through that season as well."

"Yes, but I'll be so beholden . . ."

"Now, just stop that," Elizabeth scolded kindly. "If Christian people can't help each other when one of them is

in need, then what are we all about? You'd do the same
for any of us.''

''We have some extra cloth stored at home. I'm sure
Papa won't mind giving it to you for the children,'' Sarah
added.

''My poor children! Why, Robert has had nightmares
for two nights in a row. They'll never get over this.''

Sarah sought mentally for some other subject she might
introduce to take Anetje's thoughts off her troubles, but
since the moment she walked in no other subject seemed to
be able to divert the woman from her grief. It was under-
standable but not very pleasant for a girl whose happiness
was overwhelming.

''I'll never get over it,'' Anetje went on lamenting.
''They might have left us something. Everything! My fine
silver candlesticks. The blankets and quilts I'd worked on
for years. Even Mr. Stoakes's psaltry. I think he feels
worse about that than anything. It was his grandfather's,
from Holland. A family treasure.''

''Sarah,'' said Elizabeth, ''won't you have another cup
of tea?''

Sarah, who was feeling more depressed by the minute,
took the opportunity to indicate she would be leaving.

''No, thank you. I really must be going. I promised
Deborah I'd stop in.''

''Such a shame to call this stuff tea,'' Anetje said,
ignoring Sarah. ''Loosestrife leaves! A poor substitute
indeed. How I used to enjoy my little cup of Bohea of a
night.''

''Why, there has not been any real tea in Cole's Landing since early in the war,'' Elizabeth said with indignation.

''I know. I hoarded what I had on hand when New York
fell. Made it last, too, by only enjoying a small cup now
and then. But that was burned. . . .''

She turned away, dabbing her handkerchief to her eyes.
Taking advantage of her grief over the lost tea and

Elizabeth's outrage at the hoarded contraband, Sarah made her departure. Once outside, the sunshine seemed a little less bright than when she had gone in, but that image was dispelled by the time she turned down the path to the Millers' ordinary, and her good spirits were restored. Now, if only she could find Deborah in a good mood!

Deborah Miller was in one of the public rooms, polishing glasses. In one corner two gentlemen were bent over a backgammon board, intent on their game. Young Davey was playing with a wooden spoon and mortar bowl at his mother's feet. Otherwise the room was empty, Sarah was glad to see. Sweeping off her hat, she flounced up to one of the Windsor chairs, greeting Deborah with a shining smile.

"You look like the cat that swallowed the canary," Deb Miller commented. "Did your father bring you back something nice from Fishkill?"

"No, nothing like that."

"Well, something has put a gleam in your eye. I'm glad you're here. Perhaps you'd take this child out in the garden for me for a while. He's driven me wild this morning. Under my feet every minute, getting in the way just when I've so much work to do."

"Why don't you ask one of the servants to watch him?"

"But they're busy themselves. You've no idea how much work is involved keeping a place like this going, Sarah Reed. Not all of us are fortunate enough to be a lady of the manor, leaving the work to our slaves."

"Nonsense, Deb. You know we don't have any slaves. Nor a manor either."

Deborah folded the towel and sat down beside Sarah. "Forgive me. My irritation has made me rude, and with you so happy with the world too."

"I forgive you," Sarah said, smiling. "But I warn you that having just come from listening to Anetje Stoakes sob in her kerchief I cannot take any more gloom. So be nice, or I shall flee back to my house."

Deborah enfolded her son, who had clambered to her lap the moment she sat down.

"I'll try. It's just that I have so much to do."

Sarah reached over for Davey, who willingly went into her arms. "I'll take him outside for a while. We always find pleasant things to do, don't we, Davey? Bring your little bowl and we'll fill it with flowers for your poor, overworked mother."

"Mrs. Miller . . ."

A tall gentleman stood in the doorway, beckoning to Deborah. Sarah looked up, noticed that he was a stranger, and turned back to Davey, who was pulling on her linen kerchief.

"Oh," Deborah said, jumping up and smoothing her apron. "Yes, Mr. Popham. Can I be of service?"

The man walked into the room and Sarah took the time to scrutinize him, from the top of his white-wigged head to the expensive cut of his velvet coat and buckled shoes. He swept off his hat and made the two ladies an elaborate bow.

"May I introduce Sarah Reed?" Deborah said. "Mr. Popham from the manor of Rensselaerwyck, up near Albany."

"And just arrived in your charming village," Popham said graciously. "So pleased to make your acquaintance, Miss Reed."

"You'll likely be seeing Miss Reed and her sister, Darcy, very often if you stay in the Landing long," Deborah added. "They live at the other end of the street, near the bridge."

"Though I am only here briefly on business," Popham said to Sarah, "I do hope to get to know some of the inhabitants of the town. So interesting, these little river communities."

"Do you come down here often, Mr. Popham?"

"No. This is my first visit. I hope to go on to Peekskill with a view to shipping produce from my farm in Rensselaerwyck. I was told they have a very decent harbor."

"Yes, they do. I have an aunt who lives in Peekskill and have visited her often, so I am familiar with the place. It would probably suit your needs better than our little Landing."

"Perhaps, perhaps. Forgive me for taking you away from your friend, Mrs. Miller, but I wonder if you might have a look at my accommodations. I think I would prefer to be in the room across the hall."

"Oh. Well, of course, whatever you wish. I'll come up with you. Excuse us, Sarah."

"Of course. I'll stay here and play with Davey."

She watched them leave, wondering what a visitor of Popham's obvious wealth and elegance was doing in Cole's Landing. He was sure to be a sensation if he stayed long enough to attract attention. Most gentlemen of his stamp never did.

"Good morning, Miss Reed."

Sarah looked up to see Hendrick van Tassel entering the public room, Andries Stoakes close behind him. Suppressing an urge to flee with Davey into the garden, she smiled and nodded and exchanged a few pleasantries with the two men. She still found it difficult to like van Tassel, after he had hounded her father into Newgate prison, yet since Nat's conversion to the cause of liberty he had treated her with the utmost respect and amiability. She reciprocated with a cool politeness.

Andries slumped down at one of the small tables, drumming his fingers on the top.

"Where's Miller?" he asked. "A man needs a glass in a public room, and there's no one about to serve him."

"I don't know where Noah is, but Deborah will be back in just a moment," Sarah explained.

"Well, it's a nuisance," Stoakes went on. "Come all the way from West Point and can't even get a glass."

"Now, now, Andries," van Tassel said. "Patience. I'm sure Deborah Miller will serve you as soon as she returns, as Miss Reed here says. It'll do you good to sit a moment."

Sarah, whose ears had pricked up at the mention of West Point, reached for a wooden spoon to occupy Davey's hands.

"You were at West Point this morning?" she asked offhandedly.

"Yes. I rode up to Fort Putnam to see about getting some help for rebuilding my barn and house. And little enough I got for it too, in spite of all Partherton's fine words."

"You spoke to Lieutenant Partherton?" Sarah added shyly.

"Not this morning. Yesterday. Today it was that Colonel Green. And he wasn't half so interested in helping me rebuild as the lieutenant had implied he would be. A few men, a little wood. 'But you can't rely on us too much,' he said. Not rely on them, when it was their carelessness in not finding and catching this Ferris Blunt that lost me my house in the first place!"

"Now, Andries," van Tassel said consolingly. "You are just feeling low at the moment. You'll get the help you need to rebuild. I promise it. We good patriots are well aware of the fact that it was your devotion to the cause that brought this calamity upon you. We won't let you starve because of it."

Andries gave van Tassel a murderous look. "Humph! Damned army, anyway. Always complaining about what they don't have. Well, they've got guns, haven't they, and powder? Why don't they just go on down there and chase Clinton out of New York and back to London and let us live in peace. Now they've even got the Frenchies to help them and still they do nothing."

"I'm convinced that our general would like nothing better than to strike a blow at New York," van Tassel said. "But you must remember how difficult the circumstances are. We are lacking terribly in supplies. The British have been uncommonly successful in the south, and Arnold's treason last year had a dreadfully demoralizing effect. But I'm convinced that in the end we shall triumph, because the cause of liberty and justice is the right one. You'll see."

"If I don't starve to death before it happens," Stoakes muttered.

"Now, you know we are not going to let you starve."

"Good day, gentlemen," Deborah said, breezing back into the room. "What can I get for you?"

While Deborah set about supplying the two men with rum toddies, Sarah took Davey's chubby hand and ushered him out into the garden, where she set him digging at a sandy spot with his wooden spoon and bowl. The insects buzzed around her head, and the sun was warm on her arms. She was glad she had not had the chance to speak of Neil to Deborah. Somehow her joy might be lessened by sharing it with these people who had such large, overwhelming problems. She would hug it to herself a while longer, keeping it her secret delight, sharing it only with that one person who was its source.

Dearest Neil. When would she see him again?

Four

❧

ALL THE following week Sarah waited anxiously for word
from Neil, hoping every day to see him come riding up the
path, and telling herself when he did not appear that he
must be very busy with his duties at the fort. Then, at last,
a courier on his way to the cantonment at North Castle
stopped by the Reed house to inform Sarah that Neil would
be over around noon of the following day. This news
caused a flurry of activity on the part of all three occupants
of the house. Sarah began at once to wash her hair and
spruce up her prettiest dress. Darcy slipped away to ponder
the best strategy for slipping some of Maude Sackett's
potion into Neil's drink. And Nat let it be known to his
daughters that unfortunately he had already made plans to
be away, so they would have to entertain the lieutenant
without him.

To Nat's relief this news seemed not to dampen his
daughters' enthusiasm in the slightest. Early the next
morning, several hours before Neil was expected, Nat

stepped into his fishing dingy and had Cato, his Negro
servant, row him across the river northward to a point
above Fort Putnam. An outcropping of rock there made a
natural dock, which was often used by the men from the
village who came hunting in the thick woods that made
these mountains so impenetrable and so full of game. He
wore his round felt hat, carried a leather powder bag, and
rested his long musket slung across his shoulders—a picture of a typical country gentleman off for a day's hunt.
Leaving Cato to watch the boat, he began the long, wearying climb up the side of the bluff. It was hard going, for
the woods were composed mostly of a thicket of small
trees intertwined with brambles. Several times he had to
stop, cursing a body that seemed to grow weaker every
year. For Cato's benefit he once or twice took desultory
aim at a small animal, startling a rabbit or a squirrel. The
gunfire blast resounded through the mountains and was, he
felt sure, reassuring to the servant waiting at the dock.

As he worked his way inland he knew the sound of his
gun was growing fainter, a dim echo among the trees.
After nearly two hours of climbing he finally heard what
he had been listening for the last hour—a thin echo of
another gun off to the right. Veering in that direction, Nat
walked for another thirty minutes before the sound of a
fox's cry stopped him again. It was very close and too
regular to have any but one meaning. Cupping his hands,
he made an answering call of four sharp yelps, repeated
three times. In only a few moments a form materialized
out of the woods, so soundlessly that Nat was very nearly
caught unawares.

Without saying a word Nat rose and laid his musket
over his shoulder to follow his guide back through the
thick underbrush. They walked for ten minutes before
emerging into a clearing in front of a sharp face of sheer
rock, cleft nearly in two parts, with an opening just large
enough for a man to squeeze through. Laying the handle of

his gun on the ground, Nat rested against it as the man he had come all this way to see emerged from the shadowy opening in the rock. It was amazing he could slip through it; he was so huge and thick. His face, like the rest of him, was oversize. But his eyes were pinched and narrow and had the mean, hard look of a predatory animal. The heavy jowls, the thick lips, and the stubble of black beard covering half his face did nothing to soften these fierce eyes. He stood, feet spread apart, hands on his hips, studying Nat where he leaned on the long barrel of his musket. His mouth was not exactly scowling but not smiling either.

"Hello, Ferris," Nat said, still breathing hard.

"God's eyeballs, you look as though you're going to pass out in the dirt right there where you stand. What an old woman you are, Nathanial Reed. I never thought I'd see it."

"You think it's easy to get up here to this godforsaken place! I've been climbing nearly three hours with barely a rest. If I don't get back by dusk I'll have Cato calling out the regulars at the Point to search for me. It's a hard trip."

"Posh! You're just an old woman. All right, old woman, sit yourself down here and rest. Hey there, one of you louts bring my friend Nat here a cup of ale. And hurry about it."

Nat lowered his body onto a puncheon standing wobbly before a cold campfire while one of the shadowy figures lounging nearby went scurrying off. He had never gotten to know the men in Ferris's entourage, and he had no wish to. They all had that ferrety look of outlaws and scoundrels, which most of them actually were. They lived in sufficient fear of their leader to get out of his way when someone from the outside world came to visit. There were not many men who knew how to find Ferris Blunt's forest retreat, and those who did were friends of Blunt's—if a man like Ferris could be said to have friends.

Nat himself would not have called Ferris a friend. More

like an acquaintance whose usefulness was important to the cause they both served.

Ferris slumped on a boulder opposite Nat, saying nothing until his lackey emerged from the cave with two tankards of ale. Then, when they were left alone, he took a long swig from the cup, rubbed his arm across his mouth, and leaned forward, his elbows on his knees.

"So. What is important enough to bring you all the way up here?"

"Something's afoot. I'm not certain what it is, but it's important. And it just may involve my house."

"What makes you think so?"

"A friend of my girls', one of the officers from Fort Clinton, stopped by the other day expressly to see me. Wanted to know if my house would be available for a secret meeting of some sort. Of course, I said I would be happy to accommodate him."

"Of course."

"He asked about that old passageway between the house and the river."

Ferris's head rose like an animal on the scent. "I thought no one knew about that."

"Evidently there are rumors. It was once well known in the village, but it hasn't been used in so many years I thought it was forgotten. Obviously I was wrong."

"That's a devil of a thing to be wrong about now! What did you tell him?"

"That it was blocked up and had been for years. I think he believed me. At least he didn't question it."

"Is this 'officer' the kind of man who would go snoopin' about?"

"I don't think so. He's young, and besotted with one of my daughters besides. I doubt he'd be suspicious enough to go searching.

"Which daughter? It had better not be Sarah or I'll tear his eyes out of his head myself!"

Nat squirmed uncomfortably on the bench. "No, no. I think it's Darcy. You know her—she's a little flirt if ever there was one. Wraps every young man she sees right around her finger."

"Well, I suppose that's all right." Draining the tankard, Ferris leaned back, resting one powerful arm on the rock and stretching out his thick legs. "What could be up now? It has to involve the frogs, since they're scattered from hell to breakfast all over Westchester. An attack on New York? Clinton expects it anytime. He's convinced that will be Washington's next move."

"And it probably will be. What else can he do? He doesn't dare leave the Hudson unguarded, and now he's got the French to help him. It has to be New York."

"Aye, but when? Old Clinton would give a pretty penny to know that."

"We may just be in a position to tell him if this meeting involves what I think it does. There'll be money in it too. I'd lay my soul on it. Washington's ragtag rabble is next door to throwing down their arms and lighting out for home, and it's only hard specie that will keep them with him. He knows that, Rochambeau knows it, and Congress knows it. So if there is anything afoot, it will have to involve money. And no small amount, either."

Ferris smiled. "Aye. And it would be nice to get our hands on it, wouldn't it just. I'd have old Clinton right where I wanted him, for sure, eating right out of my hand. And when the war was won, I'd be lord of the manor around here. I'd have enough to buy half these mountains, those that Farmer George didn't grant me out of gratitude."

"Humph," Nat scoffed. "It's not the money I want; it's an end to this war. And the right kind of end. Loyalty to England and the King."

"And a good thrashing for a few self-righteous Whigs who threw you into jail, too, I'll wager."

"I've got those Whigs where I want them now. Why,

they think so highly of me, the Committee on Conspiracies has agreed to let me stand surety for Christian Weiss.''

''What's Christian got himself into now?''

Nat shrugged. ''The usual nonsense. But you can be assured that the Committee would not accept me if they weren't convinced I'm as true a patriot as can be found up and down the North River.''

''All the same, a little vengeance never hurt a man.''

''You'd better hope your words don't come back to haunt you. I know a number of fellows who want nothing so much as to take a little vengeance out of your hide. Why did you have to burn Andries Stoakes's farm anyway? An unimportant little no-account like him. You could have taught him a lesson without going so far.''

Ferris glared and spit to one side of Nat's bench. ''Mangy little river rat! It was no more than he deserved. He only turned in Thomas Collins to keep his own neck out of van Tassel's noose.''

''Since when are you so sympathetic to Quakers? I thought you had nothing but contempt for them and their peaceful ways.''

''I do have contempt for them. The bastards won't fight. If it was left to them this war would never end. But even cowardice is better than a man who would sell another man to save his own skin. Besides''—Ferris grinned, if the nasty crease that fell across his face could be called a grin—''Andries had it coming. I owed him for that time in seventy-four when he wouldn't hire me to help bring in his crops.''

Nat shook his head. ''Folly! You take revenge for your old grudges and call it done in the King's name. It has made you hated up and down both sides of the North River.''

''It's made me respected. And feared.''

''That's not respect, Ferris, no matter what you may think. Just watch that you don't get caught. There is not a group of men within thirty miles who would bother with a trial or a jury. It's vengeance they want. Nothing more.''

"Bah! I'm not afraid of Whigs. Besides, how could they ever find me? Would you if you hadn't known the way?''

"No. But you cannot stay holed up here all the time. I know you take risks, not just at night but in broad daylight. And it's not as though the British were going to protect you if you did get caught. They consider you just as much of an outlaw as the Whigs.''

"Maybe so, but they're glad enough to get the information I bring them. If this meeting turns out to be what I think it may, I'll have something very important indeed to pass along.''

Nat sat reflecting in silence while Ferris walked back to the cave and brought out a pottery jug of ale, refilling first his cup then Nat's. Nat shifted on the plank bench, feeling some of his strength returning after the long climb. He would allow himself an hour's rest; then it would be time to start back, at least most of the return trip downhill. He took a swallow of the ale and glanced over the edge of his cup to see Ferris studying him.

"And what about Sarah?'' Ferris said, his voice actually softening. "What's she doing? How is she?''

Nat shrugged. "Why, she's the same. Just as pretty, just as gentle. She keeps all of us on a steady keel. Not like Darcy, with her flighty ways. I never know what that girl is going to get herself involved in next.''

"I've been thinkin'.'' Ferris abruptly sat up, elbows on knees again. "After this war is over I might settle down. Use some of the gold I've accumulated to buy a fine manor house further up the river. I'd need a wife, and it suits me to think of your eldest daughter. What do you say?''

In a nervous gesture Nathanial Reed smoothed back the frizzled hair of his wig, hoping the wide sleeve of his coat hid the expression on his face. He was not surprised. He had expected Ferris Blunt to make an offer for his daughter for some time. The problem was how to answer. This was not a man to take rejection. And when offended, he was likely as not to strike back in ways that Nat did not wish to think about. On the other hand, the idea of this gross, mean-spirited, violent man with his lovely, gentle daughter was enough to make the gorge rise in Nat's throat.

The silence was beginning to grow heavy. "Why, I haven't thought about it at all," Nat said guardedly. "Sarah is—well, she's the one who keeps us all going. I'll miss her sorely when the time comes for her to marry. But it's too soon for that, and things are too unsettled."

"Yes, but we could have an understanding. I'd like that. Not that anything would take place for a while, but one day when this business is all settled and I'm a rich man, she'd come to me. Meantime, if another man so much as looked at her . . ."

"Come now, Ferris. That's not fair to Sarah. She's a young girl and very pretty. Let her have her time of flirting and enjoying her youth. We can always work something out after the war's ended."

Ferris glared at the older man. "I don't like it. I want it settled now."

"Well," Nat hedged. "I won't say yes and I won't say no. Why don't we give it a little more time? After all, you can't even press your suit, since you can't show your face in the village. And as I remember, the times she's been around you she did not seem to be favorably impressed."

"That's because I didn't have anything then. I do now— more than I ever dreamed of having, and that's not going to be all of it by any means. I'll accept your yes and we'll let it go at that. Meantime, you keep her away from those pretty boys that flock around her."

"I'll do my best," Nat said, feeling he had not handled

the conversation at all well. With any luck Ferris and Sarah would never meet until the war was over, and perhaps by then . . .

"You'll stay and have some dinner," Ferris said without a touch of hospitality in his voice. "It's cold. Can't risk a fire." He smiled with a thin satisfaction. "In fact, it's some of Andries Stoakes's smoked ham.

"I'm obliged," Nat muttered.

"Oh, and speaking of Stoakes—there's a bag in the tunnel near your cellar. It's full of old Andries's keepsakes, some pieces of silver and pottery. Not much but probably worth something. I left it there for the next trip. Put it away, will you, just in case someone goes snooping around the tunnel."

"Was that wise? I don't expect anyone to see it, but I'd hate to for anyone to find a link between you and me and the raid on Stoakes's farm."

"Then hide it better. You can manage that much for an old friend, can't you? I'll pick it up the next time I'm down." Ferris reached out and slapped Nat on the shoulder with his paw of a hand. "And now, come and have some of Andries's ham. He'd want you to enjoy it."

When Sarah thought about Neil arriving later that day she could barely contain her happiness. All week she had been consumed with a private joy that seemed to separate her from anything hurtful or unpleasant in the world. She was not ashamed to admit to herself that such happiness was long overdue. It had seemed to her sometimes that ever since that dark day years ago when her mother had died so suddenly of yellow fever nothing had gone right. Her only sister, always a changeling child, had grown more strange and unmanageable with every passing year. Then the rebellion had begun and her father had been carried away to languish for nearly a year in a loathsome jail, leaving them to get along as best they could in a

neighborhood where half the people who used to be their
friends now abused them as traitors. That situation was
eased when Nat returned to take charge of his house and
fields once more and to convince his Whig friends of his
new patriotism. When the young men from the Continental
cantonments began to frequent their small village she had
entertained visions of dances and teas that would liven up
the quiet Landing, but that never happened. And it was
just as well, as it turned out, for Darcy's behavior seemed
to invite scandal. She was certain that had there been many
social occasions, it would not have been long before they
were no longer invited.

Then, just when she was resigned to a spinster's life in a
backwater village, a fort had been built across the river
and their dock began to be frequented by officers and their
men going back and forth between the fort and the post in
Gallows Hill. And one day Neil Partherton had ridden into
the village to be rowed across to the Point. She had been
sitting on a bench in front of the Millers' tavern just as she
had a week ago when he returned from Andries Stoakes's
farm. He had smiled at her with such kindness that nothing
had been the same since. And now she knew that he loved
her, just as she had loved him from that first moment. It
was almost more happiness than her poor heart could bear.

The only cloud to darken her joy was her concern for
her sister. It was not difficult to see that poor Darcy had
developed a young girl's infatuation for Neil, and Sarah
only hoped that when she learned of his love for her,
Darcy would not react too strongly. She was a headstrong
girl with a dark side to her nature that Sarah had seen many
times before; if only she could overcome her jealousy and
rejoice in her sister's happiness, Sarah felt certain her joy
would be complete.

By the time Neil rode up to the house in the early
afternoon Sarah had changed her dress twice and combed
her hair three different ways. She greeted him at the door,

feeling there was nothing more she could do to make herself any prettier, and the loving admiration in his eyes told her she was right. He stepped inside, looked quickly around, then gathered her into his arms and kissed her warmly. Sarah's arms went around his neck and her body melted against his. When he finally released her, she stood back, breathless and glowing with happiness.

There were no words spoken as they stood there, drinking in each other's face, smiling that secret smile of all lovers, until Darcy's call from the kitchen brought them back to an awareness of where they were. By the time they heard her quick steps in the dining room they were standing apart, composed and calm.

"Won't you come into the parlor, Lieutenant Partherton?" Sarah asked, smoothing down her dress. "Papa is not here today, but he ordered us to give you his apologies and to entertain you in his place. And he ordered *you* to have a pleasant visit with his daughters."

"That is an order I shall have no trouble complying with," Neil said lightly as he turned to give Darcy a polite bow. "Good morning, Miss Darcy. You are looking very well today."

It had no meaning beyond polite formality, Sarah knew, but it disturbed her to see Darcy's quick reaction. Her color heightened; her eyes grew bright, glistening like polished ebony. She bobbed a curtsy in Neil's direction and flashed him a brilliant smile.

"How kind of you to say so, Lieutenant Partherton. I am feeling very well, thank you."

"Come into the parlor," Sarah said, taking Neil's arm and leading him into the pleasant, sunny room. "We want to hear all about the things you've been doing. How is the war going? Have you visited the French camp yet?"

"I'm afraid my life is sadly dull," Neil answered as he took a chair near the window. "No, I haven't seen the Frenchies yet, but I expect to next week when I go down to Greenburgh. As to the war, it goes on as always. Nothing decided, nothing changed.''

"Your life has to be more exciting than ours," Darcy said with an edge of bitterness. "I declare there cannot be a more dull place on the face of the earth than Cole's Landing. Nothing ever happens here. Mercy me, Lieutenant, but you do look thirsty. Can I fix you a nice cool drink? We have some excellent perry, which we just opened. I'm sure you would find it most refreshing.''

"No, thank you, Darcy. I'm really not thirsty at all. Perhaps later.''

"Papa has gone hunting," Sarah said, sitting opposite Neil. "He planned the trip before he knew you would be stopping by, so he asked that you excuse him. He does so enjoy trekking the highlands, looking for small game. And, of course, it adds to the pleasures of our table. He always returns with several pheasant and a squirrel or rabbit or two. He enjoys Brunswick stew, so I always make him some after one of these trips.''

"It sounds delicious. I hope someday I shall be invited to share it with him.''

Sarah felt her cheeks grow warm under the blatant admiration in his gaze. "Next time, I promise.''

"Sarah is an indifferent cook," Darcy said, pulling up an upholstered footstool and sitting down at Neil's feet. "But she does make an excellent wine from pears. It was some of her perry that we just opened. I'm sure you would love it.''

Neil could not tear his eyes from Sarah's face. "I'll wager it is excellent.''

"Are you certain you won't have some?''

"Some? . . .''

"Some of Sarah's perry? I'll be more than happy to get it for you.''

"Oh, well, all right. I'd love some, thank you, Darcy.''

"Let me get it," Sarah said, making as if to rise. It

made her uncomfortable to know how much Darcy wanted to impress Neil, now that she and Neil had declared their secret love for each other.

"No, no!" Darcy cried, jumping to her feet. "I offered, and I shall bring it. You two just sit here and talk. I'll be right back."

She was out through the door before Sarah could protest. Settling back in her chair, Sarah watched her sister leave and wondered at her strange behavior.

"Sometimes I think I shall never understand Darcy," she muttered.

As soon as the door closed Neil reached for her hand. "She's just young and flighty. She'll settle down as she grows more mature."

"I hope so. She worries me at times. Her judgment seems so poor."

"My love, let's not spend our few precious moments alone talking of Darcy." He was down on his knees before her, taking both her hands and pressing them to his lips. "Oh, Sarah, I love you so. When can I speak to your father? Soon, please. Let it be soon."

"But Neil, I . . . I haven't thought. Should we tell Papa now? Isn't it too soon?"

Neil sat back, keeping tight hold of her hands. "I want to marry you now, today, but I know it would not be fair to you or to the cause I serve. Sarah, this accursed war drags on and on, yet I don't dare take a wife until I know how it is going to end. It would be so unfair to you. I might have to leave at any time. And if there were a battle, I might never come back to you at all. I won't make you a bride just to leave you a widow."

"Neil, Neil. Don't say such things. I don't want to hear them."

"But they're true. And they stand in the way of our happiness together. But at least let me speak to your father, and let us have a proper betrothal. Then I won't have to worry about another man spiriting you away."

"As if any man could." She laid her palm against his lean cheek. "You are the only man I will ever love. If I cannot marry you, then I won't ever marry. So you see, you mustn't talk about dying and leaving, because if you do, you condemn me to the life of a spinster."

"That could never be. Oh, my love, I wish this war were done with. I wish we could marry tomorrow."

His arms slipped easily around her, and he laid his head against the soft swell of her breasts. Sarah leaned her cheek against his hair, closed her eyes, and savored this special moment.

"Dearest Neil. I am so happy just knowing that you love me that I can wait for a while. If we were to marry right away, I don't think my poor heart could bear so much joy. Now," she said, breaking away from his encircling arms, "go and sit in your chair so when Darcy comes back we shall look all proper. I don't want her to know yet."

"Why not? I thought sisters were always the first to share secrets."

"No," Sarah answered gravely. "Not until we've told Papa. Then I shall tell Darcy at . . . at the right moment. Neil, do you really think the war will drag on much longer?"

Reluctantly Neil pulled himself away and back to his chair. "I don't have much hope of its ending soon. Although . . . there just may be something decisive soon. Something that might be helpful to my career as well. I cannot tell you about it yet, but suffice it to say that it could be important to our future as well as to the future of our country. But so much depends on other men that I almost dare not hope."

"The French?"

"Yes. The French, General Washington, Congress, even

General Clinton in New York. But the outcome depends as much on blind luck as on the wisdom of men. Even that wretched Ferris Blunt keeps us dancing to his tune, and we cannot stop long enough to catch him.''

"Ferris Blunt! Ugh, I hate that man. I've always hated him!"

Neil's eyes widened in surprise. "You know him?"

"Years ago he worked for my grandfather just before the mine closed. He was very young then, yet he was just as ugly and gross as now, with awful eyes that leered at everyone—including me. I could not stand him. He used to try to stroke my hair and kiss me, as young men sometimes will do to children. Ugh! It was revolting."

"Did your father know him too?"

"Papa? Yes, they went hunting together, I believe. But that was long before the rebellion began, and I haven't seen him around here in years. He wouldn't dare show his horrible face in Cole's Landing now. Not after all the terrible things he has done."

Neil was anxious to ask her more about Ferris when the door swung open and Darcy backed into the room, carrying a tray with three tankards and a plate of cakes.

"Here we are," she said in a cheery voice as she set the tray on a table by the window. Very carefully she handed each of them a mug, then pulled up the stool and resumed her place at Neil's feet, cradling her own glass in her fingers.

"Your health," Neil said, gesturing to both girls in turn. The perry had a strangely bitter flavor, which he supposed was due to the fact that each household made it differently. Still, it was tasty, and he found he was thirsty. He emptied his glass quickly.

Darcy chattered about the camp at Fort Clinton, asking him questions about his quarters and the food they ate, while Sarah sat quietly sipping her wine, unable to take her eyes from Neil's face. Nearly an hour passed before

Neil finally rose to leave, rejecting a second glass, which Darcy seemed most anxious to foist upon him. He wanted to ask Sarah more about Ferris, but she was called away by one of the servants just as Darcy was handing him his hat. He grabbed at her hand before she left, kissing it, trying not to let the love in his eyes appear too obvious. When she was gone he walked with Darcy out to the large black willow tree where his horse was tethered.

"How do you feel?" Darcy asked, slipping her hand through his arm and looking up into his face with an expression he could not fathom.

"Why, very well."

"It was lovely to have you stop by today. I do hope that you will come again very soon."

"I promise I shall. At the first opportunity."

"Did you like the perry? Did it cause you any . . . any unusual sensations?"

He could not imagine what she was talking about and was growing more annoyed by the moment that it was Darcy and not her sister walking with him to his horse.

"It was very good. Very fine. And I think that by now, after five years in the army, I can hold my liquor tolerably well."

Darcy stopped, looking up at him, her small face serious.

"That's not what I mean. How do I look to you?"

"Why, you look lovely today. I told you so before."

"Oh!" Suddenly one small arm went around his neck and she reached up to kiss him on the cheek.

He stepped back, startled. "Why, Darcy. That was kind of you, but perhaps not . . . not . . ."

Darcy stood staring up at him, waiting expectantly. When he slapped his hat on his head and turned swiftly to bound up into the saddle she stood looking after him, her face growing white.

"Good day, Miss Darcy," Neil said curtly, turning his

mount to clatter down the path toward the street. Behind him Darcy clenched her fists, rage growing like a gathering storm within her.

"Damn that Maude Sackett! Witch, indeed!"

Five

ॐ

IT WAS nearly eleven o'clock when Neil Partherton rode into the American camp at Philipsburg. He had been in the saddle since early that morning, and now all he wanted was to stable his horse, brush away the grime from his clothes, and find a bottle of good claret to wash the dust from his throat. To that end he headed straight for Major Harron's marquee. He could always count on Ian to have the best wine in camp.

This was his first glimpse of Rochambeau's army, and in spite of his weariness he was fascinated. He had deliberately ridden into the cantonment from the east so he could visit the outskirts of the French Soissonais camped nearest the Americans. His first impression was of their stunning uniforms—neat white coats with sky blue collars and yellow buttons and red lapels. Even their tents were a model of efficiency and order. After the casual confusion of an American camp, with its odd mixture of make-do uniforms, cots without mattresses, and threadbare tents,

Neil was amazed and encouraged to see that well-equipped allies were now at hand to help win the war.

After seeing to Sampson, he was directed to the marquee that Major Harron shared with three other officers. None were there when he entered, but Neil made himself at home anyway, washing up a little and stretching out on one of the cots. It was there that Ian found him when he threw back the flap fifteen minutes later and walked into the comparative coolness of the tent.

"You never know what an ill wind is going to blow in," Ian said, a broad smile on his face.

Neil sat up and stretched. "I hope that bottle is for me. I'm absolutely parched."

"It is, my friend," Ian answered, pulling out the cork as he sat down on one of the camp beds. Rummaging around on the floor, he retrieved a chest from underneath and took two glasses from a rack inside. "I've been waiting for you nearly an hour. It took you a devil of a long time to get here. Did you have any trouble?"

"No," Neil said, reaching gratefully for the wine. "Everything is rather quiet in the neutral ground now that our forces are stretched out across the southern perimeter. But General Howe sent me to Continental Village to deliver some dispatches, and that took me out of my way. I also detoured slightly just to have a closer look at our allies. I was impressed."

"You should be. They're a fine-looking lot, aren't they? They've done wonders for our morale. And they fight well, too. That little skirmish we had with the British boats at Tarrytown showed the lobsters they now have something to deal with. To Rochambeau," he said, lifting his glass.

"His health," Neil answered. "I'll gladly drink it. This is very good. Where did you find it?"

"It's part of a keg of claret sent to His Excellency by one of the French generals. He shared it with us. I tell you, Neil, since these Frenchmen arrived life has improved immeasurably. Not only are they well fitted out, but they appear to be extremely hospitable about sharing their largesse with their impoverished allies.''

"They must be shocked at the state of those allies.''

"Oh, I think appalled is a better word. You can see it in their eyes when they goggle at a detail lopping by, half of them without shoes, one uniform coat in ten. But we've earned their respect, nonetheless. They know we have the stamina to march fast and get by on very little. And we've some of the finest marksmen in the world. They've learned that already. And, God be blessed, their Comte de Rochambeau and our good General Washington have the greatest admiration and respect for each other. That is what will finally bring us victory, I'm convinced.''

"They haven't had any trouble working together, then?''

"No. They're as amicable as can be. Nothing at all like the British. Clinton and Cornwallis are so busy detesting each other and so afraid one will get the best of the other that they let golden opportunities slip right through their fingers. But come, you are going to take dinner with us, are you not?''

"I'd be honored.''

"Good. I told my good general there would be one more at mess. Finish another glass of this excellent claret and then we'll have a little walk. I don't think I want to go over the information I have for you inside a tent where you cannot see who might be listening on the other side.''

Neil smiled and reached out his glass for a refill. "I am tempted to say you are oversuspicious, but I know better. One can hardly visit the necessary house at West Point without it being relayed to the British in New York.''

"It's terrible, isn't it? We don't make a move without it being known. It's so bad that not even the officers have any idea what is being planned. We've been told so often that a decisive attack on New York is in the works that we're almost tempted to believe it will never happen. Yet the truth is, I don't think at this point even General Washington himself knows what we are going to do."

Neil drained his glass, rose to adjust his sword, and followed Ian out of the marquee down a row of smaller tents toward a small rise where young trees and shrubs grew fitfully around a huge rock at least ten feet across. In front of the tents men slouched, cleaning their muskets or tending cook-pots hung over campfires. These were the billets of the soldiery, or troops. The larger marquees of the officers, with their flags, pointed center spires, and fancier canvas, lay in the opposite direction.

Neil kept his voice low as he walked beside Ian Harron. "But His Excellency still wants to attack New York, doesn't he? I've been told he's been pressing for it from the beginning."

"He thinks it would be the wisest thing militarily, since it would force Clinton to bring back part of his army from the south. And, of course, our general would dearly love to retake the city and wipe away the stain of having lost it back in seventy-six, five years ago. Rochambeau thinks it would be wiser to attack Cornwallis in Virginia, but he insists he must defer to Washington's judgment. So, as you can see, we wait."

Ian did not speak again until they were beyond the tents and in the open ground near the huge rock. Skirting it, they headed along a stretch of thin wood interspersed with chinaberry bushes and occasional wild daisies.

"The problem is," Ian went on quietly, "that we cannot attack New York without the French fleet to support us, and no one knows where it is. Admiral de Grasse is rumored to have sailed from Brest with some twenty vessels and three thousand troops, but we've had no word on where he touched except the West Indies. His Excellency

has sent him letters urging him to sail for Sandy Hook—
you see, we have spies in camp also—but so far, nothing."

"He'll never do that. New York Harbor is too shallow
for the French men-of-war. Besides, there is a whole
British fleet lying at anchor there that would sail out to
engage him before he could even try. It sounds like a
dubious business to me."

"To me also. However, we are not the ones who decide
these things."

Major Harron was several inches shorter than Neil, but
he made up for his lack of height with a brisk step and a
ramrod stance that bespoke authority. Neil knew that in
spite of all his dark talk about deploring informers, Ian
Harron ran one of the most efficient spy services in the
entire Continental army. If Neil had not known him so
long—they had been at King's College together—he might
have discounted Ian's description of the situation as just
another set of rumors. Ian was one of the most likely
people in camp to know what was actually happening, and
unfortunately the situation he was describing was not one
to do away with fears that all this valuable French help
might be wasted. Like most American officers, Neil stood
in great awe of George Washington. Yet how many times
in this long struggle had a good general let a chance to
win slip through his fingers? It had happened so often that
it had almost come to be expected, especially with the
British.

Fifty feet beyond the first boulder they came upon a
second, even larger than the first but flatter on top. Major
Harron climbed it to the center, where he sat, knees crossed,
surveying the woods spread out below. Amused, Neil
climbed up next to him. Certainly no one could get within
hearing distance on this massive stone without being seen.
Idly he wondered how anything Ian had to confide in him
could be that important.

Pulling a linen handkerchief from the wide cuff of his sleeve, Ian Harron wiped at his damp brow.

"*Mon dieu*, but it's hot. There, they've even got me talking like one of them."

"Take care you don't pick up some of their other characteristics," Neil said teasingly.

"Why not? They know how to enjoy life. How to eat well, drink superbly, captivate the ladies—"

"I'll wager they made quite an impression in their fancy uniforms."

"A trail of broken hearts from here to Newport. Ah, but they deserve it. You should see the Duc de Luzun in his gold braid astride his magnificent charger. He was supposed to have been Marie Antoinette's lover, and it would not surprise me in the least if he was. He has only to flash that glittering smile and swagger across the room with a sword in his hand and the ladies swoon at his feet."

"Egad, I don't know how I will be able to return to the rustic backwoods of West Point after being exposed to all this civilized society. It's going to be unbearable."

Ian laughed. "Well, you will at least have a good dinner to console you. Now, my friend, let's get to the business at hand."

He drew up one leg, rested an elbow on his knee, and flicked his handkerchief at the dust on his boot. The heavy planes of his swarthy face took on a weary efficiency, as though the momentary lapses of frivolity never touched the gravity underneath.

Neil shifted his weight on the hard surface of the rock. "I should tell you that I've already found the place you asked for. It's a house on the river at the Landing. It has its own dock, though it has been unused for several years, and is far enough away from the rest of the village that a man could slip ashore unnoticed. Besides that, if it were necessary to hide somewhere, there is an entrance to an old mine around it—I've not yet been able to locate where, but I soon will. The owner is agreeable to its use. He has told me he will even take himself and his daughters away anytime we need it.''

"You mean Nathanial Reed, don't you?"

Neil nodded, and Ian ran a thin finger along his full lower lip.

"I don't know. Can the man be trusted? He was sent to prison once as a Tory sympathizer."

"Yes, but that was early in the war. Since then he has worked with great zeal for our cause. I know of no one who has done more to keep the garrison at the Point supplied than Nat Reed. He wants nothing to do with political intrigue any longer and is simply content to bring in cattle and grain from upstate to fill our depots. I believe he can be trusted."

"Your instincts are usually right," Ian said softly. "All right, I'll go along with it. But tell him only as much as you have to."

"Of course. His best quality is that he seems to want to know nothing more."

Ian leaned toward Neil and dropped his voice even lower.

"You've seen the sorry state of our troops. His Excellency fears we are going to have a repetition of last winter unless something is done very soon. The men of the line have gone so long without proper food and clothing that only one thing will keep them in the army now—a month's pay. Most of them haven't seen any hard money for three years. General Washington fears that without money they'll throw down their arms and march home now, just at the moment we need them most."

"Do you really think that is likely? The militia, perhaps, but the regulars? Most of the men I work with have some sense of loyalty even though they have been miserably treated."

"So did the mutineers of last winter. And remember,

they were regulars. But a man can only take so much. There is a feeling among us now that some kind of resolution is in sight now that the French have joined us. To lose our army now is unthinkable, especially when it would probably only take a month's pay to keep them in line.''

"Is there any chance they'll get it?"

"General Washington has written to Robert Morris in Philadelphia urging him to send several thousand pounds to make one payroll to the men. We have received word that it will be arriving soon. That's why I need your help.''

Neil leaned forward, all alert. "That's a fortune!"

"Yes. And if word of it got around, you can imagine how likely we would be to receive it intact. Somewhere between here and Philadelphia that courier would be way-laid and robbed. No one—I stress, no one—must know he is coming. There will be an escort, of course, but a small one so as not to call attention to itself. They will come by back roads and cross the river just below West Point, arriving at Cole's Landing.''

"Not King's Ferry?"

"No. That would be too obvious. It is our opinion that no one would expect such a huge sum of money to be brought across the river at an obscure landing, far above the most appropriate route.''

"I wonder that Congress ever agreed to send so much. They are usually far too parsimonious.''

Ian shrugged. "It was simply necessary. For this entire war we have gone in want of food, proper clothing, ammunition—everything needed to supply an army. It is my personal opinion that only General Washington's great stature has kept this ragged group together. While food was abundant all around us and boxes of clothing rotted on the wharves a hundred miles away, the states have done nothing to help us receive the supplies we needed. But this is the moment of decision. Whether the resolution comes in New York or in the south, it will be now or never. Congress at last has had the foresight to recognize that fact.''

"Very well. How can I help?"

Ian's voice was barely a whisper. "We will send you word when the courier and his escort are expected. It should be within the next two weeks. I want you to meet them below Fort Clinton, ferry them across the river to Reed's house, and there turn them over to an escort from this camp that will be waiting for them. We will arrive at the house separately or in pairs so as not to call attention to ourselves. That is why we need Nat Reed's house. But don't tell him that.''

"Of course not.''

"Just make certain that he and his family are well out of the way. I will send your orders to the commandant at Fort Clinton. I shall say that you will be escorting a small deputation from Philadelphia across the river, but only you will know the true nature of the group and how important it is to us. I will be counting on you, Neil, to get them safely across and into our hands.''

"I won't fail you, Ian. You have my word.''

Ian clapped a hand on Neil's shoulder. "I know you won't. Now, let's go and have that dinner I promised you. You may not eat so well again for many weeks.''

Dinner proved to be more than up to Major Harron's expectations. Neil found himself at a table with twenty-five covers, beef and lamb, vegetables and tarts, all washed down with Madeira, claret, and fine grum—a mixture of rum and water. He was more than a little startled at how well the officers ate when the men of the line were so in need, until Ian assured him that today's largesse was due to the generosity of the French and to some judicious foraging on the surrounding districts by the quartermaster's troops. He soon lost count of the healths that were drunk, and by the end of the meal he had decided to wait until morning to start back north. That evening he walked with Ian to the Soissonais camp, where he spent a lively evening visiting with several officers of the regiment, admiring their glittering retinues and exchanging questions about their respective countries. The Frenchmen were as curious about the cultural innocence of the Americans as the Americans were about the sophistication of the French. It amused Neil how Rochambeau's officers assumed that in wild, free America, untainted by centuries of feudal society, Rochambeau's "natural man" flourished in unspoiled innocence. He longed to tell them that there was just as much venality and arrogance in a natural man here as in any other place on earth. But he did not. They were too charming and hospitable; and besides, he thought, every man needs a dream. He simply enjoyed their vivid descriptions of Paris and of the tangled intrigues of the court at Versailles. He took his leave late in the evening and prepared to set off before dawn to return to the far more primitive society of West Point.

The day dawned gray and threatening, with dismal moisture weighing the air. Neil knew that by the time he reached Fort Clinton he would be soaked. He had no more than passed the Drover's Inn on the Post Road before the rain finally broke, pouring down in sheets to cloud the face of the hills around him. When he reached the river, it was tempestuous, whitecaps boiling in the wind, and the currents so strong they all but carried the boat past the wharf before the rowers could get him ashore. It was still early in the afternoon when he finally arrived at the fort, but the sky was so dark that it seemed much later. A thin stream of smoke rising over his quarters assured him there was a fire going, and after stabling a weary Sampson he headed straight for it, wanting only to strip off his wet boots and soaked coat and dry out in front of the flames.

When he stepped inside the log room he shared with three other men he was surprised to find it empty of all but one figure swathed in a dark blue cloak, sitting before the fire. Assuming it was one of his fellow officers, off duty and keeping dry, he began to pull off his dripping oilcloth cloak. "God's blood, I'm glad to be home," he muttered, throwing his cloak on a peg by the door and unfastening his sword belt. He shunted it onto his cot and headed toward the fire. His boots would be next.

But as he reached the hearth, the figure moved. Neil froze, his coat in his hand. "Darcy!"

The girl stood up, a short, slight figure swathed in the folds of the dark blue cloak. Her hair was limp from the rain, and the damp wool of her dress gave off a pungent odor where it had steamed by the fire. Her eyes were huge in her small face, as though she were afraid of how he was going to react.

"Hello, Lieutenant Partherton—Neil," she said timidly.

Neil was too stunned to speak. For a long minute he stared at her, not believing his eyes. He had never pictured either her or any other woman here in his quarters, and there was a quality of dreaming about seeing her here now. But she was no dream. She was very real.

"Darcy, what on earth—"

"I . . . I had to see you."

"How did you get here? What are you doing here? My God, this is terrible!"

Darcy looked around the empty hut. "They told me to wait here for you. They said it was all right."

"Has something happened at home? Sarah? Your father? They're all right, aren't they?"

Darcy's face slumped sullenly. "Yes, yes. They're fine. That's not why I came."

"But how did you get here? And in this weather!"

"I had Cato row me across. He's waiting over in the barracks. I told them I had an important message from my father, meant only for your ears. They believed me. It's not so unusual, you know. You and Papa are always sending each other messages."

"I hope they believed you," Neil muttered, uncomfortably aware that he was going to take a ribbing for this. He started to slip back into his coat, but it was too damp. Throwing it back on the cot beside his sword, he leaned closer to the fire, wishing he didn't have to deal with this problem at all. He was too tired and too wet; all he wanted was to get warm and dry and rested. What on earth was he going to do with this girl?

"Unfortunately, they were quite aware that if Nat really needed to send a message he would not send his youngest daughter with it."

Her chin lifted defiantly. "He might. In an emergency."

In spite of his irritation, Neil was amused by her audacity. "Yes, I suppose he might. We shall just have to concoct an emergency, then, won't we? Otherwise my reputation is going to be as besmirched as yours."

Darcy tipped her head and looked at him provocatively from under her thick lashes. "Does that mean you're not angry with me for coming?"

"Of course I'm angry with you. It was crazy! A respectable young girl of good family, coming alone to an officer's hut! Don't you care anything about your reputation? You'll be ruined."

Tossing her limp curls, Darcy resumed her seat on the bench. "Pooh. What do I care for my reputation? That's not important. What matters is that I had to see you, to talk to you."

"My dear girl, I am soaked to the skin, grimy after a long day's ride, in no fit condition to talk to anyone, especially an attractive young lady like you."

Her eyes grew round, dancing with light. "Oh, Neil, do you really think I'm attractive?"

"You know what I mean. This is hardly the time or the place . . . ." He threw up his hands. "Darcy! You should not be here!"

"My poor Neil, you *are* soaked," Darcy said, jumping up. "Here, come and sit before the fire. Let me help you with those boots," she added as she knelt in front of him. "You'll catch a chill for sure."

"Darcy, it's not proper. . . ." Neil's protests could not surmount his weariness and her determination. With the practice that came from years of helping her father out of his jackboots, she now eased Neil's feet from the stiff leather. He sat back on the bench, stretching his stockinged toes toward the fire, savoring its warmth. In a quick gesture Darcy slipped off her cloak.

"Oh, how I wish I had a warm drink to give you. That shirt. It's damp too. You really should change it."

"Darcy Reed, I am not going to remove this shirt!"

"Do your shoulders ache? Let me rub them. Papa says I have a knack for taking the tightness out in just the right places."

Before Neil could stop her she was behind him, kneading her lithe fingers into the tense muscles of his back. Her hands were strong for so slight a girl, and they felt so good that after a few moments Neil no longer wanted her to stop.

"Oh, my, you are stiff," Darcy murmured, massaging the sensitive tendons of his neck. "Papa says that hours in the saddle will do that to a man. That it is easier to walk twenty miles than to ride ten."

Neil leaned his head forward to better enjoy her relaxing ministrations, too weary to argue with her any longer. The fire crackled in the hearth, and for a few moments he was numb from the warm comfort of the otherwise silent room.

Then he suddenly felt Darcy's arms steal around his shoulders and the light, warm touch of her lips on the back of his neck.

"Oh, Neil," she sighed. "I love you so."

Abruptly he was yanked out of his lethargy. "No!" he cried, pushing her arms away and jumping to his feet.

Darcy ran quickly around the bench, throwing herself against him and clasping her arms around his waist. "I will say it," she cried. "I love you. I love you!"

He put his hands on her shoulders to push her away. "Darcy, this is insane. You musn't."

"I must. I came here today because I had to tell you. I love you, Neil. Only you. I have since the first day I saw you." Her arms went around his neck, and she rose on her toes to kiss him. Her lips were warm and inviting, and Neil found his determination wavering under the intensity of her body against his. He began to kiss her back, his arms tightening around her shoulders as he felt her insistent flesh grinding into him. Then, like a man drowning, clutching at a last hope, Sarah's face came clear in his mind.

It was enough. Violently pulling her arms away, he shoved her back.

"This has to stop, Darcy, or I am going to do something I do not want to do. Something you and I both would regret the rest of our lives."

"No! I won't regret it. I want it. I want to be yours, wholly, completely yours."

"You don't know what you are saying. You are young and infatuated."

She struggled to grasp him again. "This is not infatuation, Neil. It's love, true, warm, and complete. I'm offering it to you."

"You are being a foolish little girl," he answered, feeling more angry by the minute. He wanted her to go and was annoyed that she refused. And he was also a little disturbed by his own reaction to her wild kiss.

"Does Sarah know you are here? What would she think if she could see you carrying on this way?"

Darcy stepped abruptly back as though he had struck her.

"Sarah! Who cares what Sarah thinks? She has nothing to do with this."

"Oh, but she does. More than you know. I'm flattered that you have such strong feelings for me, and I wish I could return them. But the truth is, I am deeply in love with your sister and she with me. I cannot love you, Darcy, except as the dear sister of the girl I hope to marry. Can't you learn to think of me as a brother? A friend?"

Darcy's pretty face was suddenly transformed into an ugly, harsh scowl.

"Never! A brother! A friend! How could I think of you as either when I long for you with all the passion in my soul?"

Neil struggled to keep his voice level and calm. "In time you will. You are very young and could have any man you want. You'll forget me the first time some handsome dragoon rides through the village."

"I don't want any other man. I want you!"

Neil could see that she was about to throw herself at him again. Fending her off, he stepped to his cot and picked up his still damp coat, slipping it on.

"This is your youth speaking. Come now, I'll take you to Cato and see that you get safely back across the river. You must not be out too late in this weather. Your family will be worried."

Darcy stood in the middle of the room, immobile, as he picked up her cloak from the floor and draped it over her shoulders. For a moment she considered pulling away the laces on her jerkin and baring her bosom to him. But his firm, matter-of-fact manner told her that even then she would not win him over. He would probably just turn his back.

Neil brusquely tied the laces of her cloak and pulled the hood up over her hair. She would not look at him, but he was relieved to see there were no tears on her cheeks.

"I meant what I said, Darcy," he said, his voice kind. "I *am* flattered. And I assure you that no one will ever know what happened here today. You have my word as a gentleman."

Darcy's eyes flew to his, startling him with their icy fury.

"Gentleman! Bah!" With a quick movement of her arm she slapped him hard on the cheek, then fled to the door. Neil stood looking after her, torn between a desire to turn her over his knee to give her the spanking she deserved, and an irritated amusement at juvenile antics.

The little vixen. He hoped she got thoroughly soaked before she got home again.

Darcy's tears did not start until the boat was nearly up to the dock below her father's house, and even then she was not certain how much of the water streaming down her face was from crying and how much from the rain. The river had quieted but was still so dark and turbulent that Darcy found herself wishing the boat would capsize and she might drown her sorrows in its black oblivion. But Cato was an excellent boatman, and in spite of the bad weather he brought the small craft to the dock with a sure hand.

As they neared the shore, Darcy could make out a dark figure standing in the rain swathed in an oiled wool cloak and holding a lantern against the gathering dusk. Sarah! Her sister was prowling the bank, anxiously watching for her return. She would be all concern and kindness, Darcy thought, but it would do her no good. Already she had made up her mind that she would plead a chill and go immediately to her bed, talking to no one, least of all Sarah. She had to think, to plan. This disastrous day had proved that Neil Partherton was not going to be won by ordinary means and, quite possibly, was not going to be won at all. But her mind was made up about one thing. If she could not have him, neither would her sister. Of that she was absolutely determined.

Six

FOR THREE days without success Sarah tried to get her father alone to talk to him about Darcy. It worried her, the way her sister dragged around the house, ill-tempered and sullen, looking thinner each day. Sarah suspected that underneath Darcy's angry outbursts lay a very deep hurt, but all her attempts to draw out her sister's feelings were vehemently repulsed. It made her own happiness seem almost something to be guilty about, as though she had no right to her joy when Darcy was suffering so.

She longed to talk about the problem with Neil, but he was busy with his duties and not expected to visit them for another week. So she turned to her father only to find that Nat was preoccupied with worries of his own and convinced that his youngest daughter's moodiness was due more to her youth than to any other cause.

With Nat away most of the time and Darcy sullen and uncommunicative, life in the Reed house became more difficult as summer grew more glorious. A rare spell of beautiful weather brought to luxuriant perfection the last growth of corn and vegetables, the clusters of pears and apples in the orchard, and the grain nearly ready to be harvested in the fields. One fine morning Johnnie Tate appeared at their door ready to drive two barrels of flour to Continental Village and begging Darcy to accompany him on the ride.

"Why don't you go?" Sarah said. "You've had such blue devils lately; maybe it will perk up your spirits."

Darcy glared at her sister. "Johnnie Tate! Who wants to go anywhere with him? He's dull as dishwater and has pimples on his face. I hate him!"

"Well, perhaps he's not the best company, but it would do you good to get out in the fresh air. And Continental Village is a lively place, I'm told."

"What do you know?"

"Oh, very well then, stay home. I'll tell him you've got the headache."

Darcy jumped to her feet. "No. Wait. I'll go. Anything is better than sitting around here."

She reached for her bonnet, tying the strings under her chin as she looked at her reflection in the mirror. Actually she had been prepared to go from the first if only Sarah had kept quiet. Not that she didn't really hate Johnnie Tate—she did—but Continental Village always had plenty of young officers around, and she did enjoy flirting with them. Besides, she was tired of this house and her sister, too, whom she resented more every day. It was easy for Sarah to be a Goody Two-Shoes and Miss Pleasant. She would too if she had managed to get Neil to put his arms around her and kiss her the way she had seen him kiss Sarah that terrible night. Darcy's thin faced narrowed, looking back at her from the wavering surface of the mirror. She still had not found a way to win him away from her sister, but she would. Something would come to her, perhaps even today, riding to Continental Village. Something would come.

With Darcy out of the house, Sarah had a sudden burst of energy and set about some of the summer cleaning she had been putting off. It was a perfect day to wash down the root cellar, she decided, to clear out the last of the past year's storage, scour the stones, and lay fresh straw in preparation for the harvest soon to come. Commandeering Cato to help her, she started emptying bins and shelves, trying to ignore the unpleasant heavy odor of spoiled vegetables that lingered in the bottom of the bins. The heavy door was thrown back to let in the fresh breezes off the river and warm the dampness of the shadowed corners with bright August sunlight.

Cato had carried away the last of the spoiled foodstuffs in the bottom of the bins to the compost heap beside the barn when Sarah discovered the opening in the wall. She had pulled the largest of the empty bins away from the wall to sweep behind it when she noticed that there was a low wooden panel set in the stones. Curious, she ran her fingers around the edge and saw at once that it could be pulled loose. She worked it away from the opening just enough to peer into the dark recesses of some kind of hole. She felt a small thrill of excitement. Could this lead to the famous passageway that her grandfather had hewn out of the side of the hill when he started a mine here? How many times had she heard her father talk about playing there as a boy and wished that she and Darcy could have found it? Working the cover—no more than a few rough planks nailed together to form a crude partition, away from the stones, she threw it aside, stooped down, and squeezed her body through the opening. It was large enough inside for her to stand. The dim light from the cellar showed her that it continued on into the side of the hill. She would have to fetch a lantern if she wanted to move any farther into that inky blackness.

She started back into the cellar when her foot brushed an object lying to one side of the door. Cautiously Sarah moved her hands over what seemed to be a sack half filled with a lumpy assortment of odds and ends. Stepping back into the root cellar, she dragged the sack out into the daylight. It proved to be what she had suspected—a bag, filthy dirty and tied at the neck with heavy twine. More curious by the moment, she pulled at the cord and spread open the sack. A glint of brightness caught her eye. Reaching in, she pulled out a narrow, elaborately carved silver candlestick. Astonished, she rumaged around and found its mate. Kneeling on the ground, she upended the bag, spilling its contents on the floor and sorting through them. There were two books, both bound in red leather and expensively embossed with gold, a small lacquered box with a broken lock, a sheathed knife with a pewter handle, an assortment of tin and silver buckles, a small box containing bone, wood, and metal buttons, and an ivory comb, delicately carved.

There was a vague familiarity about some of these items. Sarah sat back on her heels, feeling a terrible panic growing inside her as she looked over the things spread out before her, all of them representing the valuable possessions of a modest household, probably accumulated with care over many years. She picked up the book, afraid to look and yet somehow sure of what she would find.

It was a copy of the Psalms written in Dutch. On the flyleaf was scrawled in fancy script: "Christian Stoakes, His Book."

Sarah threw the book down as though it burned her hand. Christain Stoakes! Andries's father was named Christian. Now she remembered those candlesticks. Once she had accompanied her father to the Stoakes's farm on business and Andries's stout wife had served her tea at the plank table in their small dining room. How often during that half hour when conversation languished had her eyes strayed to those same candlesticks standing in unused grandeur on the first shelf of the corner cupboard across the room from where she sat. All of these—the buckles, the buttons, the knife, and the books—had to be the treasured possessions of the Stoakes family carried off the night they were robbed and burned out. The lacquered box had probably held money, but that was gone with the wretched outlaws who had committed the crime. All of these things, more traceable and not so easily disposed of, had been hidden away until they could be safely sold. But how had they gotten here? And why?

Sinking to her knees, Sarah stared back through the empty hole that led from the cellar into the bluff behind it. A kind of sick sensation began to stir in her stomach, like the first warning of an illness coming on. Obviously this tunnel led somewhere, and Ferris Blunt and the the other men who had robbed Andries Stoakes knew of it. Obviously they were using it either as a means of getting to the river without being seen or else simply as a place to stow their stolen loot until they could dispose of it someplace else. But would they do that—*could* they do that—without Nat Reed's knowledge and consent?

The answer made her physically ill. Clenching her arm across her stomach, she struggled to find some other explanation. Ferris knew her father and had once worked for her grandfather. He might well be familiar with the old mine and, with his complete lack of ordinary decency, might have begun using it for his raids without saying anything to Nat. He could slip in and out of the root cellar without anyone in the house ever being aware of it. All he would need was someplace on this side of the river to stow his horses, and that he could easily work out with the families of the men who rode with him.

Surely her father would never be a party to Ferris Blunt's

brand of villainy. He was a better man than that. A better
patriot!

Yet he had not always been. At the beginning of the war
he had been such a devoted loyalist that he had gone to
prison for it. He had suffered during those months in
prison from the cold, the wetness, the lack of food. It had
left him an ill man, although he claimed now that it had
made him strong. The kind of men he found himself
imprisoned with—wealthy landlords and Anglican clergy-
men who wanted only to protect their living—had convinced him how wrong he had been. And since that time
he had worked tirelessly to help fill the commissaries of
the Continental army.

Was it possible that he was lying? That his resentment
of Hendrick van Tassel and the committeemen who had
sent him to Newgate would drive him to join forces with a
horrible man like Ferris Blunt?

There was nothing to do but to ask him. She would
confront him with the knowledge of her discovery and see
what he said. Until then it was better to put everything
back and pretend she knew nothing about it.

Sick at heart, she set to work so that by the time Cato
returned, the bin would be back in its place against the
opening in the wall, the sweeping done, and the straw laid.
Cato, she knew, liked to take advantage of Nat's being
away to get in some fishing in the inlet north of the house.
Ordinarily that meant keeping after him to finish the job at
hand. But not today, she thought, looking around the grim
little room. Today she would be as anxious as he to leave
this depressing place.

Late the following afternoon Sarah was seated on the
high, narrow bench of the hand loom when through the
narrow window she caught sight of her father striding
across the yard. Her hands paused as she watched him
enter the tack room adjacent to the barn. She waited to

make certain no one else followed him, then slid off the bench and ran downstairs and across the yard. Nat was sitting on one end of a plank table, working at a leather saddle girth with his jackknife. He was quite alone. Pushing open the door, Sarah stood on the threshold.

"May I speak with you a moment, Papa?" she asked, quietly closing the door behind her.

Nat looked up and smiled at his daughter. "Of course. Come in, my dear. You won't mind if I go on working while I'm listening, will you? I've been trying to get to this saddle girth all day. It's far too loose, and if I don't make some new holes I'm going to find myself on my back in the middle of the road someday."

Sarah leaned against the door, wondering where to begin. In his full shirtsleeves and long leather vest her father looked so handsome, so strong. She had always loved and respected him as a man of principle and honor. The thought that she might be wrong—that he might be just the opposite of honorable—was almost more than she wanted to face. Perhaps it would be better to turn and run, never to know whether her suspicions were correct or not. Yet she had to know, if for no other reason than that it was dangerous for Nat to be involved with a man like Ferris Blunt.

"You look so serious," Nat said, studying her face while his hands worked briskly at the tough leather strap. "It must be Darcy. What has that girl done now? I know she is a trial to you at times, Sarah, but she's young yet. She'll come around in time."

"It's not Darcy, Papa. I was going to have a talk about her with you, but then something else came up. Something much more important."

"What is it?"

Sarah took a deep breath. "Yesterday Cato and I cleaned out the root cellar and—"

Imperceptibly Nat's fingers stilled over the leather strap in his hand. Then he went on working without looking up.

"—and while I was sweeping behind one of the bins I found an entrance to some kind of a tunnel behind the cellar."

Nat waited silently.

"And?"

"And there was something in it. A bag. Full of . . . of things."

For the first time Nat looked up, meeting his daughter's level gaze straight on.

He knew! He was not going to pretend or deny anything. He knew!

"Those things belonged to Andries Stoakes, Papa."

"Now, how could you know that?"

"I recognized them. I remembered seeing the candlesticks in their dining room. And even if I hadn't known, I found his father's signature on the endpaper of one of the books. They were taken from his house, Papa, probably the night his farm was burned."

"Oh, Sarah." It was more a sigh than a statement.

Sarah felt the hot tears behind her eyes, and she fought not to surrender to them, knowing that the surest way to put her father off was to give way to hysterics.

Moving slowly and deliberately, Nat laid the girth aside. Getting up, he walked to the opposite corner of the room and stood fingering the bridles hanging on a peg there, keeping his back turned to his daughter's distraught face.

"You knew it was there, didn't you?" Sarah cried. "I hoped that you didn't know. That Ferris Blunt was playing one of his horrible tricks on you. But you knew."

Nat sighed. "Yes, I knew. It would serve no purpose to lie to you. I don't ever want to lie to you, Sarah. All the rest of the world, perhaps, but never you."

There was a rude bench formed of half a log standing

against the wall. Sarah let herself down on it, clenching her skirt, still fighting back tears.

"But why, Papa?" she wailed. "That terrible man! Why?"

He half turned toward her, his profile grim against the dark of the corner. "I'm glad you finally know, Sarah, and I'm doubly glad that it was you and not Darcy who discovered the tunnel. You'll do me a great service by not telling your sister about this."

"I wouldn't think of telling Darcy. She'd have it all over the village in a day. But I do wish you would explain it to me, Papa. Perhaps if I understood—"

"I'm not sure I understand it myself. All those months in that hellhole, my hate festered inside me like a sore. Van Tassel and the others of his ilk, sending men to be flogged or fined or shut up like criminals because their beliefs did not suit the ideas of some committeemen. God deliver us from all committeemen! Power-mad hypocrites, all of them. The only thing that sustained me during that long time was the thought that someday I would get even with them for the harm they had done me and my family. I swore anew every day I spent in that black hole that I'd have my revenge. It was all that kept me going until they released me."

"But you said—you claimed—"

He looked directly at her for the first time, and the depths of hate in his eyes froze the breath in her throat.

"I lied! I'd lie about anything to keep from being sent back there again. I'd lie to hold on to my home and my livelihood so that I can provide for you and your sister. I'll go on lying so as not to lose what I have, no matter which side finally wins. But I'll never forgive van Tassel or Tate or Brennon or any of the rest of those so-called patriots."

He slumped, as though the breath had gone out of him.

"When Ferris asked me for the use of my tunnel I was happy to provide it. I would never go with him to burn old

Stoakes's house, but I've nothing against allowing him the use of my place to come and go."

"But Papa, he's an awful man! A thief, a murderer—"

"I don't like him any better than you do, but I'll help him, because by doing so I reap some measure of vengeance on the men who very nearly destroyed my life. For the same reason I help the army—"

"Oh, no," Sarah groaned, remembering all the times her father had scoured the countryside for provisions. Remembering Neil . . .

"Hanging around the army, earning their trust, I sometimes learn useful information, which Ferris knows how to pass along to the right people. It just may help someday to end this rebellion and restore the King's peace. And that is my most fervent hope."

"But that makes you a spy and guilty of treason."

"Only in the eyes of those whom I consider traitors. There are others who would consider me more of a patriot than van Tassel will ever be. This is a civil strife, Sarah. There are nearly as many men against this rebellion as there are in favor of it, and there are many on both sides who are only out for what they can get for themselves. It blurs the lines between what is treasonous behavior and what is not. I don't consider myself a traitor. Spy? Well, perhaps, but for a worthy cause."

Sarah covered her face with her hands to hide her shame. What would Neil think? Neil! He must never know. Her eyes were wild when she looked back at her father.

"They would hang you, Papa, if they knew. It's too dangerous. Lieutenant Partherton coming here . . ." She had a sickening thought. "Are you using him too? Is Neil just another pawn in your game? Someone to pry useful information from? Because if he is . . ."

With maddening deliberation Nat walked to the single table in the center of the room and settled on one corner,

lightly raking the point of his knife against the rough
wood.

"I admit he was at first. But now I am beginning to be
aware of how much you both feel for each other, and I
don't want to use him unless it proves impossible not to."

"What do you mean?"

"Unless he presents me with an opportunity that I cannot allow to pass unused."

Sarah struggled to remember what Neil had told her.
Something about an important event that might make his
future and hers as well. She would have to find some way
to warn him not to confide in her father, though how she
was going to do that without telling him the truth she could
not imagine.

"Can't you try to forget what you've learned about the
tunnel, Sarah? Can't you just pretend you don't know of
its existence and ignore any suspicions you might have
about me?"

"I wish I could, Papa. My loyalties lie with Neil and
the army. But I love you, too, and I don't want to do
anything to hurt you. Promise me that you'll tell Ferris he
cannot use our house any longer. Please, Papa. Then I will
try to forget all this and pretend everything is as it was."

With a sudden motion Nat drove the end of his knife
into the table. "I'm not sure I can do that. Ferris is not a
man who accepts orders from anyone. Even if I asked him
not to use my place, he would probably pay no attention to
me."

"You must try—and you must succeed. There is simply
too much danger involved, for you and for all of us. Tell
him you are afraid for your daughters. Surely that would
reach him."

Nat gave a bitter laugh. "If he thought it might harm
you he would stop coming here in a minute, I'm certain.
He is quite fond of you."

Startled, Sarah stared at her father. "Of me? But I hardly know the man. And I've always disliked him."

"I know. But in spite of that he has an idea that you are the only woman for him. He hopes to marry you when the war is over. He told me so himself."

Sarah was so horrified at this that instinctively she jumped up from the bench, fighting an urge to run. "Papa! You didn't—?"

"No, no. Of course not. You cannot imagine that I would give a daughter of mine to such a man. Especially you! I was evasive with him."

"I wish you hadn't been. I wish you had made it very clear that I would never, ever consent to such a marriage. If he ever suggests such a thing to you again, you must state that firmly."

Nat did not answer, thinking it was best not to try to explain to Sarah how difficult taking such a position was going to be and how impossible for Ferris to accept. He'd face that later, when he had to.

Watching him, Sarah sensed something of his ambiguity, and she made up her mind that instant to tell him about Neil. Surely once he knew of her feelings for Neil and his for her, he would never allow Ferris Blunt to speak of marriage again.

"There is something I want you to know, Papa. I had not planned to tell you yet, because Neil wanted to speak to you first. Lieutenant Partherton and I are very much in love with each other, and he has asked me to marry him. Naturally it is my dearest wish that you will give your consent."

Nate gave her a sideways glance, a faint smile on his face. "I cannot say that I am surprised. I suspected matters were tending that way. You haven't made any definite plans, have you?"

"No. We decided we would wait until the war was settled, one way or another. We haven't told anyone, not even Darcy, because we wanted you to know first. But you can see this makes any idea of my marrying Ferris Blunt out of the question. You must make that clear to him if . . . when you see him again.''

''I'm glad you haven't told Darcy yet, Sarah. My advice to you is that you say nothing about this to anyone. If Ferris ever learns that Lieutenant Partherton has made a prior claim on you, it could possibly be very dangerous for him.''

Her eyes widened. ''Surely not. Why, that man has no right—''

''Ferris is not a man to be overly concerned about anyone's rights but his own. I'm just trying to be practical. Lieutenant Partherton seems a pleasant enough fellow, and, of course, I'm happy that you both care for each other. Your happiness means a great deal to me. But I think you are wise to wait until this rebellion is settled before making any plans. It won't hurt either of you to wait awhile.''

''No, I suppose not,'' Sarah answered weakly, resuming her seat. Her father seemed overly cautious, almost afraid of Ferris Blunt, and it put something of a damper on the great happiness she had felt over her betrothal. She had hoped to tell the world of her joy once Neil had spoken to her father, and now she could see that it might be months, even years, before she could share it with anyone else.

And yet the thought that Neil might come to harm through her was too terrible to contemplate. Such a thing must be avoided at all costs. The nagging suspicion that she was not going to be able to count on her father to help her avoid it made her even more anxious. Then she remembered what had brought her to the tack room in the first place.

''I promise I will not tell anyone of my relationship with Neil,'' she said, looking at Nat through eyes brimming with tears. ''But you must promise in return that you will do nothing to compromise Neil and that you will not let Ferris Blunt use our cellar for his terrible raids. Tell him it would harm me. Use my safety as the excuse. Use anything. But please, Papa, for your own safety and for Neil's, don't let him come around this house again. Make him stay away, please.''

He went to her, lifted her from the chair, and enclosed her in his huge embrace. Her arms slid around his neck, and she leaned against his firm body, feeling almost like a child again.

''I love you, Papa. So much.''

Nat laid his hands upon her shoulders and looked down into her lovely face.

''And I love you. Don't worry about me, Sarah. Just take care of yourself and your sister and think how someday you'll be keeping house for Neil Partherton. I'll handle the war and Ferris Blunt.''

Seven

❧

FOR SEVERAL days Sarah brooded over the conversation
with her father in the tack room. The idea that a man like
Ferris Blunt was using their house was bad enough, as was
the thought that he had somehow enticed Nat to work with
him; but both these things paled compared to the news that
he planned to make her his wife. Sarah went queasy at the
thought. She thought back to her childhood, trying to
remember how he looked, sorting out small details that
repelled her even as she strained to make them fresh in her
mind: the thick lips; the narrow, squinty eyes; the heavy
jowls that always looked as though they needed shaving;
the hands like hamhocks, with blunt nails, cut from
quick to quick, the flesh bulging above them; the greasy
look of his clothes; the heavy flab of his paunch.

Sarah shuddered, wondering what had ever given this
gross man the idea that she might accept him. She had
never been able to stand him to touch her—that much she
remembered vividly. He was violent, mean, and vindictive

and when crossed would strike without compunction. And she sensed, without Nat saying it, that that was what lay behind her father's ambiguity. He was afraid of Ferris. And when a man like Nat Reed was afraid, there had to be a very good reason.

Darcy had come back from her trip with John Tate more sullen and unresponsive than ever. Sarah, weary after three days of trying to be pleasant to such a bad-tempered sister, finally decided to walk into the village to spend the morning with her friend Deborah Miller. The Miller tavern near the waterside was the center of most of the town's gossip, and being there might help to take her mind off her own problems for a few hours.

Without bothering to tell her sister where she was going, Sarah threw her shawl around her shoulders, tied her straw hat under her chin, and started up the path for the road to the village.

As she neared the end of the path she saw Maude Sackett standing in her yard spreading some small clothes on bushes to dry. Accustomed to Maude's unfriendly silences, Sarah intended to pass by without so much as a nod. When Maude called to her, she stopped in the path in surprise.

"Good day, mistress," Maude cackled, bobbing up and down.

"Why, good day to you," Sarah answered, stopping in the road.

Maude took a few steps closer. "Fine day we have, ain't it?"

"Yes, it is. A fine day."

"A strong sun, a fresh breeze off the river. Good for the garden. Makes everything grow."

It occurred to Sarah that she had just heard Maude speak more words at one time then in all the years she had known her. Still wondering, she mumbled a reply as the old woman hobbled nearer.

"And how's that pretty sister of yours this fine day?"

"Darcy? Why, she's home. She's not been feeling very well lately."

"That so."

"Yes. She's had the blue devils something fierce this last week. But she'll come out of it. She always has."

"Give her a greeting for me, lass. Give her a greeting from old Maude."

The lines on Maude's worn face rearranged themselves into the suggestion of a smile. "Tell her I'd be obliged to have her come visit me. For tea. Yes, for tea. Tell her I ask about her, how she does."

"Why, thank you. I shall tell her."

"And tell her old Maude says that should she need any advice, she's only to ask. Magic doesn't always work the first time. Will you be sure to tell her that?"

Sarah nodded. "I'll be certain she gets the message."

"You won't forget, lass?"

"No, ma'am. I promise."

Maude's head bobbed up and down. Then, without any further word, she turned her back on Sarah and hobbled off toward the rear of her house. She was lost to sight almost immediately, hidden by the wide clumps of lilac bushes that grew in wild profusion around her cottage. Sarah watched after the old woman, still wondering that she had spoken to her and, still more, that she would have such a message for Darcy. She would not have thought Maude even knew who Darcy was. But then Maude was a strange old woman who probably knew more about all that went on in Cole's Landing than she ever let on.

As she stood looking after the old woman, her attention was caught by the rattle and creak of a wagon just coming across the bridge in front of Maude's house. At once she recognized the hunchbacked peddler who showed up every two weeks or so trying to sell his assorted wares to the housewives of the village. She was as little anxious to talk with this deformed man as she had been to spend time chatting with Maude, so she hurried onto the road and turned quickly toward the river, leaving the wagon to wobble along behind her.

The Green Man was a welcoming sight, dappled by the brilliant sunshine and surrounded by splashes of bright roses. Sarah found Deborah inside, scouring the round oak tables in the dining room. When she looked up and saw Sarah coming through the door, she quickly turned over her job to Annie O'Haram, the Millers' indentured servant, and ran to greet her friend.

"You can't know how happy I am to see you," Deborah said, picking up her sewing basket in one hand and grasping her baby's fat fingers in the other. "I've been looking for an excuse all morning to sit down and gossip. Let's go out in the garden, where we can have some privacy."

Sarah took Davey's other hand and they walked with the child between them outside into the garden, where they settled in the shade of one of the old chestnut trees, watching the play of light on the river and chatting aimlessly.

The garden, which stretched down to the water's edge, was cooled by a lazy breeze off the water. The tide flowed swiftly here through the steep sides of the highlands, working its way toward the great harbor of New York, thirty miles below. Its smooth quiet was broken by the constant splash of leaping fish, and its blue surface mirrored the clear sky above and the green borders of the hills on the western shore.

Although she was only two years older than Sarah, Deborah had been married to Noah Miller since she was fourteen and had long ago settled into the early maturity of a wife and mother. Working together, the Millers had taken the homestead where Noah's family had lived for two generations and converted it into a small tavern with a taproom, a dining room, and two bedrooms upstairs. Because the Landing was not large enough to attract much of the traffic crossing the river, their struggling business had come near to floundering several times until Fort Clinton was established at West Point across the Hudson. Since then, though overnight guests were still rare, their lower rooms were often crowded with officers and their men mingling among the usual assortment of townsfolk. Deborah, who had finally presented her husband with a healthy son after two still births, felt that her life was at long last falling into place. She had come to know Sarah better after the birth of her child, and her liking for the reflective, mature girl with her serene beauty grew more every year. Now, as she watched Sarah staring out to where the tide slipped smoothly by, she was disturbed by the worry that lined her face.

"Is anything wrong, Sarah?" she asked.

"Wrong? No. Why do you ask?"

"Oh, only because you look so preoccupied today and not your usual cheerful self."

Sarah made a determined effort to smile. "I was only thinking about all the work that has to be done before the fall harvest is taken in."

"I'd wager it was not the harvest that brought that faraway look to your eyes. You wouldn't be in love, would you?" Deborah said teasingly.

"Now, what would make you think that?"

"Oh, I've seen the way that lieutenant goes all self-conscious every time you're around him. He's the picture of confidence until he gets near you, and then he begins to tremble like some lovesick calf."

Sarah ducked her head to hide her eyes. "That's nonsense."

"Well, you may call it nonsense, but it just shows how little you recognize your own power. He's such a handsome gentleman. I declare, I quite envy you."

"Deborah Miller! What a thing to say. And with Noah still hanging on your every move as he does."

"Oh, no, we've been married far too long now for Noah to pay me any mind at all. All his waking thoughts are centered on this tavern and, of course, on little Davey, since he hopes to leave it to him someday." She gave a long sigh. "I'm just his housekeeper."

Sarah glanced up to catch the mirth in her eyes.

"Oh, Deborah, you're such a tease!"

Giggling, Deborah reached over and patted her hand. "Every woman should be as unhappy as I am," she said, contentment shining in her face. "But at least I got a smile out of you. I had about given up hope of doing that much today. Oh, look. There's that peddler's wagon just pulled in. How fortunate. I'm desperate for a new mortar and bowl. Come with me?"

"I don't think so. I'll just stay here and watch Davey."

"I won't hear of it," Deborah said, taking her hands and pulling her to her feet. "Come along. Perhaps he has some ribbon, and that will perk you up better than anything. Here, Davey, love. Come to Mama."

Although Sarah had a vague uneasiness about being around the unpleasant, misshapen man who drove the wagon, she gave in to Deborah's managing ways and, taking one of young David's plump hands, walked with them to the wagon. Even the peddler's poor horse looked defeated, standing and sagging as though grateful for a few moments' rest in the shade.

"Good day to ye, ladies," the man said, smiling and covering his mouth with his hand as if to hide his bad teeth. "Have some needs this morning, do ye? Wooden bowls? Fine tin pans? Just come and have a look. Don't cost nothin' to look, I always say."

Sarah ran her hand along the horse's smooth neck, patting it in what she hoped was a comforting gesture. Deborah began at once sorting through the congestion of pots and bowls hanging from the sides of the wagon, haggling over the price as only a woman used to running a struggling business can do. Still holding tightly to Davey's hand, Sarah ambled toward the rear of the heavily loaded cart, where there was usually a tray of silks and ribbons. A cursory glance told her that its contents were of poor quality and much damaged by the sun and dust.

At that moment she glanced up to see the peddler's eyes boring into her face. The intensity of his look was startling, but even more disturbing was a sudden flutter of recognition that made her stomach turn over. She knew this man. There was something very familiar and very unsettling about those eyes. When Deborah began asking him questions he looked away, and Sarah, her attention caught, was able to inspect him more closely. She peered at him as her mind sorted through memories, darting back and forth until in one horrified flash of recognition it shot home.

Ferris Blunt! There was no doubt about it. The grotesquely misshapen back did not fit, nor did the beard and the long, dirty hair, and least of all the syrupy, obsequious manner. But she remembered those eyes all too well, devouring her with that same undisguised leer. Perhaps if she had not discovered that terrible bag in the root cellar she would not have recognized him. Had she not had that conversation with her father, or had she not been trying consciously to recall what he looked like and how he acted toward her, then today she would have seen only the deformed peddler of other days. The disguise was good enough that she had never seen beneath it before. Nor had anyone else, so far as she knew. She peered closer at him, straining to strip away the mask with her eyes, wondering even now if she could be wrong—

No. She was certain. It had to be Ferris Blunt. Pulling at her hand, Davey began to cry for his mother. Deborah walked over to pick him up, grasped her purchases in her free hand, and started back inside the tavern to get her money. Instead of following as she would have done a few moments earlier, Sarah stood hesitantly beside the wagon, barely breathing, fussing with the limp ribbons on the tray while the peddler shuffled his way to her side.

"And is there something here you would like, my pretty miss?" he said, all good humor and eagerness to please.

Sarah could not look at him. Keeping her voice very low she muttered, "I know who you are."

"What was that, miss?" he said, bending toward her.

"I know it's you, Ferris Blunt, underneath all that disguise. I recognize your eyes."

"Well now, missy, I think the blue would be very pretty. Very suitable for a lady of your coloring. And quite reasonable, too."

Sarah finally met his gaze straight on, seeing at once that although he pretended not to understand her, his eyes showed he knew exactly what she was saying.

"Stop pretending! I know it's you, and I need to talk to you. It's very, very important."

Ferris reached out and rummanged around the tray as though looking for something, bending closer to Sarah. The heavy stench of him almost made her turn away.

"Where?" he whispered. "When?"

"Before you leave the village," Sarah whispered back, looking around to make sure that there was no one in hearing distance. "By the black willow on the river behind Reverend Tate's barn."

"I'm going to have a little dram inside first, for appearance's sake. I'll be there in half an hour."

Deborah came bouncing back toward them down the walkway between the trellised roses and wisteria. "No, I don't think I want any today," Sarah said, raising her voice. "The color is not right. Perhaps next time."

"I'll have some new colors with me the next time I drive around, missy," Ferris said in an unrecognizable voice. "You save your pennies and you'll find just what you want."

"Now, if you two have finished with the ribbons, perhaps I can get back to my wooden bowls," Deborah said cheerfully. Ferris turned away to help her, and Sarah walked back under the trellis of the tavern walkway, keeping her back to the two people haggling by the wagon. She felt sick inside, and her knees were trembling so much that she had to grip the trellis to keep from swaying. Yet at the same time she felt that this was such a piece of luck as she never dreamed could happen. She had almost no hope of her father dealing with Blunt—she could tell that from the way he hemmed and hawed about the matter just talking to her. Now she would be able to settle it herself, face to face with the horrible man. It was a blessing she would never have even thought to pray for.

Fifteen minutes later, claiming that her head ached from the sun's glare, Sarah left Deborah and made her way to the Tates' old barn. Since it was one of the few buildings that stood near the river, where the rocky bank was impractical for fishing, she hoped it would afford her the privacy she needed to talk to Ferris Blunt. As she strolled across the thick grass, she was relieved to see there was no one about. The black willow standing only a few feet from the edge of the bank was so large that she felt sure if she sat directly in front of it no one would see her, should they bother to look at all. Leaning her back against the rough bark of the trunk, she gazed out at the water. The sun's dancing pattern on its silver surface did indeed make her eyes ache—fate's retribution for her little lie. She was so anxious to help her father that the moments seemed to drag by, yet when she thought of facing Ferris Blunt—openly arguing with him, pleading with him—she wanted only to get up and run to the safety of her house.

When finally she heard his shuffling walk, she steeled herself to stand her ground for her father's sake. He came up to her without hurrying, as though enjoying the serene beauty of the day. When he got close he doffed his battered round hat and for a horrified moment looked as if he was about to plop his deformed body down beside her. The anxiously aloof glare she turned on him seemed to change his mind, and instead he stood with one hand propped on the tree for support.

"You're a clever lass," he muttered in a low voice. "Many a time I've come through this village, and no one has ever recognized me before today. How did you know?"

"Never mind that. I want to talk to you about my father. I know he has been helping you. I found your bag with Andries Stoakes's belongings in the tunnel behind our root cellar."

That seemed to surprise him. "Clever indeed," he muttered, rubbing a finger along his broad nose. "Or maybe just too curious for your own good."

"You must stop involving him in your schemes, Mr. Blunt. You could get him into a lot of trouble. He has suffered enough already."

Before her eyes he seemed to change. The disguise was still there, but the real man oozed through—his authority, his brute strength, his cruelty. Sarah could almost see the Ferris she remembered as she watched him.

"Now, I don't hear Nat sayin' anything about not being involved. In fact, he's been a willing helper right along. Who is it, do you think, supplies the information I need to strike in the right places?" Ferris gave a low, humorless chuckle and continued, "Why don't you ask your father who it was that told me about how Andries Stoakes set that high and mighty Committee onto Quaker Thomas? Who gave me the information last month about—"

"Stop it! I don't want to hear any more. If Papa did tell you those things it was because he resents it so that the Committee sent him to prison. But you must understand

that if they ever find he's mixed up with you after what
he's already been through, he could even be hanged.''

"We could all be hanged. In fact, I think old van Tassel
would much rather see a noose around my neck than
Nat's, given the choice.''

Sarah threw a look at him that said she would prefer it
too.

"I need Nat Reed," Ferris went on, his voice quiet but
hard. "Between us we are helping to keep this devilish
rebellion at bay.''

"Rebellion!" Sarah spat out the word. "My father may
believe that what he is doing is for a worthy cause, but
you—all you want is the stolen loot you take from innocent people. And some kind of horrible satisfaction from
hurting them.''

Ferris's dark little eyes went cold as winter ice. "Those
be strong words, missy. I wouldn't stand here and let
anybody else in the whole world say them to my face. It is
only because of my regard for you—''

"And that's another thing." Sarah struggled to keep her
angry voice low. "Papa told me what you said about me,
and I want you to know that such a thing is absolutely out
of the question. I want nothing to do with you. Ever. You
must not think of me in that way at all, for it will bring you
nothing but disappointment.''

Her impassioned speech did not have the effect she
intended, for when she finally looked up, expecting to see
a forlorn lover, she found him standing there grinning
evilly at her.

"I mean it, Mr. Blunt.''

"Oh, I'm quite certain you do. But there's time yet to
change your mind. Plenty of time. For one thing . . .''

Sarah shrank back as Ferris actually leaned down and
squatted next to her.

"For one thing," he went on, his lips still smiling,

though his eyes were not, "we might strike something in the nature of a bargain."

"I want no bargain with you."

Hidden behind the wide bulk of the tree Ferris lost all shred of the peddler's obsequiousness. "Well, it appears that you have asked something of me—or, rather, demanded something. You want me to protect your father by not involving him in my . . . 'little schemes,' I believe was the way you put it. For my part, well, I would like to look forward to the time when you might change your mind about me."

She longed to scream "Never!" at him, but the thought of her father made her hold her tongue.

"Would you tell Papa that you don't want his help any longer?"

"Will you agree to marry me?"

He had swiveled on one knee in front of her so that her back was against the willow and she was imprisoned by his body. Glancing nervously to either side, Sarah saw a few fishermen standing by the dock, but so far away as to be out of hearing. She tried to edge to one side, but Ferris swiftly put out one arm against the trunk, pinning her in.

Trying not to meet his eyes, Sarah mentally turned over her choices. What he was suggesting was intolerable. But she needn't say that now. If she could make him think she would consider his proposition, it might at least buy her a little time—and in the meantime, her father would be safe. She forced herself to sit still, pushing back against the tree trunk so forcefully that the rough bark cut through the thin fabric of her dress.

"I cannot agree to marry you now. Things are too unsettled. The war and all . . . I'm . . . I'm still young. I want to enjoy myself for a while." She prayed that the revulsion that filled her was not too obvious.

"Is there some other man? Because if there is . . ."

The look on his face was enough to chill her blood.

"No. No," she said hurriedly. "There's no one else. Just harmless little flirtations."

"No flirtations. If you're going to be my wife, you'll keep yourself pure. Just let another man look at you the wrong way and I'll kill him with my bare hands."

He leaned close into her face. With his grotesque makeup, false beard, and lank hair, his thick lips flecked with moisture, Sarah feared for a moment that she was going to retch. How had she gotten herself in such a position? All she had intended was to demand that he leave her father alone, and now here she was, making flimsy excuses as to why she couldn't marry him right away! The man was a monster with a fatal way of maneuvering people where he wanted them.

Reaching out a thick finger, he lightly stroked her throat. "We'll have an understanding, my girl," he murmured, his pudgy lips only a few inches away from hers. "We won't call it a betrothal yet, or cry the banns, but you and I will know it is all arranged."

Sarah felt a shudder go through her body at his touch. Turning her head to one side, she tried to blot out the image of that leering face.

"And my father?"

For an answer he suddenly gripped her chin, twisting her face around and forcing his wet lips against hers. She struggled to pull away, filled with shock and revulsion. When she began to feel his tongue flicking against her tight lips, trying to force them apart, panic took over. Twisting and squirming she shoved against him, pushing him off balance long enough to jump to her feet and run far enough away to be out of his reach.

"How dare you! How . . . how dare you!"

Ferris stared up at her, admiring the fury that made her fair skin pink and mottled. Then he laughed.

"Never touch me again! Do you hear? Never!"

The angrier she grew, the more it seemed to amuse him.

"Now, is that any way for an intended bride to speak? Come now. It was only a harmless little kiss. Why, some-day you'll be beggin' me for more."

This was hopeless. She was never going to save her father by pretending to go along with this creature. She would have to find another way.

"You vile man. I wouldn't marry you if you were the last man left on earth. I would as soon make a bargain with the Devil himself as with you. I'm warning you—leave my father alone or I'll find some other way to protect him."

Slowly Ferris rose to his feet. Now he was the peddler again, his body shriveling before her eyes, the hump on his shoulder growing larger.

"Why don't you go now and run to tell the Reverend Tate and the holy Mr. van Tassel that the terrible outlaw Ferris Blunt is here in the village? Go on. It would be quite a triumph for you, catching that black devil not twenty rods from your own door."

Sarah stood rigidly staring at him. She never wanted anything so much in her life as to act on his suggestion and bring the people of the town out to unmask this imposter. Yet she could not move.

"I'll tell you why," Ferris went on, grinning evilly. "Because I'd have old Nat up there swinging beside me before you ever knew what happened. Make no mistake, my beauty. Your father and I are together in this like two chickens in a pot. There's only one way to get me to help him, and you know what that is."

"I won't do it. Go on with your masquerade and your thievery and murder. I can't stop you. But I'll find some way to protect my father, and I'll do it without making an unholy promise to you."

She turned and ran, wanting only to put as much dis-tance between Ferris and herself as possible. Catching up her skirts to free her ankles, she ran, feeling her heart thumping in her chest and the wind hot on her face. She was not aware of crossing the path or of flying up the stairwell until she found herself standing against the door to her bedroom, gasping in long, deep breaths of air. She longed to rush to wash her face, hoping to blot out all physical traces of those horrible wet lips on her skin. If only there were some way to erase the memory from her brain . . . but she knew it would be there forever, coming on her when she least expected, to raise the hairs on her neck and send shudders down her spine.

She was scrubbing her face at the washstand when she heard voices below. A man's tenor followed by the hesitant murmur of Jurie, the housemaid. For one terrible moment Sarah feared that Blunt had followed her back to the house. Then she recognized the temperate tones of this man's voice as nothing like Ferris's cynical bass. Blotting her face with a towel, she walked into the hall and looked down to where Jurie stood in the entranceway. Behind her, standing on the front stoop, was the tall, shadowed figure of a gentleman wearing a long cloak and tricorn hat.

"I'll have to see if Miss Sarah will talk to you," Sarah heard Jurie saying. How like the girl. She could rarely handle the smallest question herself without looking for guidance from someone in the house, usually Sarah, since Darcy had so little interest in anything not directly concerning her.

"Who is it, Jurie?" Sarah called from the stairwell.

"Oh, Miss Sarah," Jurie said. "It's a gentleman to see Mr. Nathanial. Maybe you'd be good enough to speak with him."

Sarah hesitated, wondering if she was up to this. "All right. Ask him to step inside. I'll be down in a moment."

She stepped back into her room to smooth her dress and straighten her hair. Then she descended the stairs. The tall figure, with his back to the light, was indistinct in the shadows.

"Good morning, mistress," he said in a cultured voice. "I was told Nathanial Reed lives in this house. Is that correct?"

"Yes. This is Mr. Reed's house. I am his daughter, Sarah."

"Why, Miss Reed. Of course. Mr. Popham, ma'am," he said, sweeping her a rather formal bow. "William Popham from Rensselaerwyck. I have business with your father."

"Oh, yes. I remember you, Mr. Popham. We met once at the Green Man. My father is expecting you, then?"

"No. We've unfortunately never been introduced, though I have long thought an acquaintanceship might be profitable to us both. Since I was once again in the vicinity, I took the opportunity to call and introduce myself."

"Well, won't you come in, please, Mr. Popham?"

"Thank you, mistress. That's very considerate of you."

Sarah stood aside to allow Popham to pass by. Once he was standing inside he seemed even taller, his hat nearly touching the low ceiling of the entranceway. He swept it off at once, revealing a head of thick, wavy blond hair, pulled back and tied in a ribboned queue.

"May I just lay my cloak here on this chair?" he asked pleasantly.

"Of course," Sarah answered, walking past him into the parlor.

Motioning him to one of the crewelwork-upholstered chairs in the parlor, she took the opposite one.

"My father is out at the moment, but he should return soon. He is often away during the morning hours but is always back in time for dinner. Perhaps you would like to join us?"

Mr. Popham smiled at her while obviously mulling this over. He has a very pleasant face, Sarah thought, watching him. Perhaps it was just that right now anyone with a normally good disposition would look beautiful to her after Ferris Blunt disguised as a malformed peddler. But no. This gentleman did have a good face—long, lean lines, sculptured lips, expressive eyes that seemed to have an amused twinkle hovering behind their ice blue surface. It was an easy face to like.

"That is very gracious of you, ma'am. Perhaps I will stay, if you are certain it will cause you no inconvenience. I don't get down this far very often, and I did hope to meet your father."

"It is no inconvenience at all, Mr. Popham. You are from Rensselaerwyck, did you say?"

"Yes. Near Albany."

"That is beautiful country. I journeyed up the river with my father several times before the war began. It's curious. . . ."

"Yes?"

"Oh, nothing. I was just remembering that there were quite a lot of people of Dutch descent there."

"You are thinking I do not sound as though I came from that part of the country."

"Well, perhaps," Sarah said lamely, embarrassed that her thoughts were so transparent.

"You would not be the first to say so. You see, I traveled widely and spent some years in England before this rebellion broke out. Once it came to open war, I hurried home to protect my inheritance. My father was able to put together a sizable and valuable farm near the banks of the river, raising mostly cattle and sheep. I did not wish to see it all lost. That is why I am here today. I have been informed that Nat Reed is always looking for a source of beef and mutton to purchase for the army, and I think I can be of service in supplying him with what he needs. God knows the men are desperate enough for it."

He crossed his legs and touched his fingers together, making a pyramid, and looked at her over the pinnacle with a frank, pleased appraisal. At his mention of the army Sarah realized that something about him reminded her of

Neil. In fact, he was a lot like Neil. They would probably like each other if they ever chanced to meet.

"I am sure my father will be happy to know this, Mr. Popham. He spends a great deal of time searching for supplies and seeing that they get to the right place. He is devoted to the cause—the patriot cause."

She could not look him in the eye. Please, God, she thought, don't let it show that I am lying. If good people like this man ever learn that Papa is playing both sides . . .

"Tell me something about yourself, Miss Sarah. Have you lived here at Cole's Landing very long?"

Sarah murmured her response, gradually allowing herself to relax as she talked more about herself and thought less about her father and Ferris Blunt. William Popham was an expert conversationalist, and by the time half an hour had gone by and Nat Reed came swinging down the path toward the house, she was feeling more like her old self. When at last Popham was face to face with her father he became all business. Sarah politely left them to discuss cattle and sheep while she went to see to the laying of the table. By the time the two men concluded their affairs and withdrew to the dining room for dinner, Darcy had also come in to join them. Sarah sat next to her sister at the highly polished mahogany table and across from William Popham, who listened with bowed head as Nat recited the grace from his place at the head of the table. Though Sarah tried to keep her mind on the long prayer, her thoughts continually bounced between memories of the morning, the attractive way Popham's blond hair fell in a wave over one side of his high forehead, and her sister, quietly subdued at her side. It was not like Darcy to be this quiet about anything, especially when there was an attractive man present. Suddenly Sarah remembered that strange comment of Maude Sackett's earlier this morning. She must remember to speak to Darcy about that.

During the course of the meal, William Popham seemed to develop an interest in drawing Darcy from her shell. How curious, Sarah thought, that when for once Darcy did not openly attempt to captivate a man, it seemed to make him more interested in her. Sarah was grateful to Popham, for if anything could restore her sister's vivacity, it was the undivided attention of an attractive gentleman. By the end of the meal, when he had begun to regale them with tales of life in London, Darcy had begun to show traces of her normal behavior, and she went happily off to walk their guest around the garden, tossing her head a little arrogantly in her pleasure that she had been singled out instead of Sarah.

As she helped Jurie clear the table, Sarah daydreamed of Darcy happily settled with a cultured gentleman like William Popham. After all, he had said nothing to suggest that he was married, and he would be just what a girl like Darcy needed. If only she could dream of being settled with Neil, she thought, and a pain shot through her chest. If only everything were not so confused. If only her father were safe, then she and Neil could cry their love to the world. She did not dare tell anyone of it now for fear that Ferris might find out and go searching for Neil. She slammed a stack of slipware plates on the table a little too emphatically for such chippable pottery. Oh, why did life have to be so complicated!

Eight

∽

FROM THE deck of a boat on the river, the high wall of thicket and rock behind the Reed house stood like an impenetrable barrier. But Darcy Reed had known for years that there was a path through the thick woods that circled up and around the steep sides of the bluff, a path that emerged at the other end on the edge of a small cove hidden by clusters of overhanging branches from any view from the river.

Darcy came here often when she was feeling particularly angry or confused. It was one place that was hers alone. No one else seemed to remember the circuitous path. Years ago someone had left an old half-rotted skiff tied partway up on the bank, and though it was near total decay she could still manage to sit on one of the wooden slats across the stern, often dangling her feet in the water.

She was not a reflective girl by nature, and often she found that after a few moments of solitude she grew restless and bored in the deadly quiet. Still, those moments seemed to restore some vague strength that enabled her to cope with the endless sameness of her life. In some way she could never define, a sense of purpose and equilibrium was put back into focus.

She came here today, the morning after William Popham's visit, for two reasons: to avoid her sister, who was anxious to talk to her about something, and to try to figure out what to do about Neil Partherton. At the thought of Neil her cheeks began to flame. When she remembered how she had bared her heart to him and he had all but laughed at her for it, her shame was almost too much to bear. Not that she was ashamed of what she had done—those were honest feelings; it was his rejection of them that filled her with such chagrin. Yet even in her anger she could not really blame Neil. It was Sarah's fault. Sarah, who always got what she wanted, who was always in everyone's good graces, who took without any thought that what she was taking might be something her sister wanted and needed.

How was she going to win Neil away from Sarah? Over and over she had examined ideas and then discarded them for not having a chance of success. She had gone over every possible thing she might do to entice him, even to returning to Maude Sackett for one of her foolish charms. In the end she had to face the fact that nothing was going to turn Neil's heart away from her sister. Nothing except one thing.

If Sarah should reject Neil, then it would be the most plausible thing in the world for him to turn to her for solace. It was her only chance. But how to get Sarah to do this? Tears and pleading would never work. She might take to her bed and threaten never to rise until Sarah gave him up, but that would be as hard a threat for her to carry out as it would be for Sarah to accept. No, there was only one way. Somehow she must trick the two of them into believing the other one had stopped caring. But how?

She leaned forward, her arms on her knees, so intent on

her thoughts that she watched without seeing her toes wiggling in the cool water. When she finally heard the snapping of branches on the path behind her it was too late to get up and run into the woods. Swiveling around on the old seat, Darcy looked up in time to see her sister emerge from the path and step out near the water's edge.

"There you are," Sarah said, a little too brightly. "How did you ever remember this old path? I haven't thought of it for years."

"How did you know I was here?" Darcy said, unable to keep the annoyance from her voice.

"I saw you when you started up it from the other end in the garden. I was hoping to find you when I saw you disappear into the woods. I hope you don't mind that I followed, but it's important that we talk."

Darcy turned back, observing her toes. Though she did not voice her displeasure at being interrupted in the only private place she knew, her feelings were evident in every attitude of her body.

"I don't want to talk," she muttered, splashing the shallow water with her feet.

Sarah, fully aware of her sister's hostility yet determined to get at what was bothering her now that she had come this far, sat down on a flat rock far enough from the edge of river to avoid getting her shoes damp.

"Darcy, what's wrong? You've been going around for the last week in a blue melancholy, angry with everyone and looking as though you lost your last friend. Has someone hurt you? Is there anything I can do?"

The glare Darcy threw at her sister did away with any hopes Sarah had that her concern might heal the breach between them. For the first time Sarah began to sense that she was part of the problem.

"What have I done?" she said. "If I've hurt you, I'm sorry. It's just that there is so much on my mind right now."

"Why should you have so much on your mind?" Darcy said dryly.

"I'm terribly worried about Papa."

That was a relief. Darcy had half expected Sarah to say something about Neil. "Papa? Why? What's the matter with him?"

"Oh, well, I can't exactly express what it is. It's just that he's so involved in this business of finding supplies for the army and he . . . looks so tired sometimes. I'm concerned about his health."

"He looks fine to me. I think you're just searching for something to worry about. You do that often, you know."

For a moment Sarah looked as though she was going to get up and leave. Then she resolutely squared her chin and went on.

"And I'm worried about you as well."

Now it comes, thought Darcy.

"The other morning I passed Maude Sackett laying out clothes, and she said something to me that was very curious.

"Oh? What did she say?"

"Something like, 'Tell your young sister that the magic doesn't always work the first time. Tell her I'd be obliged to have her come for tea.' What did she mean, Darcy? Surely you haven't gone to call on that old woman, have you?"

Darcy looked around, her eyes narrow with belligerence. "And what if I did? It's not against the law, you know. It might even be my Christian duty to be kind."

"Darcy, if you went to see Maude Sackett it was certainly not out of Christian duty! I know you better than that. Why did you go see her?"

"I wanted the benefit of her advice. She has a lot of knowledge. It's the same as going to see old Dr. Talbot."

Sarah's voice was beginning to rise with alarm. "It's not the same at all. Did she give you anything?"

"I don't know why you're getting all excited about this."

"Did she?"

"Well, what if she did?"

Reaching out suddenly, Sarah gripped her sister's arm. "What? Was it some kind of charm?"

"Ow! You're pinching my arm. Let go, Sarah."

The boat began to rock.

"Tell me!"

"Yes! She gave me a potion."

"Oh, Darcy, how could you be so foolish?"

"I don't see what all the fuss is about," Darcy said, rubbing at her arm. "I asked her for something that would make someone think better of me. It was only a silly love potion. And it didn't do a bit of good, either. That old woman is a fraud."

"Oh, Darcy, don't you know half the people of the town believe she's a witch? It's been eighty years since they burned all those witches in Salem village, and I don't think anything like that could happen now. But she *is* crazy, and people fear her and wonder if she does have some kind of evil power. If they knew you were having anything to do with her it could bring trouble down on all our heads. And Papa doesn't need any more trouble right now."

"So what if she is crazy. So is Jamie Earing, and people aren't afraid of him."

"That's not the same thing."

In the silence Darcy felt her sister's eyes on her, studying her. When Sarah spoke again her voice had softened.

"Are you that much in love with someone, Darcy? Who is he? Do you want to talk about it?"

"No. I don't want to talk about it. You don't know him."

"Someone you met in Continental Village?"

"Yes."

"Well, I'm sorry that it makes you so unhappy. You are young and still have plenty of time to find the right gentleman. I had even hoped that Mr. Popham might appeal to you. He seems to like you well enough."

Darcy tossed her head. "Oh, he was all right. But my heart is quite fixed. It will never be free for anyone else. That's why I went to see Maude. I was desperate."

"I hope you learned that those potions and magic charms are useless. There's nothing in them. Love is a gift and cannot be bought or manipulated. Perhaps this man will come to his senses and see you for the girl you are. Then he will really love you."

Darcy stared into her sister's eyes. "Even if he thinks he loves someone else?"

"Oh, I don't know. People do sometimes change their minds. But how sad for you. No wonder you've been so unhappy."

"You don't need to waste your sympathy on me. I'll manage." Some of her anger had subsided in spite of all her attempts to hold on to it. All at once Darcy was filled with a terrible longing to lay her head on her sister's shoulder and cry out her misery. Resolutely she fought it back.

Smoothing down her skirt, Sarah made as if to rise.

"Well, if there's any way I can help, you know you've only to ask. Meanwhile, it will be very helpful to Papa if you will be careful to do nothing that could bring down the criticism of the Committee. I don't think they really trust him yet. All they would need is one little thing to hold against him. Please promise me you won't go to see that woman again."

For the first time Sarah's concern for their father began to sound as if it might have some basis. Darcy nodded her head. "I promise. It wouldn't change anything for me anyway."

"That's my girl." Impulsively Sarah leaned forward,

laying her hand on her sister's unyielding shoulder in a
brief gesture of affection. Then she turned and started back
up the path toward the house, disappearing almost at once
into the thick underbrush. Darcy stared after her long after
the faintest glimpse of her blue skirt had gone from view.
With an effort she forced the budding response to Sarah's
goodwill back down underneath her bitter anger.

"I'm not your girl!" she muttered.

In the early afternoon, a longboat from Fort Clinton
pulled up to the dock at the foot of the Millers' tavern and
Neil Partherton stepped out onto the unsteady planks that
jutted out into the river. He had not been to Sarah's house
since that awful day when Darcy surprised him at the fort.
He walked down the village street, filled with a longing
to see Sarah and yet hating the thought of coming face to
face with her sister. As he turned down the narrow path to
the Reed house he saw Sarah pruning the rosebushes in
front of the door. She spotted him walking down the path,
and, throwing down her shears, she ran to him, so happy
to see him again that for the moment all concern about
what people might think was forgotten.

All thought of Darcy fled Neil's mind in his delight at
seeing Sarah running toward him, her dark hair flying
behind her, her hat bobbing by its long strings. Catching
her hands, he pulled her into the shadow of the tack room
only a few feet away and kissed her soundly.

She clung to him, gaining strength from the good feel of
his solid body, longing to pour out all her worries about
Nat and Ferris Blunt, yet knowing she dared not speak.

He put his hands on her shoulders and stood back,
drinking in the contours of her face.

"My dearest girl. How have you been? I missed you
so."

"Oh, Neil. I was beginning to think you would never

come. I've longed to see you these last few days so much. So very much."

He kissed her again, long and hard, running his hands over the soft, pliant contours of her body.

"I couldn't come sooner, though I wanted to desperately. Things are happening, Sarah. Momentous things. I can't tell you about them, but—"

Laying a finger on his lips, she stopped his words. "I don't want to know. Don't tell me anything, please. Just hold me tightly. Don't let me go. Make me forget war and everything bad!"

Though she tried to hold them back, the tears spilled down her face, part relief and part anguish. Neil held her tightly in his arms.

"Why, what's wrong? My poor dear. Has something happened to hurt you?"

"No, no. It's nothing. Just happiness at seeing you again."

Would he believe her? He must. She wiped at her eyes and made a determined effort to appear cheerful.

"Come into the house. I've some very good juniper wine that was made last year and that Papa only just opened. And some delicious almond cakes that Jurie made. That girl is nearly hopeless about most things, but she can bake." She pressed the palms of his hands to her lips. "Now, kiss me once more, then let's go in and act presentable."

"I don't want to go in and be presentable. I want to stay here with you, forever."

Breaking away from his embrace but clinging to his hand, she tried to laugh. "You'd get weary of that very soon, I fear. Please, my love. If we don't go now, I won't want to leave either."

"All right. But soon . . . soon. This damned war has to end, and, pray God, it won't be much longer. Then we'll never have to care what anyone thinks again."

Sarah threw her arms around his neck and pressed against him. "Do you really think so?"

"Yes, I do. Listen, Sarah. Some great things are happening. . . ."

"No! I don't want to know. The excitement in your eyes tells me enough. I don't want to know any details. Come now. Let's go inside. Papa is in the kitchen, and he'll want to visit with you, I know."

Reluctantly, Neil followed her into the house, clinging to one of her hands while she tried to smooth down her mussed hair with the other. By the time they walked into the parlor, where Nat was sitting smoking a pipe with his feet on a footstool, they were both composed enough to feel their secret well hidden. They were not able to realize that their love for each other was so obviously written on their faces that it brought a knowing smile to Nat's lips.

"Lieutenant Partherton," Nat said, laying down his pipe and rising to take Neil's hand. "It's been some time since you were here. It's good to see you again."

"Thank you, sir. They keep me very busy running between West Point and White Plains. But I came by the first opportunity I had."

"Have a seat here, opposite me. Would you like a pipe?"

"No, thank you, sir."

"Sarah, run and fetch the lieutenant some of that good wine we opened last night. He'll enjoy that. Don't know where that lazy Jurie is—she's never around when you need her."

"Of course, Papa," Sarah said reluctantly, wondering if it was safe to leave the two men alone. Would her father try to worm information out of Neil for Ferris Blunt the minute she was out of the room? She closed the door behind her and leaned against it for a moment, trying to hear what they were saying. In the indistinct murmur of voices she could not make out any clear words. Oh dear, she thought, her heart sinking. Is this what it is going to be like always, now that I know about Papa? I wish I had never found that terrible bag.

The door had hardly closed behind his daughter when Nat, scrutinizing the young officer in the opposite chair, began to struggle with his own demons. This was the young man who wanted to marry his daughter, who wanted to be his son-in-law someday; who carried in his head information that might be helpful in destroying the very cause for which he was devoted; who trusted him, Nathanial Reed, as a man who claimed to care for the same cause. He had given his word to Sarah that he would try not to use this young man. But it was difficult. He was being forced to choose between his own daughter and his beliefs.

"I'm delighted to see you, sir," Neil said, leaning forward and resting his elbows on his knees. "It's good to be able to talk with someone I can trust outside of the military."

Nat sucked on his pipe. "Oh? And how are things going?"

"Bad and good. The bad news is that reinforcements have arrived in New York City. A whole regiment of three thousand Hessians to strengthen Clinton's British army. They sailed into the harbor yesterday morning. We had word of it right away—in fact, for a time His Excellency was convinced they were part of de Grasse's fleet, come to blockade New York Harbor."

If Neil was surprised at the mild response he got from Nat Reed, he did not betray it.

"Is de Grasse expected to blockade New York, then?"

"We don't know. He's left the West Indies, but where he is headed is anyone's guess. It is no secret, however, that General Washington devoutly hopes he is on his way to New York. Or that he was very disappointed when those ships turned out to be carrying reinforcements for the British. Very disappointed indeed."

Nat puffed at his pipe and stared at the toes of his slippers. "I suppose now it will be more difficult than ever to mount an attack on the city."

"Well, of course, such an attack is our general's dearest wish. Rumor has it that he will go ahead with it in spite of the arrival of those Hessians and in the face of General Rochambeau's reluctance. Just last week we began building some very large forage depots in the Jerseys. That was one of the things I wanted to see you about. We will be needing some fresh supplies of pickled beef, if you can get them."

"That should not be a problem. Yesterday I met a gentleman from upstate who has both mutton and beef to sell."

"We're also to begin constructing ovens near Chatham way, so flour would be welcome as well."

"Depots . . . ovens . . . it sounds as though General Washington is determined to retake New York no matter where de Grasse and his fleet may be."

"Yes, it does, doesn't it?"

"But a full-scale attack would require an enormous amount of troops. Wouldn't we have to recall some of our Continental regiments from the south?"

"Perhaps he intends to. No one knows for sure yet what he plans. Of course, with our French allies we have quite a sizable force now."

A loud knock at the front door was followed by voices in the hall. Neil stiffened as he recognized one of them as Darcy's. Leaning toward Nat, he spoke in a low voice.

"I should have some word soon on that rendezvous I spoke to you about. It cannot be much longer. Are you still willing to allow us to use your house?"

Nat gave him a long, intense look. Behind his placid expression his mind was churning. Now was the time to say no and be done with it. End the danger, the hurt to his gentle daughter, the risk of bringing Ferris Blunt into the affairs of his family. One small word of protest, of reluctance to take the chance, and his conscience would be clear, his family intact. The word was nearly on his lips when the cold dampness of the walls of Newgate prison pushed into his consciousness. He looked away from Neil's earnest, open face, staring back at the toe of his shoe on the footstool, feeling again the clammy hopelessness of those months in the dark.

"Just let me know when you need it."

There was a low murmur of voices beyond the door. Sarah was returning with the wine and refreshments.

"It should only be a matter of days, but as soon as I am sure, I will get word to you. I don't need to mention the need for absolute secrecy."

Nat managed a thin smile. "Of course. You have my word."

The door was thrust open, and Sarah entered, bearing a tray. Behind her, Darcy, smiling and vibrant, came bouncing through, followed by a tall gentleman with blond hair and a long, narrow face.

Neil, caught between embarrassment at seeing Darcy and curiosity at who this imposing stranger might be, rose slowly to his feet. Darcy had been laughing as she entered the room, but as Neil materialized before the hearth near where her father was seated, she stopped, stricken, all the color draining from her face.

"Good evening, Miss Darcy," Neil said politely, meeting trouble head on. "You are well, I hope."

"Tolerably, Lieutenant Partherton. And you?"

"Very well, thank you."

Sarah laid the tray on the table and, since Darcy was standing mannerless as a statue, led Popham forward.

"Lieutenant Partherton, may I present Mr. William Popham, from up Albany way? Mr. Popham is a business associate of Papa's who has now become a friend of the family."

"I'm pleased to meet you, Mr. Popham," Neil said, bowing politely.

"Likewise, sir." Popham bowed back. "It is always an honor to know one of the brave fellows who so nobly defend the cause of liberty. Are you at the camp nearby?"

"Yes. Across the river at Fort Clinton." Neil dragged up one of the side chairs for the gentleman, who sat down with a flourish while Sarah poured the dark aromatic liquid into their glasses.

"Ah, yes. That would be West Point, the cantonment that replaced those two forts lost in October of seventy-seven, would it not? Such a terrible thing, that loss. It was never supposed to happen that way. Ah, thank you, my dear Miss Reed," he said, reaching out one long, almost delicate hand to take the wineglass from Sarah's hand.

"There are always surprises in wartime," Neil answered laconically, looking Popham over. "General Washington feels the river can be much better guarded with the fort where it now is. He never believed those two lower ones were safe, though he was overruled by others. I don't think there will ever be a repetition of that former disgrace. There is no way the British could attack West Point from the rear."

"No, I don't suppose there is," Popham said, running a long finger down the stem of his glass. "Fortunately for us."

"Mr. Popham here is going to supply us with some hogsheads of pickled beef," Nat said, breaking off the end of his clay pipe. "At a very fair price, too. It's an answer to a prayer, him appearing just now."

Popham looked curiously from one man to the other. "I understood there was a continuing need for supplies for the army. Is there some special reason why they are more urgent now?"

"Oh, well . . ."

"Darcy," Sarah interrupted, "why don't you pass around

these almond cakes? Jurie made them,'' she said to the men, ''and Jurie makes the most delicious cakes you ever tasted. She's not much good anywhere else, but I have to give her credit. . . .''

She went chatting on while Neil smiled thinly to himself, recognizing how she was turning the conversation away from dangerous shoals. There was really no reason why this Popham, who for all his pleasant manners somehow did not seem quite rustic enough for a country farmer, should be trusted with the knowledge that Washington was preparing for an assault on New York. Spies were everywhere these days, and even random events held too much importance. The less said about the upcoming campaign the better.

As if he sensed what Neil was thinking, William Popham followed Sarah's lead, leaning forward to take one of the cakes from the plate a scowling Darcy put before him.

''I had a servant like that just recently. An indentured woman who, I trust, would never have made it out of old England had anyone ever tried her in a home before she was bound. Couldn't do the simplest tasks. But just give her a needle and thread and she would present you with the most delicately hemmed shirts and ruffles you ever saw. A veritable wonder with her stitchery. Do you sew, Miss Darcy? I'll wager you are very proficient at it.''

''Ha!'' Darcy could not help exclaiming. ''Ask Sarah. She'll tell you that 'stitchery' is not one of my most wondrous accomplishments.''

''That is true,'' Sarah replied. ''But there are other things you do well.''

''I would be very interested in knowing what they are,'' Popham said, smiling at Darcy. ''I'll wager that whatever they are, you do them extremely well.''

There was such suggestiveness in his voice that Darcy almost forgot her irritation with Neil. She smiled at Popham provocatively and lifted one shoulder. "I shall have to show you someday."

Yet she could not help shunting her eyes around to see if Neil was impressed with her flirtation. When she caught him thoughtfully staring at his wine instead of at her, her heart hardened again, and she was filled with such a pain that it nearly made her keel over. How could she still love him after the way he treated her? He was selfish, unfeeling! And yet, even while she tried to flutter her eyes at Popham and impress him with the way she held her body and tilted her head, all the while her feelings went out in waves of longing to the solitary figure in the blue coat sitting opposite her father. She never wanted anything so much as she wanted at that moment to go over and put her arms around his neck, her lips on the lean curve of his cheek. . . .

"You're not hearing me, Miss Darcy," Popham said, leaning toward her.

Darcy tore her eyes away from Neil's profile.

"Oh, forgive me. I'm sorry. What did you say?"

"Only that I should be honored sometime to have you and your sister come up and visit my farm in Rensselaerwyck. You've never been up that way, have you?"

"No. Sarah has, but I have not. That is very kind of you."

"Let me tell you something about it. . . ."

Popham's voice, friendly, flirtatious, obviously enjoying himself, droned on while Sarah sat, oblivious to her sister and her lover, her eyes fastened on her father puffing away at his pipe. Had Neil said anything to him while she was out of the room that would be dangerous to the patriots if it got back to Ferris Blunt and his spies? If only she had not had to leave! Yet Nat had promised her that he would not compromise Neil, and, God willing, he had been careful to keep his word. But what would she do if he had not? If Neil should be hurt or . . . killed because of her father . . .

Quickly she took a long sip of her wine. Somehow she must warn Neil never to tell Papa anything that would hurt the American cause. Yet how was she going to do that without somehow giving away the fact that her father was secretly sympathetic to the loyalists? Could she confide in him? He would never hold it against her, and he might be in a position to protect Nat if he wanted to. But would he want to?

Oh, dear God, how was she ever going to be able to protect her father and her lover at the same time? It was too difficult!

Although the time seemed endless to Sarah, yet it was actually only about half an hour before Neil finished his wine and stood up to leave, claiming that there was much to do. He made his apologies to Popham and Nat, lightly kissed Darcy's cold hand, avoiding her eyes, which looked as alive to him as a pit of vipers, and coolly walked with Sarah to the door.

"Who is this William Popham?" he whispered as he took up his hat. "I never heard of him before. Has your father known him long?"

"No. He just appeared yesterday, and tomorrow he is to go back to Albany. He says he heard of Papa's work and took the opportunity to introduce himself while he was down here."

"He's a very cultured gentleman for an Albany patroon."

"He lived in England for a long time. He told us he only returned when the rebellion broke out to save what his father had built for him."

"In England? That might explain it, but . . . I don't know. I'd be careful around him. Are you sure he's a patriot?"

"He claims to be. But Neil, how can anyone know where a person's loyalties lie except by what they say. Or . . . or do."

Neil clamped his hat on his head. "That's the trouble.

There is so much lying right now that you have to go by what they do, not what they say."

"Neil . . ." She hesitated. Now was the time to warn him, yet she could not say the dreadful words, *My father may be lying too.* How could she betray her father even to Neil? She could not do it.

"What is it, my love? Is something wrong?"

He laid an arm around her shoulder and pulled her to him. Gratefully she leaned against him, burying her face in his coat.

"It's nothing. Only be careful, my dear. And come back soon. I love you so."

Neil tipped up her face and kissed her soft, yielding lips.

"As soon as I can. I promise."

Nine

❦

BY THE time Nat Reed set out for the meeting at Four Corners early that evening, a light drizzle was coming down and the distant rumble of thunder could be heard rolling from the hills across the river. The dismal weather was a perfect backdrop to his mood, Nat thought as his horse plodded along the road. Nothing but his fondness for Christian Weiss would have induced him ever again to attend a meeting of the Committee of Conspiracies, so painful were the memories he carried of the last time he stood before them, threatened, accused, and convicted without a scrap of hard evidence. He had vowed then that he would die by his own hand before he would ever again be delivered into theirs, and now here he was, volunteering to walk back into their midst. It was only because he knew so well how Christian felt that he had agreed to go and stand surety for him. Each mile that brought him closer to the old farmhouse where the meeting was to be held seemed to increase his reluctance. His only hope was

that with any luck, Christian's case would come up first
and he could get in and out quickly enough to keep the
anger and pain he felt from rising to the surface.

He had not been inside the Mandeville house since old
Israel Putnam had held his headquarters there that disastrous autumn of '77. Mandeville, one of the first settlers in
the area, had been a tenant of Adolph Philipse more than
thirty years ago, and until Beverley Robinson married
Mary Philipse and built his fine house not half a mile
away, his venerable old farm had been the best house in the
district. Mandeville was dead now, and Beverley Robinson
was off fighting with the British loyalists in New York, so
both houses had been appropriated by the American generals passing through the area. As Nat turned his horse down
the long, tree-covered path that wound through the woods
to the porch, he found that even the sight of the yellow
lights in the windows, flickering like fireflies in the dusk,
seemed more ominous than welcoming. The post outside
the porch was lined with horses, their tails swishing at the
late-evening flies, heads bowed in mindless reverie. He
tied his mount next to one he recognized as Christian's
and, boots crunching on the crushed-shell walkway, ap-
proached the front door.

Smoking pipes and swatting at the mosquitoes, several
men lounged on the two high-backed benches that flanked
the front door. Nat recognized one of them as the smith
from Cole's Landing, Coenradt Johannes, a taciturn, burly
man with a perpetual worried frown who nodded politely
in his direction. Inside the spacious hall all the straight-
backed chairs along the three walls were filled. Glancing
around, Nat saw that all the men there were familiar
except one, a small fellow in a dirty farmer's smock sitting
beside the cold hearth sucking on a straw. He nodded to
Christian, who was sitting next to Barnet Sindon, the
miller, and took the one empty chair next to Andries

Stoakes, wondering absently what had brought each of them there.

The committeemen were already gathered in the dining room off the hall, a small room furnished with one table and several ladder-back chairs. Through the open door Nat recognized Hendrick van Tassel and Reverend Tate sitting behind the table. Between them sat a portly man in a grizzled bagwig, pinching snuff between the fingers of one hand and applying it to his thick nose. Removing his hat, Nat wiped at his warm brow with his handkerchief, searching his mind for the heavyset gentleman's name. By the time the man picked up the gavel and began pounding it on the table it had come to him—William Hargrave, a bellicose lawyer who lived near King's Ferry but who liked to go up and down the Highland Patent, soliciting customers. Looking over these three committeemen, Nat's heart began to sink: Hendrick van Tassel, whose pompous self-importance was fueled by his zeal for independence; Harmon Tate, looking every other moment toward van Tassel, as though to take his lead from the more dominant man; and, worst of all, Hargrave, a man who had just enough knowledge of the law to use it to justify repression and to intimidate ignorant men. Nat settled back in his chair, his tricorn hat in his lap, thinking how it promised to be a very long evening.

Because the night was so warm, the door was left open, and Nat, sitting near it, was able to see and hear the proceedings just as though he were in the room itself. The first name called turned out not to be Christian's but Barnet Sindon's, the miller who lived not far from Mandeville's farm. Nat gave the miller a thin, encouraging smile as he shuffled through the door to stand before the table. Barnet Sindon was an industrious, gentle man; Nat could not imagine him involved in anything that smacked of conspiracy.

"Barnet Sindon," van Tassel intoned. "Is that your name?"

Sindon's head was as bowed as his shoulders, but he answered sullenly, "Ye know right well it is."

Hargrave's gavel clattered against the table. "Just answer civilly, if you please. This is a legal proceeding. State your name and occupation."

"Barnet Sindon, miller, and I'd like to know why—"

The gavel interrupted him. "All in good time. Just your name and occupation, if you please."

"I said, Barnet Sindon. Miller."

Van Tassel leafed through a stack of papers on the desk in front of him. "Now, Mr. Sindon," he said, "we have brought you before this Committee tonight to have you answer some charges which have been preferred against you."

Sindon's head came up. "What charges! I'm an honest man, as you well know and have known for years. Have I ever been known to cheat a man? Are my weights fixed? Has anyone ever said I give less than is paid for? I've been an honest miller all my life and—"

"The charges have nothing to do with your occupation."

"What, then? And who? Who charges me?"

"Yes, we'd better have him up." Van Tassel waved a hand and called a name and Andries Stoakes rose from his chair to hurry into the room toward the table. Barnet turned first in surprise, then glaring angrily.

"Now, Andries Stoakes here has made the charge against you of evil practices against the state."

"I cannot believe this!"

"Brother," Reverend Tate said gently, "we are only here to discern the truth. Please hear the charges and then you will be given an opportunity to answer."

"Evil practices against the state," van Tassel went on. "He accuses you of frequent complaints against the government and states that not only he but several of the other well-affected inhabitants of this patent have heard you make these complaints."

"I only said—"

"Further," van Tassel went on, reading from a paper in his hand, "that by your conduct and conversation you daily disturb the public peace and attempt to dissuade the friends of the American cause from taking up arms in the defense of their liberties."

Barnet's face turned the color of raw beef. "It's a lie. I never said nothin' of the kind."

Andries took a few steps toward him. "Don't deny it. Didn't I hear you just the other day saying to three or four of us who were waiting for flour that we were fools to enlist in the Continental forces? Those were your very words."

"Yes, but we were talkin' about how the war might be over soon. I only said—"

"You said it! You did!" Stoakes shouted.

"You miserable runt! Who gave you a whole sack of flour when your house was burned and never asked for a penny in compensation!"

The loud clatter of the gavel silenced the shouts of the two men. "Now, see here," Hargrave said with deadly seriousness. "These are civil proceedings. No more shouting from either of you. Barnet Sindon, did you or did you not advise against taking up arms in defense of liberty?"

"I may have said it, but it was only—"

"And did you say it on more than one occasion?"

"How would I know? Standing around the mill I talk to everybody all the time. How do I remember what I say? You can't expect me to remember everything I say."

"And have you knowingly ridiculed and maligned the American army and the noble attempts they have undertaken to drive the enemies of liberty from these shores?"

"I suppose I criticized them a little at times, but so does everybody else."

"I think this man should be sentenced to jail," Hargraves pronounced, leaning back in his chair.

While Barnet stood sputtering in outrage, Tate and van Tassel leaned toward the lawyer, the three of them with their heads close together while they whispered loudly to each other. At length they sat back and van Tassel addressed the hapless miller.

"Barnet Sindon, you are found guilty as charged of making seditious comments against the state. However, our main business here is to protect the cause of liberty against those who would strive to overthrow it and who would give solace and assistance to the enemy. While your comments are foolish and misguided, we do not consider them to be dangerous enough to condemn you to jail. We will allow you to go back to your work on the condition that you find a trustworthy man to stand surety for you and that you pay a fine of one hundred pounds."

At the mention of such a vast sum of money Sindon's face turned as pale as the flour he handled daily.

"We also trust that you will in the future curb your tongue and make no further criticisms of the state, or attempt to prevent any good citizen from taking up arms. Is this agreeable?"

"And what if I don't?"

"Then there is no alternative but to issue a mittimus for your arrest and sentence you to a term in prison."

Barnet stared sullenly at the three men.

"Come on, man," Tate interjected kindly. "It's your only choice."

Grudgingly Sindon nodded while Hargrave banged the gavel once against the table.

"Released on recognizance of good behavior. Pay the fine to the clerk outside the door. Next case."

Nat watched while Sindon stood struggling between an urge to pour forth his fury at the three men behind the table and his very real concern over fear of what they

might do to him. At length caution won over anger, and
with one last furious glare at Stoakes he shuffled from the
room, his eyes fixed on the polished floor.

It was with some surprise that Nat realized his heart was
thumping like a drumbeat. Rage, forced down and quieted,
was boiling deep within him. He longed to run after
Sindon, grab his arm, and declare his willingness to beat
these three within an inch of their lives. It was that kind of
a rage—a blind lashing out with fists and cudgels because
reason had long since been swept away. He couldn't even
look at Andries Stoakes, who had resumed his chair, ready
to be entertained by the rest of the evening's proceedings.
Why had he done this? Was his own life so warped by
loss that he could only find satisfaction in making other
men suffer? One thing was certain—it was not zeal for the
cause of liberty that led him to accuse the kindly miller,
though he would in all likelihood say that it was.

"Coenradt Johannes," the lawyer's voice intoned.

The local blacksmith—a huge, muscular man whose
head seemed almost too small for his wide body, ambled
in from the porch, glancing sheepishly at Nat as he moved
through the door to stand before the table.

"Name and occupation."

"Coenradt Johannes, smithy," he answered, a thin smile
at the corners of his lips at so obvious a question.

Van Tassel rummaged through the papers in front of him
and drew one forth.

"Coenradt Johannes, you have made application to the
board on behalf of your brother, Robert, who is now in jail
in White Plains."

"That's right, Hendrick—Mr. van Tassel."

"On what question?" Hargrave said.

"Well, your honor, sir, my brother, Robert, he was
always a true supporter of liberty."

"Humph, that is difficult to believe when we look at his
record. He is accused of making inflammatory statements

about patriots and, even worse, of being involved in several robberies.

"Yes, but your honor, that was when he was younger. He has better sense now, and being in jail has developed his character something wondrous. He'll behave himself now. I'll see that he does. It's my ma, you see. She's not well, and she really needs him to be home."

"That is all well and fine, but your brother must be considered a dangerous fellow."

Van Tassel folded the paper and tapped the edges on the table. "Robert Johannes was confined in jail by an order of this Committee. I remember well when he came before it." He glanced at Hargrave. "It might not hurt to reprieve him. He's been there many months."

The three men put their heads together once again, whispering while the other men in the hall tried not to look at each other. When they sat back, Coenradt stiffened automatically.

This time it was Hargrave who spoke. "Mr. Johannes, while the Committee would like to grant your request, nevertheless it finds that in this present critical situation of public affairs it would not be in the interest of liberty to consent to your brother's release. Request denied."

Nat stared at the corners of the hat lying in his lap. It was his devout hope that Christian would be called next, for he was not certain how much longer he could sit listening to these proceedings. But when the next person's name was read, it proved to be one Jellis LeGrange from Albany, the one stranger he had noticed when he entered the hall.

LeGrange was a wizened little man with a face like a dried prune, one of those malcontents who found pleasure in disturbing other people's lives. Nat almost laughed out loud when he heard Jellis proclaim that Cole's Landing harbored a notorious disaffected person by the name of Jamie Earing, whom he had heard with his own ears declare himself a King's man who loved Farmer George dearly and thought the British officers wore handsome scarlet uniforms. Even Hargrave began to look embarrassed.

"Jamie Earing is an idiot. Everyone knows he does not possess all his faculties. Had you been a native of these parts, Mr. LeGrange, and not merely passing through, you would certainly be aware of that."

"Even an idiot ought not to be allowed to babble such treason," LeGrange said sourly. Then he went on, his voice rising, "Besides, I was through that village long enough to see more than you locals do. There's spies everywhere. British officers disguise themselves and walk through the lines, picking up all they can about the American forces while being harbored by enemies of the state, assisting robbers to carry their stolen goods to New York for hard money. It ain't right. Somethin' ought to be done about all these wicked Tories."

"Mr. LeGrange," van Tassel said evenly, "you ought to be reporting such things to your own committeemen in Albany."

"Oh, but I do. I'm before 'em all the time. They know me well."

"I thought as much."

"It happens all up and down the river. And the closer to New York, the more the danger."

"Perhaps. But I think you can trust us to weed out the Tories and loyalist criminals in our midst."

"They're one and the same!"

Nat turned to stare at the darkness outside the window. He was beginning to feel sick with the bottled rage within him. It was men like this—wastrels, failures, fanatics who bit like insects at the bodies of better men—who drove him further every day into the service of the King. What had begun for him as a reasonable assumption of tradition and loyalty had now been twisted by such men as these into a burning hatred. He was about to get up and leave when he heard Christian Weiss's name called at last.

With half an ear he listened as Christian's crime was read out—that he had offered to exchange the paper money lately issued by Congress for hard specie at the rate of three to one, a dastardly attempt to depreciate both the money and the Congress. This when every man in the room knew that Congress did not have the means to make good on the specie they issued and three to one was probably more than a fair exchange.

When he was bid to face the Committee and agree to stand surety for Christian's good behavior, he rose and did so, deliberately saying nothing but the bare assent required of him. Christian turned almost as white as Barnet had when his fine was set at 100 pounds, but he quickly agreed to pay it rather than be sentenced to jail. Mercifully then, with a snap of the gavel, the meeting was closed.

Nat spoke a few words to Christian and fled the room before he was forced to make conversation with the members of the Committee. With their words still ringing in his ears—words of what a loyal subject he was, words of how his true devotion to the cause of patriotism made him the ideal choice for Christian's surety—he set his horse along the road home, thankful that it was so familiar he barely need guide her.

He had been almost ready to sacrifice his beliefs for the sake of his daughter and the young man she loved. Tonight's events had turned him from that forever. For better or worse, he would be true to his own heart, no matter who would be hurt by it.

Ten

~

SHORTLY AFTER dawn the next day, Neil was called from the parapet where he was supervising the cleaning of one of the six-pounders to receive a message brought by a courier from White Plains. The thick dust that layered the young officer's clothes and the foam on his horse indicated the speed of his journey. Inviting the man inside, Neil poured him a glass of porter, then broke open the seal on the letter.

Quickly he ran his eyes down the page, half listening while the courier complained about the steepness of his climb from the ferry. The letter was from Ian Harron, informing him that the couriers from the south would be arriving in two days, probably in the late afternoon or early evening, and he was to be prepared to deliver them safely across the river for their meeting with the general.

"Wouldn't be surprised if I knew what was in that epistle," the young man said rather smugly.

Neil's eyes flew to his face. "Oh?"

"Only because the whole camp's full of it. Buzzing like a hive of bees no matter how much the good generals try to keep everything secret."

"What are you talking about?" Neil said, his heart sinking. If a shipment of so large a sum of money was public knowledge there would be almost no way he could guard it.

The courier balanced his lean body on a corner of the table and rested one arm on his knee.

"Why, the letter from Admiral Barras, of course. It came just yesterday and set His Excellency in a rare taking."

Neil folded the paper in his hand, almost sighing with relief. "Tell me what you know. This message is so brief I can barely make sense of it."

The young lieutenant needed no urging. "Barras has finally heard from Admiral de Grasse. He's on his way to the Chesapeake with an army of three thousand men. Now we can finally take some decisive action after all this waiting and wondering."

"He's not headed for New York, then?"

"Not at all. He's going after Cornwallis in Virginia, and the whole camp is betting that we'll soon set out to join him there."

With a studied nonchalance, Neil poured himself a glass of porter. "That must be a grievous disappointment to General Washington. It's common knowledge he is itching to attack New York. We've begun building campsites surrounding the city. I think you gentlemen are letting rumors cloud your judgment."

"Well . . ." the lieutenant said, a little deflated. "General Rochambeau always was for Virginia, you know, and it's only out of deference to His Excellency that he's not insisted we be off before this. Now that they know de Grasse is headed there—"

"Good God!" Neil exploded. "I hope you are not this

rash in discussing policy everywhere you go! Why don't you simply run a dispatch down to New York so the British can be as well informed?''

"But sir,'' the lieutenant said, stepping quickly to his feet. "But you are—''

"Yes, I am an American officer. But don't you know there are spies everywhere, men who are just waiting for news like this to inform Clinton how the game goes? He'll prevent any move we might make for the south unless he's convinced we don't intend to make one. I would advise you to rein in your tongue, lieutenant, even in camp!''

The young man seemed to wither under Neil's reprimand.

"Yes, sir.''

"If there is this much open speculation in the camp at White Plains, I tremble to think how far the information has already gone.''

"Yes, sir. Sorry, sir. Is there a letter to be returned, sir?''

"No, I don't think so. Just tell Major Harron that his message was delivered. And don't linger too long before starting back.''

"Yes, sir.''

Neil stopped the man at the door. "And need I say, don't mention Admiral Barras's letter while you are here. I cannot vouch for all the people around this post.''

As he hurried down to the ferry landing a short time later, he thought back over his words to the courier. The truth was he could trust no one—not even Nat Reed, really. Yet he had to take some chances. There was no way to be effective without occasionally bringing in help from outside. And Sarah, he knew, was as true and honest as the day was long. He would simply have to trust Nat and hope he was not blundering as badly as that talkative courier from White Plains.

*   *   *

By a stroke of luck Nat was in the house alone when Neil found him. He had been working over his books, and his fingers were stained with ink. The desk before him was littered with papers and sand, and scattered on the floor were two or three broken turkey quills.

When Jurie led Neil into the room, Nat pushed his round steel glasses up onto his forehead and rose to greet him, thankful to stop for a while.

"Won't you have some refreshment?" Nat asked, cordially. "The girls are down at the tavern, gossiping with that flightly little Deborah Miller. I've been trying to catch up on these books without the help of my good Sarah, and it's difficult, I must confess. Don't know how I'm going to manage when she marries and moves away."

Neil smiled at the thought. He had been so full of the army's concerns that Sarah had slipped from his mind. Now, in this pleasant house, she was suddenly very real to him once more, and he found he felt something of the warm anticipation he was so accustomed to feeling when he came to the Reed home.

"Nothing, thank you, sir," he answered Nat, taking a chair opposite the desk. "I cannot stay long. I'm glad Sarah and Darcy are not here, since I've come about that matter we mentioned between ourselves. It looks as though it is about to take place at last."

"Oh?" Nat sat back in his chair, his body tensing.

Leaning forward, Neil lowered his voice to a near whisper. "Tomorrow afternoon or evening. If you could manage to be away with your family it would be most helpful."

Nat rubbed a finger along his heavy underlip. "Well, it won't be easy, but I'll find a way. What about Jurie and Cato?"

"It would be best if they were gone too."

"That will be a little more difficult, but I'll think of something. I confess I'd like to be here myself to meet your 'significant guests.' Yet I can understand the need for secrecy. Very well. You can count on my help.''

"Thank you, sir. I cannot say much about this, of course, but I can tell you it is a most important meeting— one that might well make the difference between the survival of our cause and its eventual failure.''

"In that case, you may doubly count on my help. I am honored that you should have chosen my home.''

Something about his stance reminded Neil of the courier. "I am putting a great deal of trust in your word, Mr. Reed. You have served us faithfully these past two years. If matters work out as I hope, perhaps you will be rewarded for that service very soon.''

Nat moved uncomfortably in his chair. "My best reward will be the liberty of our country.''

"One thing more. I think it wise perhaps to take Sarah into our confidence. To tell the truth, I am more worried about Darcy interfering than anyone, and I'd like to count on Sarah to keep her out of the way. Is that agreeable with you?''

"Of course. Though both girls will obey me in this if I ask them to leave.''

"I know, but it might not hurt for Sarah to be aware of just how important it is that they stay away. If you will excuse me, I think I will walk on down to the Green Man now and have a word with her before I ride on. I've an errand at Continental Village this afternoon.''

"By all means, my boy. Go ahead. And be confident that when you arrive tomorrow you will find the house empty and the door unlatched. Good luck.''

Neil bowed slightly, set his hat on his head, and left the room. A moment later Nat watched him from the window bounding jauntily down the path toward the village, full of confidence and youth, brimming with obvious happiness at the prospect of seeing Sarah.

Would he himself ever feel so full of grace again? he

wondered. He was more disturbed by Neil's mention of "trust" than he wished to be. At times like these it was difficult to remember the cold, gnawing anger that had driven him to Ferris Blunt in the first place. Was it still worth it? Especially when he might be damaging the relationship between a beloved daughter and this prospective son-in-law—a young man he would have so welcomed under normal circumstances.

The memory of Hargrave's stern face at the Committee meeting came bounding back. It was too late for these ruminations. He was caught fast in the bounds of circumstance and had long ago passed the point of tearing himself out of them.

Closing the ledgers, he laid the quills on the inkwell and called to Jurie to tell Cato to saddle his horse. There was business to attend to.

It was such a lovely day that the women took their sewing out into the garden once the midday meal was over. Sarah and Darcy, along with Helena Earing and Elizabeth Tate, had all gathered in Deborah's garden to help one another with the annual job of making rag carpets. Each woman had arrived earlier that morning with a basket of remnants, bone needles, and silks of every color, along with half a pie or a piece of cheese tucked inside. This was the first of several such "frolics." It would take quite a few before each of them finally carried home two or three new carpets to adorn the floors of their homes. The widow Earing and Mrs. Tate represented the older generation; Deborah, Sarah, and Darcy, the younger. But for all of them, pleasant conversation and good company made the boring, tedious work more palatable. For Darcy, who was an indifferent seamstress at best, it was the only thing that made the day worthwhile. That and the close proximity of the tavern.

Sarah had always enjoyed these gatherings, and the delightful atmosphere of the Millers' extensive garden made this one even more pleasant. The river was calm and a silvery blue. The pungent fragrance of honeysuckle and roses perfumed the air around them. Voices and laughter drifting from the open windows of the taproom made the world seem peaceful and serene.

And yet she could not enjoy all this pleasantness, because of the anxiety that lay just below the surface of her thoughts. It was nothing she could define. It had no reason or substance that she could name, but it was there all the same. It had been there since the conversation with her father in the tack room, and she was powerless to ignore or dispel it, try as she might.

Darcy sat next to her, pricking her finger with her needle and exclaiming in exasperation over the refusal of her material to perform as it should. With each new round of laughter from the window she would lift her head and peer toward the tavern. Sarah knew she longed to be inside. One of the easiest voices to identify was the high tenor of William Popham. Sarah, smiling to herself, thought this was the magnet that drew Darcy's attention. It pleased her, for it gave her hope that her solemn sister might at last take that gentleman's suit seriously.

"Those men have a good lot to laugh about, it seems," Helena Earing commented as she sorted through her basket for a red remnant to go alongside the blue and gold pieces she had just used.

"Perhaps it is not the jokes so much as the porter," Elizabeth Tate said sourly. "My Harmon says a powerful lot of it is consumed of late, and early in the day, too. Can't be good for those of us who have to put in a full day's work."

"Oh, I don't know," Deborah said, tossing her head. "Noah won't truck with drunkenness, you know, but he thinks wettin' down a man's thirst is as good a service as

one can offer. And in these hard times it's a consolation
for many as well.''

"Too much of a consolation sometimes," Elizabeth
added. Though she was fond of the good-natured Deborah,
she also felt it was her duty to put in a word in support of
her husband, who, as the local cleric, was often at odds
with Noah Miller over the way he ran his taproom.

"Egad!" Darcy exclaimed, shaking her hand and pop-
ping a finger briefly in her mouth. "I'm all thumbs today.
That's the tenth time I've pricked my finger. At this rate
we won't have this carpet done before Christmas.''

"That's all right, dear," Sarah said, taking the cloth
from her sister's hand. "We'll give this one to Jurie for
her room. Here, let me see if I can get these together, then
you can take it from there.''

Darcy gladly relinquished her remnants, rose to her feet,
and stretched her arms above her head. "Oh, this sun feels
so good!" she said, turning her face into it. "It's good to
stretch after sitting so long.''

"You should be more careful of the direct sun, Darcy
child," Helena said. "It's very bad for the complexion.''

"Yes, freckles are so unbecoming," Elizabeth added.

"I don't care," Darcy said, shrugging. "It feels so
nice. However, it *is* warm. Perhaps I will just duck inside
for a moment and ask Noah to send us out a pitcher of
lemonade. Would anyone else like some?''

Sarah smiled at her sister's obviousness. "Now that you
mention it, I would," she said. "It is rather a warm day.''

"So should I," Deborah said. "Would you like me to
go with you?''

Darcy was already down the path. "No, no. I can
manage. I'll be right back.''

The two older women, bent over their stitches, barely
noticed she was gone.

"When I was a girl," Helena said, "we would rub

white paste on our faces to make our skin look creamy and pale. Why, a freckle was a disaster."

" 'Tis only the whores that paint their faces now," Elizabeth said. "I've heard that down in New York they promenade on the Trinity mall around the ruins of the old church as brazen as you please, faces painted up with paste and French rouge and all kinds of patches. Imagine!"

"Now, how would you know that," Deborah said in all innocence, "since no one here can get into New York unless he be a Tory or a British spy?"

Elizabeth Tate looked down her long nose at the girl. "I was told it by Mrs. Granger herself, she who lives over near the village of Peekskill and who went there to fetch her son from one of those wretched British prisons. If you have a pass you can move through the neutral ground. I should think anyone would know that."

Deborah felt a mild flush redden her cheeks. "Yes, that is true," she murmured, inwardly cursing her careless tongue. Mrs. Tate had a good heart, but, as the wife of the local clergyman, she was inclined to be more judgmental than most.

"Oh, look, Sarah," Helena said, glad to change the subject. "Isn't that the young man who visits you at your house so often?"

With a small startled intake of breath Sarah looked up to see Neil coming down the path from the tavern, Darcy hanging on to his arm. The blatant joy on her face did away with any hopes Sarah had that she might have gone inside to speak with Popham.

"Look who I found just entering the taproom," Darcy said gaily. "You'd think he would want to have a glass with the men, but nothing would do but he must come outside and speak to the ladies."

Sarah laid aside her sewing and gave Neil her hand, which he raised to his lips. "Good afternoon, Miss Reed," he said, giving her a secret smile before bowing to the other ladies. "You have picked a very congenial spot for your work this lovely afternoon."

The ladies, pleased to have the handsome young officer as a diversion, exclaimed over Neil and chatted happily with him for the next ten minutes. After that he was able to draw Sarah away for a few moments' conversation alone, leaving a frowning Darcy behind them.

Walking down to the river's edge, he managed to pull her behind a large growth of boxwood away from the peering eyes of the ladies in the garden.

"I was anxious to have a private word with you," Neil said softly, subduing an urge to take her in his arms and kiss her. "I've just come from seeing your father. He has agreed to allow us the use of his house tomorrow evening for a very important meeting between some of the officers of our army and a group coming up from Philadelphia."

"Oh, Neil," Sarah said, her heart sinking.

"We need your help, however, to make sure that Darcy is out of the house. He plans to take you both away, but it seems Darcy might not leave if she had any idea that something was up. I convinced him to take you into our confidence."

"But Neil, why our house? Are you sure it would be safe? Why not use the Robinson house or Mr. Mandeville's? They've both been used by the commandants, and you know they can be well guarded."

"Because this is a very secret meeting and both those houses are too heavily occupied. No, I'm convinced the location and innocence of your home will make it the best place. No one would suspect that anything of importance would be going on there. But you'll have to be gone, all of you. I would not want to put you in any danger, my love."

"Does Papa know what you are planning?"

"Not everything. Just that it is of the utmost secrecy and significance."

Sarah twisted her hands in the folds of her skirt, desperately wondering how to tell Neil that he could not trust Nat. Her face was etched with misery.

"I've told you, my dearest," he went on, "because I know you are as trustworthy as your father. If you can manage to keep Darcy away without arousing her suspicions, you will be doing our cause a great service."

"I want to help, but . . ."

Neil caught both her hands and raised them to his lips. "I knew I could count on you. Oh, Sarah. How glad I'll be when all this is over and we can show the world our love, openly and honestly."

"When will I see you again?" Sarah managed to say. So many thoughts tumbled about in her mind, and none of them could she share with him.

"I'll be back through the village later today, but I won't have time to stop by your house. If all goes as planned I should be able to come back over and spend the afternoon with you the day after tomorrow. Perhaps we could take a box and go up the hill for a picnic. Would you like that?"

"Yes . . . no. I don't know. Neil . . ."

"What's the matter, my dearest? What's bothering you? You look as though tears are about to wash you away."

"Nothing. I'm just . . . overwhelmed by everything. Don't worry about tomorrow. I'll do what I can. But don't tell Papa too much about it."

"I shan't say any more than I have already," he said, kissing her again. "Now come. We'd better go back before we give your friends something to gossip about."

Sarah went back to her sewing, trying to concentrate on the stitches while watching Neil walk back toward the inn, Darcy once again clinging to his arm. It was some time before her sister reappeared, this time followed by William Popham. Sarah bent over her needle, her mind churning, saying almost nothing. What was she to do? she wondered. If her father knew about the meeting that was planned, it

was almost certain he would tell Ferris Blunt, and that
meant danger for everyone, especially for Neil. Even if he
were not hurt in a fight between Ferris and the army, the
disgrace at being betrayed was likely to harm his career.
Yet what could she do without being disloyal to her father?
For another half hour she endured the shallow conversation
of Popham and her friends, mulling back and forth the
dilemma she faced. Looking up, she caught Darcy intently
watching her. Finally she threw down her needle in disgust
and gathered up her basket.

"I can do no more," she cried. "It's no use. Better to
wait until next time than have to go back and sew everything over again. Will you ladies excuse me?"

"Of course, Sarah," Helena said sympathetically. "I've
noticed that this past hour you've barely spoken a word.
Perhaps the sun has given you the headache."

"Yes, that must be it. I think I will just go on home and
lie down for a while. Thank you for your hospitality,
Deborah. It has been a lovely day."

For a moment Darcy looked as though she would accompany her, but to Sarah's relief she finally decided that Mr.
Popham's company was preferable to no gentleman's at
all. Carrying her basket, Sarah hurriedly walked back
down the village street to her house, where without meeting even one of the servants she went straight to her room
and paced the floor, wringing her hands. Over and over
she mentally tallied her choices, unable to find one that
would not hurt someone she loved. Finally, after nearly an
hour, she threw herself down on the coverlet and broke
into furious tears. She never heard Darcy enter the house
or open her door and was startled when someone touched
her on the shoulder and she looked up into her sister's
face.

"Why, Sarah, what in the world is wrong? Does your
head bother you that much?"

Alarmed at being caught like this, Sarah rubbed her sleeve against her eyes and tried to make light of it.

"No, no. It's nothing."

"Well, of course it's something or you wouldn't be so distressed. Come now," Darcy added, pulling up a chair to the bed. "I do think you will have to confide in me. After all, if you cannot trust your own sister . . ."

"I can't, Darcy. I cannot tell you. This is something I must handle by myself."

"Nonsense. Things are twice as difficult when you try to go them alone. Come now, it cannot be anything so terrible. Nothing ever is for you; you are such a nice person."

Sarah smiled thinly at her sister. "But it is. Oh, I wish I could share it with you. Perhaps you could help, and certainly I have not been able to come up with a solution."

"Then that is what you must do. Here, take this damp cloth and wipe your face. Then tell me what's causing you so much pain."

"But it is for your own good that I can't speak. I want to protect you from knowing anything that might hurt you. And . . . it is so terrible!"

She burst into fresh sobs. Yet at the same time she felt some measure of relief in being able at last to share some of her anxiety with another person.

"It cannot be that bad," Darcy said a little petulantly. She could think of no catastrophe severe enough to cause the usually unflappable Sarah so much pain. Unless . . . unless it had to do with Neil. Maybe something between them was amiss. A stab of hope shot through her breast. Gently she laid a hand on Sarah's shoulder.

"Come now, Sarah, you're getting your coverlet all wet. Calm yourself and tell me what this is all about. Between us, I'll wager we'll find a simple answer."

Sarah sat up and wiped at her eyes.

"I cannot tell you how I know, but Papa has some kind of connection with Ferris Blunt."

"The outlaw?"

"Yes. Papa has only been pretending that he believes in the patriot cause. He is really at heart just as much a Tory as ever, even to helping Ferris in his persecutions of the Whigs in the neighborhood. It is because he is still so bitter about being unjustly imprisoned years ago."

Darcy sat back, dismayed at Sarah's words. In her own detached way she was fond of her father, and the thought of him being involved in treachery and dishonor was frightening—not only because of the risks he was running to himself but also because it could bring down harsh repercussions upon his daughters as well.

Intent on her thoughts, the sudden mention of Neil in her sister's rambling conversation brought her back to the present.

"Neil trusts him, you see," Sarah was saying. "That is why he has set up this whole dangerous thing."

"What dangerous thing?"

"Neil has arranged with Papa to use our house tomorrow night for some kind of important meeting between several Continental officers and some men coming up from Philadelphia. I'm sure it has something to do with the plans for the campaign. Oh, Darcy, I'm so afraid Papa will tell Ferris about it and he'll come here with his men and raid the place. Neil could be killed! Papa could . . . Oh, Darcy. It's all so terrible!"

"Calm yourself, Sarah. There must be something we can do."

"I don't know what it is. I've looked at it every way I know and I cannot see how to prevent it without betraying either Papa or Neil. And I don't want to do either!"

Darcy bit at her fleshy underlip. Thoughts were churning in her fertile mind—intriguing, delightful, terrible thoughts. The faintest touch of a smile lifted the corners of her mouth. What kind of a person was she to use a sister's pain to her own advantage? A girl madly, desperately in love, the answer came without a momentary pause.

"Have you said anything to Papa about this?"

"I haven't seen him since Neil told me. But I did speak to him once before, when I first learned about his connection with Ferris. It did no good. He's so bitter and angry, he no longer cares about danger and dishonor. I never thought to see Papa this way."

"Look here, Sarah. There must be some way to convince him. He could cause you and me a lot of trouble. If the Committee ever learned, it wouldn't be only Papa who would feel their heavy hand. You and I would suffer as well. We might even lose our home."

Sarah's first hysterical reactions slowly began to subside as she shared her pain and confusion with a sympathetic listener. Her mind seemed clearer now, and her determination stronger. She had not known what to do alone, but surely now, with Darcy to help her think it out, they would find an answer that would save both her father and Neil. That was all she cared about. Their home meant nothing compared to the safety of those she loved best.

"He told me he would stop helping Ferris, but I don't think he really meant it. Oh, that Ferris Blunt! How I hate him. He is such a terrible man. He even has some wild idea of asking Papa for my hand. Have you ever heard of anything so foolish? I'd rather die!"

"Perhaps trying to convince Papa is the wrong way to go about this. If you talked to Ferris, you might be able to get him to leave Papa alone."

"I tried that," Sarah said, grimacing as she remembered the scene by the riverbank. "It did no good at all. He's . . . he's a cruel, crude man, and I never want to have anything to do with him again. He as much as laughed at me. He said the only way Papa would be safe from his influence was if I would agree to become his betrothed. Can you imagine!''

Darcy waited a moment before speaking. Her voice was very low and full of feeling, and her eyes looked everywhere around the room except directly into her sister's face.

''Perhaps if you agreed . . .''

''What!''

''Oh, you don't have to really mean it. Just make him think you mean it. ''

''Darcy!'' Sarah cried. ''I cannot believe you'd ask such a sacrifice of me, your own sister.''

Darcy tried to sound very matter-of-fact. ''Would it be such a sacrifice? All you have to do is convince Ferris that you intend to marry him long enough to get Papa out of this crisis. If he agrees for your sake not to raid the house tomorrow, sparing Neil and the other Continental officers, wouldn't it be worth it? Later you can break it off. The war has to end someday, and you'd never have to really marry him. Think about it, Sarah. It might be a way out.''

As if to escape from her sister's terrible words, Sarah rose and walked to the washstand, where she poured a little water into the bowl. Dipping her cloth in its depths, she wiped at her face. The dampness seemed to ease the tightness and confusion of her mind.

''I would be as dishonorable as Papa has been,'' she said quietly.

''Posh! With a man like Ferris, an outlaw and a thief and a murderer? Why, he has long ago put himself outside the bounds of honor. Besides, expediency is sometimes more important than the niceties of manners, especially in wartime. Think how you will feel if you don't do this and disaster comes tomorrow night.''

Sarah leaned against the window frame, dejection in every line of her supple body. Relentlessly Darcy went on.

''I would do it myself in a moment except that he has no

fondness for me." She moved to her sister and laid a soft hand on Sarah's shoulder. "It's the only way out, Sarah. The only way I can see."

"But I hate him," Sarah moaned. "And . . ." And there's someone else, she longed to say. Someone I am already betrothed to. Yet something held the words back. To even think of the happiness she had shared with Neil made the grim prospect of pretending to a relationship with Ferris more terrible. It broke her heart. It was against everything she wanted to be, everything she had believed herself to be.

"I'm afraid," she said in a tentative voice. "Afraid that if I even pretend to such a betrothal, it might really come to pass. I couldn't stand that, Darcy. I'd kill myself."

"Now, why should it ever come to pass? You know Papa would never force you to marry him—not you, his favorite daughter. It would only be a pretense. A deception. Long enough to get Papa out of the clutches of this evil man. I wish I could do it."

Her voice was so full of fervor that Sarah never doubted that if she were the one Ferris wanted, she would be on her way that moment to offer herself to him. It made her ashamed of her reluctance. There were always sacrifices to be made in times like these. Why had she thought she would never be required to make any?

"All right," she said, so low Darcy could barely hear her. "All right. I'll do it. Perhaps it will save Papa and . . . and Neil. If it does, then it will be worth all the shame. But it will be hard. So hard."

With her back still to her sister, she could not see the small, triumphant smile that passed across Darcy's lips. She only felt the strong arm that hugged her shoulders.

"That's my brave Sarah," Darcy said in her ear. "Now, wash your face and make yourself look pretty. We'll have to find some way to speak to Papa and to Ferris Blunt right away. The sooner we get all this arranged, the better for everyone."

Sarah turned and poured more water in the bowl.

Everyone but me, she thought sadly.

Nat did not find Ferris at his camp that morning. Leaving a message that he must talk with him, he returned to his house at Cole's Landing by late afternoon to find Ferris there waiting for him, disguised in his role of the peddler. As the two of them sat in Nat's study going over their plans for the raid the following evening, there was a sharp rap at the door. Ferris, momentarily startled, reached for his battered old hat, yanking it down around his face. Pulling forward some scribbled bills of lading, Nat called, "Who is it?"

At once the door opened and his eldest daughter stood on the threshold, dark half-moons under her eyes and an unaccustomed sober scowl on her face.

"Why, Sarah . . ." Nat began, glancing uncomfortably at Ferris.

Sarah looked around the room, taking in the peddler and making sure there was no one else. Stepping inside, she quietly closed the door behind her.

"It's all right, Papa. I know who this gentleman is, and it's just as well he is here, since what I have to say is something both of you should hear."

Nat started to protest, but his daughter's angry, determined look held him back. Ferris, he noticed, only smiled at Sarah, making no attempt to disguise his real identity.

"I never expected to have such pleasant company when I came here today," he said, his voice full of insinuation.

"Nor would you have," Sarah said bitterly, "except that I have no other way to put a stop to something that will surely end in disaster for us all. I cannot say I'm glad you're here, but it does make my task easier." She turned to her father. "I've come to insist—nay, even beg you both to stay away from this house tomorrow evening."

"Why, Sarah," Nat said in surprise, "I don't know what you mean. I have already made plans for you and Darcy and me to visit old Auntie Emerson in Peekskill. She was such a good friend of your mother's, and we see her so seldom."

Sarah glowered at her father, and Ferris gave a short laugh.

"No use pretending, Nat. I'll wager the girl knows everything. Right, my pretty?"

"Don't call me that! Yes, I know there are some people coming here tomorrow, and I'll stake my life that you and your scurvy gang are planning the same kind of reception that you gave Andries Stoakes. You cannot do it. You must not."

There was a brief flash of rage in Ferris's narrow eyes. "I'm not accustomed to being told what I can or cannot do," he said coldly.

"All right, then," Sarah answered, looking quickly away. "I ask you not to come here tomorrow. For the sake of the friendship you shared with my father."

Ferris chuckled, low in his throat. He's enjoying this, Sarah thought, resentment spreading through her. He's enjoying watching me debase myself! She glanced over at her father, who was staring absently at the papers in his hand, his face strained. He had already backed off, leaving the field to her. I wonder if he knows that I'm only doing this for him, Sarah thought bitterly.

"Oh, of course, Nat has always been such a good friend," Ferris said, settling back easily in his chair. "Such a very good friend."

"Papa, please. If you love me, listen to me. Don't do anything to disturb the men who are coming here tomorrow. Let them come and finish their business and go away again. Please, Papa."

"You were not supposed to mention this to anyone," Nat said in a voice little more than a whisper.

"More important," Ferris added, "have you told anyone else?"

"No. I have said nothing to anyone. But . . . but I might. I could tell Mr. van Tassel."

To her dismay this threat only made Ferris chuckle louder.

"I doubt that, my pretty miss, since to do so would put a rope around your good father's neck. No, I don't think we have anything to fear from that source."

"Neil never should have told you," Nat said, looking directly at his daughter for the first time.

"Neil? Ferris's voice was cold. Neil who?"

"He didn't," Sarah lied, knowing that somehow she had to keep Neil's name out of this. "I cannot tell you who told me, except to say that it was someone who is not involved at all."

Nat did not mistake the panic in her eyes. "It could have been Popham," he said, looking at Ferris. "Though how would he know of it? There's a lot of mystery about the man."

"It doesn't matter," Ferris answered, his eyes devouring Sarah. "Look here, Miss Reed. There are larger matters at work here than you know of. Your pa and I have poured a lot of effort and time, not to mention the risk to our necks, into furthering a cause we both believe in. And you're asking us to forgo one of the best opportunities we've ever had because you're afraid someone will get hurt."

Sarah turned to him, her eyes blazing. " 'Cause!' You don't believe in any cause! That's just empty cant to disguise your self-serving crimes. Robbery and murder are all you believe in!"

"Sarah!" Nat gasped.

There were two angry red spots on her white cheeks.

But she forced down her bitter resentment at the scowling man opposite her and held her tongue. It would do her no good to send him stalking out the door. That would accomplish nothing.

Although Ferris had to curb an urge to strike her, his overpowering reaction once again was to be full of admiration at how beautiful Sarah looked with the color in her face and her dark eyes alive with fury.

"Mistress Sarah is upset," he said patronizingly to Nat. Then, leaning forward in his chair, he reached out a long finger and lightly touched Sarah's wrist.

"There is only one way I might be persuaded," he said, his voice dripping with honey. "And you know what that is."

Snatching her hand away, Sarah felt a stab of cold in her chest.

"Nat here knows," Ferris went on, "how I feel about you. I've already spoken to him. Maybe this is as good a time as any to make everything official." Shrinking back, Sarah felt as though a pit were opening at her feet. She had hoped desperately that she might be able to persuade Ferris without resorting to this, and now, here he was, dragging it in himself. Yet might that not suggest how susceptible he would be to the proposition?

"Mistress Sarah here is most anxious for me to do her a great service, one that will be some cost to myself. Very well, then. I'll do her a service in exchange for one she does me."

Resisting an overpowering urge to get up and run to the door, Sarah grimly concentrated on the image of Neil's face.

"What do you mean?" Nat said, looking between the two of them.

Ferris's voice went on relentlessly. "I'll agree to leave the officers to their own affairs tomorrow if Sarah here will agree to marry me."

"Oh, now Ferris," Nat said lamely. "I don't think—"

"What about it, mistress?"

Sarah clenched her hands and closed her eyes tightly against his leering, horrible face. Desperately she tried to concentrate on Neil even as his features grew foggy and dim. Must she do this? Was there any other choice?

"At once," Ferris added.

Sarah's eyes flew open. "What?"

"Yes. The sooner the better. I'm not near so young as you, my pretty, and I've wearied of waiting. Besides, I wouldn't want any other man looking at you, knowing you were soon to be mine."

"Oh, no, not so soon. When the war's over, perhaps."

"That won't do."

"Papa," she said, looking beseechingly at Nat. He looked as sick as she felt, and she knew this was not the marriage he had wanted for his daughter. Yet, while the moments seeped slowly by and her father protested nothing, all hope died for Sarah. He was not going to protect her, and there was only one way she could protect him.

Trying to put a good face on it, she turned back to Ferris, lifting her chin and staring haughtily down on him, saying with every gesture how completely beneath her she felt him to be.

"Do I have your solemn promise that you will stay away from this house tomorrow evening?"

"Aye."

There was a worn old Bible on the window seat. Sarah grabbed it up and thrust it at him.

"Swear. Swear on this holy book."

"First you swear that you'll be my bride."

She hadn't bargained for this. She was caught now in the very same strands that made his oath secure. Laying her hand on the book, she said in a stifled voice, "I swear by this holy word that if you keep your promise I will marry you."

A triumphant light spread across Ferris's face. Grabbing the book from her hand, he held it between his. "And I swear I will not enter this house tomorrow evening."

"Or come near to it . . ."

He hesitated a moment, then added, "Or come near to it."

Sarah's knees turned to water and she slumped in her chair, not even daring to think about what she had just done.

"Well, Nat, it seems you're to be my father-in-law," Ferris said, smiling broadly.

Without a word, Nat moved to the door and, wrenching it open, stalked from the room, slamming the door behind him. Sarah would have followed, but Ferris reached out and grabbed her by the wrist.

"Come now, dearie, and give your betrothed a kiss."

"No." Sarah cried. "I've made a bargain with you, but you'll find it does not include affection or tenderness. Getting a wife by force is going to bring you very little warmth, Mr. Blunt."

With a quick jerk of his arm, Ferris pulled her to him.

"You'll be warm enough in bed, missy, and that's where it matters."

Filled with revulsion, Sarah endured the horrible pressure of his body against hers and the revolting wetness of his lips against her cheek. Then, wrenching free, she ran to the door. Her hand was on the latch when she turned back.

"I'll keep my promise. You see that you keep yours."

Eleven

❧

THE AFTERNOON air was close, encouraging tiny rivulets of perspiration down Darcy's cheeks as she hurried along the road. With so much of the way uphill, she had to stop several times to catch her breath and wipe at her brow with the hem of her apron. How she wished she had dared take one of Nat's old horses, but that would have been too obvious. She wanted no one to know she had left the village.

Parallel to the dusty road a brook tumbled along just inside the surrounding woods. Darcy stopped long enough to dash some of its cold water briskly on her face, then started off again, a little slower this time. It would do no good to find Neil if she was so weary and worn out that she could not keep her wits about her. Besides, she wanted to look as pretty as possible—not all sweaty and hot like some field hand.

When she reached the crest of the road she began searching for a likely spot to wait. It must be overgrown enough to afford her shade and privacy yet allow her a good view of the road ahead. She walked for another half mile, then found the perfect place, a grassy knoll shadowed by cool beech and maple trees. The gray trunk of the beech was wide enough to put her arms around, and she knew that if anyone else came down the road she could quickly hide behind it. Sitting on the grass, she leaned back against the rough trunk, fanning away the gnats with her bonnet while some of the heat of her exertions faded. When she heard a faint rattle on the road ahead, she jumped up to hide behind the tree. Peering around the trunk, she saw Johnnie Tate prodding his old milk cow and her calf toward the village. Darcy kept very still, for Johnnie was the last person she wished to see just now. When quiet descended and the dust kicked up by the cows had settled, she took her place again and almost drifted off to sleep in the warm, soft afternoon air.

Almost but not quite. The truth was she was much too excited to be lulled asleep. When she caught the faint jingle of a horses's harness she jumped up again, alert and wide awake. Then at last she spotted Neil cantering slowly down the path, his hat pulled down over his eyes.

Darcy waited until he was almost to where she stood, then stepped quickly from the trees into the middle of the narrow road. The horse gave a whinny as Neil reined in sharply, pulling Sampson sideways to keep from running over her.

"By God, Darcy!" he exclaimed, turning his startled horse in the path. "I thought you were a ghost. What do you mean jumping out at me like that?"

Reaching for the bridle, Darcy helped to steady Neil's mount, looking up into his face with such intensity that at once he jumped to the conclusion there had been some terrible accident at home.

"Neil, I must talk to you," she cried.

Above Sampson's tossing mane, Neil scowled down at her.

"Now see here," he said, beginning to grow annoyed. "You've got to stop this, Darcy. I can't have you jumping out at me like this, God knows where and when. You could have talked to me when I was at the tavern this morning."

The horse grew still, standing quietly while Darcy ran up and pressed against Neil's boots in the stirrup, her hand clutching at his arm.

"But I didn't know then . . . Oh, Neil, it's of the utmost importance."

"If this is about your feelings for me again . . ."

"No," she lied. "It's about all of us, Sarah, Papa. . . ."

Neil hesitated, wondering if somehow Darcy had learned about the plans for tomorrow and knew some difficulty about them he did not. It might be wise to hear what she had to say just in case it had a bearing on that important event. Moreover, if anything had happened to Sarah . . .

Darcy looked up at him, her eyes brimming. Whatever this was, it had moved her deeply.

"All right, but just for a moment."

Swinging out of the saddle, he tied his horse to a branch of the maple and followed Darcy, who had gone back to where the overhanging limbs could shield them from any travelers on the road.

"Now, what is this about?" he said impatiently. "Whatever it is, you must find a better way to get a man alone than to leap out at him from the most unexpected places. Really, Darcy!"

She dipped her head as if to hide her tears, and his complaints died on his lips. He was being too harsh on the girl, he thought, remembering her youth.

"What is it?" he said more gently.

Sinking to the ground, Darcy leaned her head against the tree, turning her back to him. Though he could not see her face, every attitude of her body was so full of despair that his heart was moved. He knelt beside her and laid a hand on her shoulder.

"Whatever is the matter, Darcy? It cannot be so terrible."

With a sudden motion she turned and flung herself against him, burrowing her head in the hollow of his neck.

"Oh, Neil, it *is* terrible. I don't even know how to tell you."

Neil hesitated only a moment before laying his arm around her shoulders and resting his head against the soft waves of her hair. She smelled pleasantly of cinnamon and lavender.

"I just can't believe she would do such a thing!" Darcy went on, her voice choking back a sob. "She's always been so gentle and so . . . so fragile. To give herself to that horrible, horrible man!"

Neil's hand arrested on Darcy's back as a coldness steeped into him.

"Who? What man?"

"My sister," Darcy cried, flinging her hands over her face. "My own dear Sarah. Betrothed. Betrothed to . . ."

Neil could not speak. Filled with apprehension, he waited.

". . . To Ferris Blunt!"

His fingers dug into Darcy's shoulders as he put her away from him. "That's absurd! She doesn't even know the man. And even if she did, she'd never do such a thing!"

"But she did. It's true, I swear it. He was there at the house not an hour ago. I heard her tell him so myself. She's going to marry him."

Wanting to laugh, Neil was stopped by the earnest despair in Darcy's eyes.

"But he's an outlaw. He'd never just walk into your house. Your father would have nothing to do with him. Sarah would never . . ."

"He *was* there. I saw him and heard them both say his

name several times. He was talking with Papa in his study
and Sarah joined them. I heard her say she'd marry him. I
couldn't believe my own ears, but before God, I heard it.''

"But why? Why would he be talking to Nat? Why
would Sarah agree to such a preposterous marriage?"

"I don't know why.''

"And how did you hear all this? You were listening at
the door, weren't you?"

Darcy glanced quickly away. "Yes, but only because I
saw the man come in and he looked so suspicious. I was
afraid it might be something about you, and I wanted to
protect you. It was for your own good.''

Releasing her with a sudden motion, Neil rose and
walked to the other side of the knoll. He could barely
believe Darcy's story, yet neither could he dismiss it offhand.
Suppose Nat was not to be trusted. If he had some sort of
connection with Blunt and had informed the outlaw about
the meeting to be held there the following evening . . . It
was too terrible a possibility to shrug off.

And Sarah? Would she be a part of such treachery?
Why? Was she more loyal to her father than to him? Had
she been leading him along all this time, just to pass along
information to the enemy? Was all her talk of love just a
pretense?

Slipping up behind Neil, Darcy put her arms around his
waist and leaned against his broad back.

"Oh, my poor Neil. It breaks my heart to be the one to
tell you all this, but I felt I had to. You know how much
you mean to me—I tried once before to explain how much
I love you. Will you believe me now when I betray my
own flesh and blood to keep you safe?"

"What do you mean?"

"I heard them all talking about something that was
going to happen at our house tomorrow evening. I couldn't
tell what it meant except that it was some sort of conspiracy which will bring trouble on the American army. I

never wanted to have to cause you so much pain, but I knew it would be better than saying nothing and seeing you come to harm.''

''She could never have told that man she would marry him!'' The words were like gall in his throat. She loves *me*. She loves *me*! he wanted to scream, and yet now more than ever he dared not reveal to Darcy the extent of his involvement with her sister.

''But she did tell him. I heard her myself. If you ask her she'll tell you so. Ask her, Neil. Ask her yourself. Then you'll believe me.''

Sick at heart, he barely even felt Darcy's arms around his body. When he turned and she leaned against him, he rested his arms around her in an automatic response, all his thoughts on Sarah. As her lips began teasingly tasting his cheek, moving with smooth silkiness toward his own mouth, he was almost unaware of it until the sudden blaze of her passion kindled a spark deep within him. Wildly she kissed him, her lips opening under his until he felt a fire, hot and growing, consuming the blackness of his heart. One moment more and he would have thrown her on the ground and taken her right there on the verdant grass.

But this was not Sarah. These pointed, catlike features were not the soft, sweet ones he saw so vividly in his mind's eye.

Summoning an angry forcefulness, he was able to push her away. ''Leave me be!'' he cried, moving away. Darcy, gulping in her breath, leaned against the rough bark of the tree and watched him go. Even as the flame within her subsided, she was filled with happiness, for she had felt the wild response of his body to hers. He could not yet give in to her completely, but he would, oh, he would. She knew that now. She had only to be patient.

''My poor dear,'' she said gently. ''I want only to comfort you.''

''I don't need comfort,'' Neil muttered without conviction.

"I shall speak to Sarah myself. You must be wrong about this. Come along. Let's get back to the Landing."

She retrieved her hat while Neil untied his horse's bridle. With strong hands he lifted her into the saddle, then vaulted up behind her. They started down the path back toward the village at a brisker pace than Darcy wished, yet she was not unhappy, since it was too delicious to be in the tight circle of his arms, feeling the hard firmness of his body moving against her with the rhythm of his horse.

When they clattered onto the bridge, she looked up to see Maude Sackett's cottage straight before them. Maude was in the garden, scratching her hoe at the dry earth. Glancing sideways at her as they cantered by, Darcy fancied the old woman gave her a sly smile, though she made no gesture of recognition.

The old witch! She knew everything. Her charms had worked after all, though not in the way Darcy had expected. But what did that matter so long as the result was the same? Neil would be hers now; she felt it in her bones. Her smile was one of triumph as they clattered into the stableyard of her father's house.

For a long while Nat sat on the bench outside his stable, struggling to get his emotions under control. Something within him grew sick as he remembered the smug triumph in Ferris Blunt's eyes. The idea of Ferris as a son-in-law was repugnant to him, and yet his dogged determination to wreak vengeance on the men of Cole's Landing who had hurt him so badly was even stronger. He could see no way of putting Ferris off without losing his help, and that he was not willing to do. Especially not at this critical point. Perhaps once the victory was won and the enemy defeated there would be time enough to save his daughter from a marriage that would destroy her.

When at last he returned to his study he found Ferris still there, standing at the window watching Sarah, who had escaped to the seclusion of her roses in front of the house.

"I thought you might have gone," Nat said sourly, closing the door behind him.

"We've not finished with tomorrow yet."

"But I thought . . ."

Ferris shrugged and resumed his seat. "This is too important an opportunity to pass up even for such a delicacy as your lovely daughter. It's enough to make her think I'll accept her terms. I can straighten her out later."

Something within Nat's heavy heart lightened. If Ferris had no intention of keeping his promise to Sarah, then it made her promise to him less binding. In a way it was to his advantage, since the opportunity would not be lost and his lovely Sarah would not be compromised. They discussed and discarded several ways of handling the raid, until they finally settled on one that suited them both. Nat would be out of the house completely, taking his girls with him. Ferris and his men would slip in through the tunnel, wait until they were certain the Americans were there, then burst in to take prisoners without the guard outside ever suspecting. If things went right, they might capture a high-ranking officer, possibly even Washington himself. There would be no killing and no burning, nothing to give away the fact that a raid had taken place inside the house. They would exit the way they came without ever having been seen except by the officers they were taking prisoner.

"And you're certain no one else knows about the tunnel?" Ferris asked Nat for the fourth time, his tiny eyes glinting in the dusk of the afternoon.

"No one. I've told everyone that it was closed years ago and never reopened. You should be able to get away completely if you're quiet about it. No pistols fired, no shouts to the guard."

"Don't worry about that. I'll make sure the first man

that makes a sound chokes on it. In his own blood if necessary.''

When at last Ferris took up his battered hat and assumed the stooping obsequiousness of the peddler, it was late afternoon. Nat walked with him to the front door, where his wagon was parked in the path. As they stepped outside, Sarah, who was kneeling on the grass, weeding the rows of flowers by the gate, looked up and met Ferris's eyes briefly before deliberately turning back to her work.

Ferris hesitated as though he were debating whether or not to go over and speak to her when the clatter of a horse caught his attention and he paused, standing beside Nat at the doorway.

Looking up, Sarah's heart gave a leap as she saw Neil riding into the stableyard with Darcy before him on the saddle. She caught the cry that rose in her throat and glanced quickly back at Ferris in the doorway. He was examining the new arrivals with annoyed interest.

To her horror, Neil dismounted, helped Darcy down, and walked straight toward her.

"I want to talk with you, Sarah," he said in none too polite a tone.

She rose, filled with panic. Throwing him a warning glance, she tried to sound politely indifferent as she answered, "Good afternoon, Lieutenant Partherton. I see you've brought Darcy home. How very kind of you."

Confused, Neil laid a hand on her arm, saying with some force, "See here, Sarah, there's something we need to clear up, you and I."

At the terror in her eyes he glanced up to see Nat and the mangy old peddler standing at the doorway watching them. He could see no reason to be disturbed about that. Nat already knew of their relationship, and surely the old peddler could not matter.

Turning her back to the house, Sarah whispered through clenched teeth. "Keep your voice down, please!" Then louder: "Why, of course, Lieutenant. I suppose you want to know about the sage tea. Darcy told me you were asking about it. I've made it special myself for years."

Neil lowered his voice, though his anger was still apparent. "To hell with sage tea. Darcy tells me you've pledged yourself to Ferris Blunt, the outlaw. It's not true, is it? I cannot believe it could be true."

What could she say, standing there with her father and Ferris looking on? If Ferris ever suspected that Neil was the man she really cared for he would kill him on the spot. If not now, certainly later.

"It is quite good for the flux. We've used it for years. I'm sure it would be very beneficial to your poor soldiers, since they are suffering so with it."

"What are you talking about?" Neil said roughly, his impatience and concern growing by the minute. "I thought you were pledged to me."

Reaching out, he gripped her shoudlers. Panic flamed in her eyes, and she jerked away, stepping back several paces from him.

"Don't touch me!" she hissed.

A hardness settled over Neil's face. She could see the anger and disappointment growing in his dark eyes. Pleading silently, she tried to make her voice light.

"I'll be happy to give you the recipe, of course. Just give me a little time to write it down."

"So. That is how it is," he said bitterly. "Well, you needn't fear. I won't bother you again."

Turning on his heel, he stalked away toward the stable. Sarah watched him go, the tears that she dared not shed hot behind her eyes. She looked back to see Ferris bend his head and whisper something to her father. Nat answered him, gesturing with his hands. Oh, dear God, Sarah prayed. Don't let him suspect.

Gathering up her basket, she walked toward the side of the house, where she could lose herself in the shrubbery of the garden, trying not to move too fast or to let the despair that filled her heart be obvious to the two men at the gate. At the end of the path Neil angrily snatched at the bridle of his horse while Darcy grabbed his arm, looking up into his angry face with eyes brimming with sympathy.

"Oh, my dear, I can tell how much she hurt you."

"Let me go," Neil snapped. "I don't want to talk about it."

"No, of course not. But come to me soon, my dear. I can help you forget, my Neil. Come to me. I'll show you."

Laying a hand on the saddle, Neil put a foot in the stirrup and was about to spring up when Darcy caught him again.

"Say you'll come. It's all I ask."

He looked into her pleading face for a moment, so openly wanton and inviting. Swiftly, roughly, he grabbed her and kissed her eager lips hard and violently, then vaulted into his saddle. Without a word he turned Sampson and clattered out of the yard.

Darcy waved after him, glowing with her triumph, oblivious to the sad figure on the other side of the garden or the glaring eyes of the old peddler beside the gate.

That kiss stayed with Neil far into the night while he lay on his cot, too restless and unhappy to allow sleep to ease his misery. Finally, in the early hours of the morning, he rose, threw a tunic over his loose shirt, pulled on his boots, and walked out to roam the parapet, hoping the cool night air might clear his mind. Speaking briefly to the corporal on watch, who for all his responsibilities seemed far closer to nodding off than Neil, he stepped up onto the wooden platform to lean against the wall and look out over the dark panorama stretching below. The full moon gave a pale glow to the dark thread of the river, enfolded by the black mass of the hills that lined its shore. Far in the distance an owl hooted, followed by an answering call close by. Neil leaned his elbows on the rough sill, his chin in his hands, and wished he could appreciate the beauty of the scene. His mind kept slipping back to a pair of wide soft eyes, their thick lashes shading the love and gentleness within. Then they faded to another pair, narrower, inviting, thick with desire.

Why had he kissed those eager lips when he knew in his heart he cared nothing for them? Because they *were* so eager, so near, so enticing? No. Because he hoped Sarah was looking and would see him do it. Because he hoped to hurt her the way she had hurt him. Because if she could play at love, then turn to someone else, so could he.

And yet it had given him no comfort to get even with her. All he had done was to further encourage Darcy in her wanton ways and make himself miserable to boot. He was just as sick at heart as before. Just as disappointed, just as hurt.

Why had Sarah done it? He would swear she was not a fickle, flighty girl, out to make the best match for herself. Ferris Blunt was no doubt a wealthy man, but it was all ill-gotten. The only way he would ever live to enjoy his money was if the revolution failed and British rule was restored.

Was that what was behind all this? Had Sarah become convinced that the war was lost and she should align herself with the victors? Yet he would swear her love for him was not based on his loyalties, but was for himself alone. He would have staked his life on that. Sarah Reed was not an opportunist to change sides with the prevailing winds of fortune.

What, then? Why had she talked so strangely, and even yanked back from his touch as though it was repugnant to her?

In the quiet of the night no answers came. Neil ran his fingers through his hair, remembering that he must be at his best tomorrow and this was not helping. Somehow he had to put Sarah and Darcy both from his mind until after tomorrow's important business was completed. Then he would face Sarah squarely and seek out the truth. And if she had truly deceived him and really planned to marry this Ferris Blunt, then he might take another long look at Darcy Reed. A nubile young girl like Darcy who made no secret of her strong passion for him might be just what was needed to help ease his wounded heart.

Somehow the thought gave him little joy.

While Neil stood on the parapet overlooking the river, Sarah lay on her own bed, staring at the ceiling of her room, as unable to embrace the comfort of sleep as Neil had been. Of all the terrible complications that might have upset her careful plans, this afternoon's had been the worst. How tragic that Neil had appeared right at the moment Ferris and her father were watching. Over and over she thought back to other ways she might have handled the scene and could find nothing that she might have done differently. If only they had been alone she could have explained, but as it was, the last thing she could allow was to let Ferris know of her feelings for Neil. But the sight of the anger in his eyes, the surprise followed by the bitterness—it was almost more than she could bear. She had not even been able to watch him leave, knowing that he was riding away believing her to be faithless and fickle. And now she did not dare send him so much as a note to say how wrong he was. The risk was too great.

After tomorrow she would explain it all. If only Neil could come safely through tomorrow's meeting, all this would be straightened out.

But would it? How was Ferris Blunt going to react when he learned that she had tricked him and never intended to marry him? Would she ever dare announce her betrothal to Neil afterward? Ferris was a vengeful and evil man.

Wouldn't he go after Neil someday, no matter how far in the future, once he knew that he was the man she loved?

She rolled over on her feather mattress with a sickness in her soul. Was she ever going to find a way out of this? Had her lie to save Neil and her father entrapped her forever? Ferris was like a spider. One lie had caught her in his web, and the more she struggled, the more deeply enmeshed she became, until . . .

Sarah groaned, burying her face in the pillow. There must be some way out. Tomorrow. Just get through tomorrow, then face it squarely and make everything right again. She'd find a way. She had to.

But oh, if only Neil had not come riding up at that very moment with Darcy before him on his saddle!

It never occurred to her to wonder how Darcy had come to be there.

The darkness of the dining room in the Millers' ordinary was broken by a small pool of yellow light on a table in a corner. Bending so close to it that the gold of his hair gleamed with the candle's reflection, William Popham dipped his quill in the inkwell and moved his hand along the paper on the table. The soft scratching of his pen echoed loudly in the silent room. He frowned, struggling to see clearly in the gloom, yet unwilling to light another candle, since it might attract too much attention. With a sharp thrust, he put a period to the end of his sentence, sprinkled sand over the paper, then held it close to the flame to read over what he had written.

"Why, Mr. Popham . . ."

At the sudden voice behind him, Popham jumped and turned to see Noah Miller standing in his nightshirt, holding up a lantern. His bare feet and knobby knees gave him an almost comical look.

"Why, sir, I didn't know it was you. I saw the light and wondered who'd be about at this hour."

"I'm so sorry I disturbed you, Mr. Miller," Popham said, carefully folding his letter. "It was difficult to write in the room upstairs, so I took the liberty of using your dining room. I shall be happy to have the cost of the candle added to my account."

Noah sat his lantern down on one of the tables and reached for a round iron circle, thick with keys, hanging on a peg.

"No matter at all. Just like to make sure nobody's breaking in. Since we're both awake, why don't I just open the cage here and we'll have a little nightcap?"

"Why, that would be very pleasant." Popham spread a blob of wax on the paper and pressed the seal of his ring deeply into it.

"That is, if you're done," Noah added, pulling back the caged rack that covered his store of wine and ale.

"As a matter of fact I was just finishing. There were some instructions I needed to send to my overseer at home. You know how these people are. If you don't keep on top of them everything goes to pieces. I like him to be sure that even though I'm not there, I'm very much aware of what should be happening. It's the only proper way to run an estate."

"I wouldn't know, myself," Noah said as he pulled out a squat green jug and yanked at the stopper. "My home-made porter suit your fancy?"

At Popham's barely concealed frown he quickly added, "Or would wine be more to your taste?"

"I believe I'd prefer the wine, thank you," Popham said, slipping the letter into his writing box and closing the lid and locking it with a small gold key he pulled from his fob.

The wine, the key, and the beautifully painted box—all the trappings of a gentleman. But give me good homemade ale any day, Noah thought to himself.

"There's a sloop coming through just after dawn bound

for Albany. You'll want to get your letter on board, I expect," he said, pouring the wine into a stemmed glass and the porter into a large tankard. Handing Popham the glass, he leaned his elbows on the bar and took a long swig of the porter.

"That will be perfect. I've been much impressed by the amount of traffic up and down the river while I've stayed here. The war surely hasn't hurt it much, has it?"

"You should have seen it before the lobsters took New York," Miller said, gesturing to the south. "The farms near Albany kept New York in foodstuffs. But I shouldn't have to tell you that. Your markets must have been hard hit once the city fell."

"Somewhat. But since I deal mostly in sheep and beef, the needs of the army more than made up for any losses."

"Some of that beef probably found its way into English stomachs," Miller said, grimacing. 'Why, they say nearly a third of the families in the neutral ground have moved away. Starved out, burned out, their crops and livestock stolen—they had no other choice. It's an outrage."

Popham tapped a long finger on the rough planks of the table. "Tell me, Mr. Miller, what's this Reed family like? Lovely girls there."

"Oh ho! So that's what you're hanging around for," Noah said, poking Popham's shoulder. "Well, you couldn't do better. Nat's all right now, anyway, though for a while he was in the bad graces of the Committee for calling the rebellion treason. A few months in Newgate seemed to straighten him out, and now he's as good a patriot as you could find. Sarah, she's a beauty, but my Deborah tells me she's much taken with one of the officers from the Point over there across the river. Now, Darcy, she's more to my liking. That girl was made for bed sport, if you take my meaning. As neat a little piece of flimsy as you could find."

One eyebrow on Popham's lean face inched upward. "I

think you do the young lady a disservice by such remarks,'' he said in a rather clipped tone. "I find her altogether charming. In fact, I'm surprised that some of the local fellows have not already laid claim to her heart.''

Noah wiped his sleeve across his lips. "They've tried hard enough.''

"With no success?''

"None. She wants something livelier, no doubt. Now me—''

"Noah!''

Deborah Miller's angry voice sounded from abovestairs. "Noah Miller, are you down there drinking? You get up here and back to bed right away!''

Noah frowned at the dark hall beyond the dining room. "I'll come when I'm ready!'' he called angrily, but he quickly downed the rest of his tankard and moved to lock up the cage with more energy than he had shown unlocking it. Popham smiled to himself and finished his own glass.

"What about that young officer from the fort—Partherton, I believe his name is?''

"Don't know much about him,'' Noah said, pattering to the hall. "Seems nice enough. Spends a lot of time over here and at the Reed house. Well, best I get to bed. Good night, sir.''

"Yes. Good night. And thank you for the wine.''

He snuffed out the candle, throwing the room into a darkness lit only by the soft glow of the moon through the window. Still smiling, he picked up his writing box, set it under his arm, and started up the stairs. Miller was already out of sight.

Twelve

BY TEN o'clock the next morning Nat had Sarah and Darcy bundled in the wagon for the trip to Peekskill. In the boot lay a large basket filled with preserves and fresh vegetables and a side of pickled beef. Old Mistress Emerson lived pretty much on the charity of the village, and on the rare occasions when Nat dragged himself down to visit her, he always made sure he brought a generous amount of the farm's provisions with him.

Sarah usually enjoyed visiting Miss Emerson, since she was one of the few people who could talk to her about her mother. The elderly lady lived in a cramped cottage only a few fields away from the Peekskill dock, and the boats and sloops which put in there were even more interesting and varied than those at Cole's Landing. But today Sarah's mind was too unsettled to enjoy anything. There was a lingering sadness when she remembered Neil's face the afternoon before, and as yet she had no idea how to convince him that she had not meant what she said. Neither could she take any comfort from the fact that Nat was taking them away from the village. If Ferris Blunt's promise could be believed, she should feel confident that Neil could go ahead with his plans in safety. The trouble was she did not really trust Ferris, and some nagging little voice kept whispering to her that while she was away the disaster she feared might happen anyway. She said little as the wagon rocked its way down the slopes toward the village and across the creek where the eagles and seagulls dipped and soared above the high marsh grass. When at last they pulled into Miss Emerson's tiny, weed-choked yard, her sense of unease was almost too much to bear.

Abigail Emerson was a tiny woman with a skin like old parchment. Crippled with arthritis, she wobbled with a cane out into her yard to give her visitors a warm welcome, unable to keep her eyes from straying toward the back of the wagon. Ushering them inside, where she exclaimed with delight over the welcome provisions, she set about with Sarah's help to fix up a dinner, while Nat unhitched the horse and put it to graze. It was nearly mid-afternoon when they finally sat down to enjoy the beef and vegetables, along with some of Miss Emerson's bread and the preserves Sarah had made herself. After that, Nat took up his hat to walk into the village and mix with the stragglers at Mandeville's Tavern, a custom he enjoyed so much that Sarah sometimes wondered if that was not perhaps the real reason he came to see Abigail Emerson. She and Darcy joined the old lady on the porch, where Abigail soon began nodding off.

"Why does she always do that?" Darcy said, sitting on the step and leaning her chin on her hands.

"She's not accustomed to company or having to make conversation," Sarah answered. "It tires her, I think."

"Yes, but she goes to sleep every time we come to visit. It's not very polite, you know. And it's so boring. I wish Papa would come back."

"Papa won't be back for hours," Sarah said, remembering his customary schedule when they came to Peekskill. If only she could relax, let go of her anxiety over Neil and the coming evening. The hours ahead seemed endless, and the feeling that she ought to be home grew more pronounced with each one that passed.

"Why don't we walk down to the dock?" said Darcy. "It would be something to do, anyway."

Sarah looked down to where the masts of the sloops gently bobbed above the tops of the trees. Perhaps one or two of them might be headed upriver—might even plan to put in at Cole's Landing. There was a strong wind out of the south. If they got aboard, they would be home by dusk instead of hours later by wagon.

"Sarah! Are you listening to me?"

"Yes. I heard everything you said." She pursed her lips together. Her father would be angry. It was probably silly—a ridiculous waste of time and money. But on the other hand, if anything did go wrong, she would be there, and there was no one else who had any kind of a hold over Ferris Blunt.

"Come on," she said suddenly, grabbing up her bonnet. Shaking Miss Emerson's shoulder, she yelled in her ear, "Tell Papa we've gone home on the boat," and ran down off the porch, leaving the startled old lady to watch bleary-eyed after her.

Darcy, quickly catching up, tied the strings on her hat as she hurried along beside her sister. "My goodness, I only thought to come down to look and pass the time."

"I know," Sarah said. "But I want to get home. I have this feeling that I ought to be there."

"But you don't even know if you can get aboard a boat to Cole's Landing."

"There's bound to be one headed upriver. I have a little money with me. I'll pay them to stop at the Landing if there's no other way."

"But why? I thought everything was worked out."

Sarah stopped briefly to dislodge a stone from her slipper. "It's supposed to be, but—oh, Darcy, I don't know. I just don't trust Papa or Ferris Blunt at all. And something Papa said at dinner makes me fear that they have both tricked us. I just want to be there."

"But Sarah, you can't just go barging in on an army matter. What will Neil think?"

"I won't barge in. I'll just make sure the house is safe, then go away, back to the Millers' tavern or somewhere out of sight. I just want to be sure everything goes safely."

Darcy could tell by the determined set of her sister's chin that her mind was made up. Well, why not go with her? There were certain to be some young men at the Green Man, and any kind of entertainment would be better than sitting here listening to Aunt Emerson snore. Skipping along the path, she followed Sarah down to the river's edge.

They found a boat easily, the sloop *Wind Haven* ready to leave on the incoming tide for stops at all the main towns between Peekskill and Albany. There was a good wind out of the south, carrying the heavy presentiment of a storm to come, but it helped them to make record time through the Horse Race, between the high bluffs of Anthony's Nose, and up to the Landing. Although the master had not planned to put in there, he decided that with such a favorable wind and tide it would not slow him too much to set ashore two such lovely young ladies.

The sun was a vermilion ball hanging over the tops of the dusky hills when they saw the low rooftops of the village appear over the undulating surface of the marsh grass lining the shore like fields of grain. Sarah stood at the rail as the boat dropped anchor long enough to send them in a dinghy to the wharf. In the gathering darkness she could clearly see the lumpy shape of the Millers' ordinary, and, straining her eyes, she thought she could make out the moving shadows of horses tied before it. Her heart gave a leap. Neil might already be there. Was she foolish to have come hurrying back like this? Would he chide her for her fears?

No. He was still too angry with her, she knew, to chide her about anything. Very well, then. She had nothing to lose. For her own sake she would be certain that he was safe.

The sun had disappeared when Neil, sitting astride his horse at a crossroads below West Point, finally saw the expected riders approaching in the distance. He had been waiting nearly an hour, watching every approaching horseman with anticipation that soon turned to disappointment. There was no misjudging this group, however. There had to be five or six of them, and they were covered with the dust that told of miles traveled since daylight. As they drew near he recognized the two plain gold straps of the staff officers of the Continental Light Dragoons. Pulling up, they stopped a few feet away, waiting until he called to them.

"Lieutenant Partherton of the Third New York."

The lead rider cantered up to Neil. "Lieutenant Sulley from Philadelphia," he answered, saluting. "With dispatches for His Excellency General Washington."

"I know," Neil said. "We've been expecting you. Everything is arranged."

"Haven't got a dram on you, have you? My throat feels as dry as the road itself."

"Here," Neil answered, handing him his canteen. "You'll have a chance to rest once we're across the river."

The lieutenant took a long swig at the canteen, then handed it to the trooper behind him. "Can't be soon enough," he replied, wiping his sleeve across his mouth. "We've been riding straight for two days."

Neil looked around, searching the dark outline of the forest for any unlikely movement.

"We'd better get down to the ferry," he said, trying not to sound anxious. The truth was that if Ferris and his men were looking for the most isolated place to jump them, this would be it.

"As you wish," the lieutenant answered, turning his mount in the road to follow Neil down a steeply sloping path toward the river, gray as pewter in the gathering darkness. The others fell in behind them as they started down the uneven path. Neil kept a watchful eye on the woods until they broke clear of them, then cantered up to where the flatboat lay pulled up on the sand. Allowing himself a sigh of relief, he helped load the horses on the boat and jumped in after the others as it pushed off from the shore. On the other side, dim lights like fireflies dotted the increasing dark, marking the tavern and the houses clustered around the wharf at the Landing. Farther up, he noticed, there was nothing but blackness where the Reed house lay. That was as it should be, he thought, beginning now to relax some of the tension he had been feeling all day.

The lieutenant had slumped down against the sides of the boat with his saddlebags over his lap, and was leaning on them with his arms across his knees and his hat down over his eyes. He looked to be already asleep. Neil sat down beside him and nudged him on the shoulder.

"There's a house on the other side, just above the village, where you'll be met," he said softly. "I expect a detachment from the camp at Greenburgh to be there to receive your dispatches."

Pushing up his cap, the lieutenant gave him a surprised glance. "The great man himself?"

"I believe so."

"Well, well. I knew I was carrying something of importance, but I never thought it merited that much attention. What do you suppose it is?"

"I think you'd do better not to wonder," Neil said cryptically.

The officer nodded and drew up his knees, as if to protect the saddlebags even more. A wind was rising with the coming of night, and Neil, lifting his face into it, thought a storm was brewing. The sooner they got this large sum of money transferred, the better, he thought. The idea of going into Nat Reed's house, even when none of the family would be there, was something he did not relish. So much of his life was tangled with their lives and in ways that seemed ever more complicated. But this was not the time to think about those things. There would be time enough to face them squarely once this night's work was safely over. That was all that mattered now.

As Neil and the courier from Philadelphia were stepping onto the flatboat on the western shore of the river, Sarah and Darcy were clambering out of the *Wind Haven*'s dinghy onto the wharf at the Landing. Sarah's sense of urgency and unease had increased as the sloop neared the village, though she had no way of knowing why. She ran down the wharf and toward the path, dragging a protesting Darcy along behind her, intent only on reaching home before darkness set in completely. The gloom was so dense that without realizing it she bounded into the shadowy form of a gentleman standing in the path before the Millers' ordinary, nearly knocking him down.

"Whoa, there," said a pleasant voice, and Sarah felt her arms gripped.

"Oh, dear, Mr. Popham, I'm so sorry. Did I hurt you?"

"No, no," Popham said, brushing his sleeve. "Only, my gracious, mistress, what fire are you running off to?"

"Why, Mr. Popham," Darcy said, stepping in front of her sister. "I must apologize for Sarah. I don't know what's the matter with her tonight, but she's been like a donkey with a burr under its saddle all evening. Do please forgive her."

"Why, it's nothing. Nothing at all. Is there some service I could render, Miss Reed? I mean if there is anything wrong and I could be of assistance, you know it would give me the greatest pleasure."

"No, nothing," Sarah murmured, anxious only to be away.

"Why, then won't you ladies come inside and be my guests for a glass of Madeira? There's a bit of a wind coming up, and a soothing glass of wine might be just the thing. I could see you home later."

"Oh, that sounds lovely," Darcy said, smiling up into his face.

"You must excuse me," Sarah muttered, "but I have a touch of the headache. I'll just go along home, if you don't mind. But Darcy, why don't you stay?"

"Well, if you think it would be proper . . ."

"But Miss Reed, I dislike the thought of you taking this road alone, and in this wind."

Sarah was already dancing down the path, burning to get away.

"I've done it all my life, thank you, Mr. Popham. And it's not so far, really. I'll be grateful if you'll watch out for Darcy," she called back to him. She was swallowed by the darkness before he could protest any further.

Popham stood looking tentatively after her as though caught in a bind of his own making. Slipping an arm through his, Darcy looked up into his face, smiling deliciously.

"I declare I don't know what's got into that girl. I think a glass of wine in a warm taproom sounds like the very thing. How nice of you to ask me."

Popham patted her hand. "Yes, well, why don't we go and enjoy it? I confess I feel worried about your sister and think we ought to follow along after her as soon as possible. She is acting very strange."

Darcy tossed her head in irritation. Sarah, always Sarah. Was she never going to be around a man who had no thought for her older sister? Leaning toward Popham so that her small breasts rubbed against his arm, they entered the tavern. She'd soon make him forget Sarah.

It seemed to Sarah that the wind picked up with every step that carried her closer to her father's house. There was a keening in the trees around her that filled the night with eerie mystery. Tree limbs dipped and shook and small branches flew against her feet, tripping her up as she half ran down the path. The tiny points of light behind the windows of Helena Earing's house and the Tates' rectory held a welcoming warmth which seemed to shut her out, leaving her isolated in the leaf-strewn darkness outside. She made the turn on the path to her house, noticing how it loomed like a black shape in the distance with no light at all.

But that was encouraging. Perhaps it meant she had been wrong all along. No one was inside, waiting. Neil might have already come and gone. All her fears were silly and groundless.

And yet somehow she knew they were not. This overwhelming sense of urgency had to come from somewhere, and she knew it was not just a figment of her imagination. There were too many signs, too much uneasiness. And, ultimately, wasn't betrayal what she might expect from a creature like Ferris Blunt?

She had to know. Even if she was wrong, she had to be sure. Lifting her skirts, she ran the last few yards to the front door. With her hand on the latch she paused, then lifted it to discover with relief that it had been left unlocked. That meant Neil hadn't yet arrived, surely. The door creaked as she pushed it open, standing on the stoop waiting for some indication of movement inside.

But there was only darkness and silence. Sarah waited a moment to let her thumping heart subside, and her breath grow more even. She was here at last. Now she could afford to go slowly, to be careful, to carefully inspect the house that was supposed to be empty and waiting.

A tin candle holder sat on the table in the hall. Striking a flint, Sarah lit it to help her in her inspection of the house. Waiting until she was certain there was no movement or sound, she slowly edged her way up the staircase to look over the bedrooms above. They were empty, cavernous in their silence and darkness. She stood in the hall, straining for any sound. The house creaked and sighed in the wind, and Sarah began to wonder if she had not let her heightened feelings lead her a song and dance. Yet, having come this far, it was better to be certain. So, quietly, feeling a little silly, she edged her way back down the stairs. She stood at the foot of the stairs, peering into the gray gloom of the empty parlor. With a startling roar, thunder crashed over the river, echoing and reechoing endlessly across the mountains outside, and Sarah realized that the quickly dropping darkness was not just the ordinary coming of night but the herald of a storm. The rain would be on them soon. Perhaps it would at least help to keep Blunt away.

Once she was assured the house was empty she would go upstairs and hide in the darkness until Neil and his party had come and gone. She had only to inspect the rest of the downstairs rooms and the kitchen, and that should easily be accomplished before the rain started.

Moving softly down the hall, she held up the candle to peer around the dining room. Satisfied, she moved down the low stairs to the kitchen, the candle before her lighting the way. The room was quiet and still and she felt almost certain now that her fears had been foolish.

Then her arm was grabbed, ruthlessly, jerked back so suddenly that the candle flew out of her hand and clattered on the stone floor. With a cry Sarah felt herself yanked through the door and into the kitchen, shoved up against the wall, a heavy body pressed against hers, a fetid breath in her face.

"Let me go," she cried, squirming against the ruthless grip pressing her back against the wall. At the sound of her voice the tightness seemed to slacken and the heavy body moved away slightly.

"Oh, so it's you. I might have known."

Her arm was released. Slumping against the cold, rough surface of the stones, she rubbed at the bruise, sensing rather than seeing the heavy form of her assailant still blocking her way.

"I thought you might be here, Ferris Blunt," she said, glaring at him. "Liar! Traitor!"

Ferris gave one of his humorless chuckles. "And you're better, I suppose. Seems I remember you promised you'd be out of this house tonight."

"So did you."

"So then, we're two of a kind."

"Don't compare me to you. I came here because I suspected your word was not to be trusted, and I was right."

She tried to slip outside the confining closeness of his body, but he shot out his arm, leaning his hand on the stones and blocking her way.

"Must be something mighty important going on here tonight to make you so anxious. I don't flatter myself you were concerned for my safety."

"Ha! That's the last thing I'd be concerned about."

"Well, then," he said with phony smoothness. "Someone else's safety, then. Whose?"

For the first time Sarah was glad of the darkness. "You know very well it is my father I'm worried about."

His hand gripped her hair, twining the strands tightly around his thick fingers. "I knew that's what you say."

"Let me go. Please," she said, trying once more to

squirm out of his grip. "I cannot talk like this. Can't we sit down and discuss these things rationally?"

"Oh, but I rather like being close to you like this," he said, leaning into her face. For a horrible moment she thought he was going to kiss her mouth, but instead he dropped his head and slobbered against the open neck of her blouse. Shrinking back, Sarah endured it, her mind frantically wondering what to do. Was Neil close by? Would he arrive any minute? Did Ferris have his men waiting back in the root cellar, ready to appear at his call?

Enjoying the feel of the soft body he had wanted for so long, Ferris dropped his hand to circle her waist. At that instant Sarah pushed against him, shoving him backward long enough to break free. Moving by instinct, she ran into the dining room, making it as far as the entrance before he caught her again. With a hard jerk, he slammed her against the wall once more and pressed against her.

"That wasn't nice," he muttered, his voice thick with the lust of violence as well as arousal. "But I like a lass with spirit."

Desperate for anything that would make him drop his guard, Sarah forced her body to go slack. If he liked spirit, then she would have none. She stood limp, allowing his hands to roam over her shoulders and down under the laces of her bodice. Her head twisted as far away from his wet lips as she could strain, while her mind working frantically. There was an unreal quality about what was happening, as if her body were participating while her spirit stood aside, looking on. She wondered how he could want her enough to forget that any moment the soldiers might arrive.

But he must have remembered. His hands slackened, his head came up. "Not now," he muttered thickly, almost as if he could not bear the thought. "But later."

Looking around, his eyes white in the darkness, Sarah knew he was trying to decide where he could lock her up until he could take advantage of the fact that they were in the house alone.

"Root cellar."

Grabbing her arm, he pulled her back toward the dining room. She grabbed at the door handle wildly, holding on.

"No," she cried. "Don't do it, Ferris. Please. Go away now. Leave this house and I promise I'll go with you."

He pried at her fingers, glaring at her. "Must be something of great importance happening here with you so almighty anxious to get me away. Well, you don't have to pretend. I know who's coming here tonight and what for, and I intend to be in on it. I'll tend to you later. Right now, you're just a distraction."

"No, I'm not. Look, I'll help. I'll be the Tory rather than Papa. Tell me what to do. Where are the rest of your men? Use me."

"I'll use you, all right, but not in this matter. Let go, damn you, you she-wolf."

All of a sudden his hand stilled and he paused, listening. In the quiet Sarah caught the distant sound that had stopped him. Horses. Clattering down the village road. The clink of harness, leather, and brass.

Thunder crashed over the house, obliterating all other sounds. Ferris jumped, turning toward the window, where there was a sudden ribbon of lightning yellowing the black sky.

Viciously, Sarah kicked at his leg, catching him just below the knee with the hard toe of her shoe. He yelled, releasing her just long enough for her to break free of his grasp. Tearing into the hall, she yanked the front door open and fled into the night. Feeling him behind her, close enough to give her a head start, she lifted her skirts and ran down the path toward the gate to throw it open. The latch was caught. She tugged at it frantically. Down the walk where the path met the village road she could see the dark shadows of the riders approaching and hear the clatter of their horses' hooves. Neil! He was coming.

It was dark by the time the flatboat drew up to the wharf at the Landing. One of the oarsmen held a lantern aloft while the front panel was lowered and the horses were led off onto the muddy ground around the dock. Inside the Millers' tavern Neil could see through the windows and hear sudden shouts of laughter punctuating the murmur of friendly conversation. Hopefully the click of harness and the infrequent neighing of a complaining horse wouldn't draw their attention to the Landing. Not that there was anything to hide, but it was better to come and go with as little notice as possible.

Within minutes they were mounted. "How far to the rendezvous?" asked the young courier who pulled up beside Neil, looking longingly at the open doors of the tavern where light spilled out onto the dark path.

"The other end of the village," Neil said quietly. "With any luck the contingent from Greenburgh will have arrived and be waiting for us."

"And then how far?"

"Oh, another three hours at least, unless His Excellency plans to stop somewhere in between. I wouldn't know about that. Once I turn you over to him, my job is finished."

The young man made a clucking noise with his tongue while Neil kicked his mount and pulled away, leading the group toward the village street. He glanced uneasily up and down the darkened path, noting that it looked unusually empty and quiet for a warm summer evening, even one with a storm brewing. As they rode past the rectory he could hear the sonorous voice of Reverend Tate reading the Bible aloud to his gathered family. A little farther on Jamie Earing sat in the dust before his cottage, while inside, beyond the open door, Neil glimpsed Helena moving about her kitchen. Jamie looked up as they cantered past him, babbling some unintelligible words and jumping to his feet as if to follow. Neil slowed long enough to make sure the boy stayed where he was, then moved up again to lead the group toward the end of the road where the path turned toward the river and the Reed house.

They paused there only a moment, Neil reining his horse to look over the silent massiveness of the dark house. It looked as though Ian's contingent had not yet arrived, although it was possible that they were waiting in the dark. Possible, but not likely. General Washington would probably want a light and a glass at the end of so long and dusty a ride. But at least everything looked peaceful.

"Is that the house?" the courier said.

"Yes. The stable is just this side of it. We'll put the horses there until . . . listen."

Both men turned to look toward the bridge, where the sounds of horses and harnesses had been barely perceptible on the heels of the thunder. Neil turned his mount, straining in the dark to make out the forms of several riders clattering over the bridge. Then from the distant house came a sudden crash. A scream pierced the silent night, shrieking his name on the wind.

"Neil! Go back! It's a trap!"

A crashing blast of thunder drowned the voice. Sampson, his ears laid back, danced nervously in the road while Neil struggled to hold him. Surely that was Sarah's voice!

"What the devil? . . ."

"Who was that? What's happening here?"

There was a second scream: "Neil, Go back!" and this time there was no mistaking the anguish and terror in Sarah's voice. Leaning out of the saddle, Neil grasped the courier's bridle and turned it toward the bridge.

"Ride that way—toward the bridge. The troops from Greenburgh are there now. Hurry."

"But what's going on? That sounded like a girl, and in trouble. Shouldn't we—"

"No! My job is to turn you safely over to those troops. Take your men and join them, and hurry. I'll see to the girl."

"Are you sure?"

"For God's sake, Lieutenant, just go!"

The lieutenant took one look back at the dark blur of the house, then kicked his mount and galloped off in the direction of the bridge. Neil waited for a moment, listening for the sounds of voices barely perceptible on the growing howl of the wind, while Sampson danced circles in the narrow path. Through the darkness he could just make out the two groups of men merging together. He waited only long enough to be certain, then dug in his spurs and tore wildly down the path to the Reed house.

Sarah pulled at the gate, straining to open it, but her frantic efforts only succeeded in jamming it more tightly,

"Neil! Go back! Go—"

A hand closed over her mouth, jerking her head back viciously. Furious, Ferris dragged her struggling body away from the gate and back down the path into the house. She tried to bite the thick flesh that covered her mouth and stilled her words, but soon realized it was hopeless. She flailed her arms uselessly while he pulled her back inside the house, slamming the door behind him.

"This is most pleasant, Miss Darcy," William Popham said, leaning across the table toward Darcy, his arms crossed before him. "It is unfortunate that your sister was not well enough to join us, and yet I am rather glad of the opportunity to be alone with you for a little while."

Darcy frowned into her wineglass, too worried to give this compliment her customary coquettish response. She was having second thoughts about accepting Popham's invitation. Sarah's behavior this evening had been very

strange, not at all like her usual complacent self. To leave
Peekskill so suddenly and without her father's consent—
that was something she, Darcy, might do but never her
dutiful older sister. And the way she had been so anxious
to get to the house. It was as though she was expecting to
meet someone. She even seemed glad to have Popham
waylay them as he did, and detain her sister here. She
glanced up at Popham's handsome, amused face, thinking
how ordinarily she might enjoy an interlude like this.

"I'm so sorry. What did you say?"

One eyebrow on William Popham's face inched upward.
"It doesn't matter. I was saying how very pretty you look
this evening," he said with that air of detached amusement
that was so habitual with him.

Darcy laughed. "Oh, I think not or else I would surely
have heard that."

"Yes, I fancy you would. You know, I really enjoy
you, Miss Darcy. You have a natural gift for leading a
gentleman on which I think is quite wasted in this backwater hamlet."

"And would be more useful on an upriver plantation, I
suppose," Darcy said, smiling at him from beneath her long
lashes.

"Well, no, but there are other places in the world where
it might. Don't you ever long to see them?"

"Oh, yes! The Landing is so dull, and sometimes I
think I shall simply die if I have to spend my life sitting
and spinning here. The only consolation would be to spend
it with the right person. Then perhaps it might be bearable."

"Someone like young Master Tate?"

"Oh, good heavens, no! I might as well tie a millstone
around my neck and throw myself in the river. In fact, that
is what I would do were I forced to marry a pimply-faced
boy like him."

"That would be a waste. Someone else, then? Someone

like that noble lieutenant you're always batting your eyelashes at?''

In spite of herself Darcy blushed. "Well, perhaps you consider someone like yourself more enticing," she answered, tossing her head.

"It is not entirely outside the realm of possibility," he answered dryly.

"Why, Mr. Popham, you surprise me. I did not fancy you the marrying kind. Or, at the most, I thought you might have a plump, dull *hausfrau* tucked away in some corner of that upriver sheep farm.''

For once Popham lost his bemused smile. "You are a perceptive young lady, Miss Darcy, but I think you have not looked closely enough at me to pass judgment. Or is it that your vision is too occupied elsewhere?''

Darcy concentrated on sipping her wine. But his words brought a frown to her face as she remembered Sarah. What could have been wrong with her?

Popham studied the frown. "You do seem unusually preoccupied this evening, Miss Darcy. I hope nothing is wrong.''

"Oh, no. That is, I'm not sure. My sister has me a little worried, that's all.''

"Miss Sarah? Why, I should have thought she was quite able to care for herself, no matter what the problem.''

"She is. It's just that I'm afraid something is going on that she has not told me about and it has upset her.''

"Oh? Do you have any idea what it might be?''

Darcy hesitated, wondering how much she could trust this man.

"No. Well, perhaps. Listen. What is that?''

She slipped from her chair to the open window near their table. Leaning her hands on the wide sill, Darcy leaned out, peering toward the wharf, where she had caught the sound of a familiar voice.

Soldiers were gathered around the wharf, leading their horses off a flatboat that had just arrived. One of them held a lantern aloft, and in the dim glow she recognized Neil's profile and the sound of his low voice. She caught her breath, so intent on peering at the group that she did not notice that Popham had come up to stand behind her. As the men mounted and cantered past the window, Darcy was certain that it was Neil she had recognized. She watched until they were swallowed by the night as they turned on the road that led into the village.

William Popham touched her elbow lightly, guiding her back to their table.

"You haven't yet finished your wine, Miss Darcy. Perhaps you would take a little supper with it. I would be most honored . . ."

"No, no, thank you, Mr. Popham," Darcy muttered, all her interest having ridden off with Neil. She was almost certain now that his arrival had something to do with Sarah's peculiar behavior, and her anxiety to get to her house and see what this was all about grew with every passing minute.

"I really find that my head is aching. From the voyage upriver, I suppose. Would you mind terribly if I went along home? I know it's inexcusable, but . . ."

"Why, I shall be deeply disappointed, mistress. However, I would not dream of detaining you when you don't feel well." He picked up his hat and cloak, which were lying carelessly on a bench. "But you will allow me to escort you there, I trust."

"That is really not necessary. I am quite capable of finding my way by myself."

"I'm sure you are, yet I would not hear of letting you set off when your head is aching so severely that you cannot enjoy a glass of the Millers' best Madeira. Come along, then."

Darcy started to protest but saw that it would get her

nowhere. Reluctantly she agreed. The important thing, after all, was to get to the house. If Popham insisted on coming along, well, let him. As long as he did not get in her way, she cared little.

"All right, Mr. Popham, but you will have to hurry some to keep up with me."

He followed her through the room and out the door into the night. Fat drops of rain were just beginning to dot the flagstone walk.

Popham glared up at the black sky, threw his cloak around his shoulders, and slapped his hat on his impeccably arranged hair. "I'm sure I will, Miss Darcy. I'm sure I will."

Uncontrollable rage set the blood pounding in Ferris Blunt's head. Violence and fury, like a white heat behind his eyes, blotted out the crashing thunder over the river and driving rain of the storm breaking around him. Gripping one arm like an iron vise around Sarah's waist, digging the fingers of his other hand into the soft flesh around her mouth, he half dragged, half carried her squirming body back into the house. Once inside the hallway he threw her across the dining room with such force that she crashed into the highboy, rattling the stacks of china cups and plates inside. Then, slamming the door shut behind him, he stalked across the room, grabbed her by the hair, and jerked her up to her knees, slapping her violently across the face.

"Damn you, you interfering bitch!"

How had he allowed her to scream like that, to warn away the courier with the money and the troops from White Plains, to ruin all he had hoped to accomplish this night! And who was Neil? Her lover? Some damned Whig to whom she had given her heart? Interfering, faithless slut!

Sarah, stunned from the blow against the highboy, suddenly began to gain back her senses. She was trapped in this house with a maniac who was trying to kill her, but at least she had warned Neil. Had he turned back? She could not be sure. She felt her head jerked back as Blunt grabbed a handful of her hair and yanked her up, raising his huge hand to strike her again. Pulling away from him, Sarah began to scream, wildly, hysterically, hopelessly. He was going to kill her, this crazy man, and there was nothing she could do but fight him until she was beaten unconscious. She flailed with her arms, striking at him wherever she could reach her fists, struggling to squirm out of his iron grip. She heard a tearing rip as he grabbed at the bodice of her dress and tore it away. In a panic, she screamed louder. With the full force of his arm Ferris slapped her again, knocking her head sideways. Careening down on one knee over her, he slammed her down against the plank floor. Sarah, numb and reeling from the blows on her face, felt his heavy weight come down on her and all her strength melted away. Like a drowning woman, she fell against the floor, too dizzy and in too much pain to care what happened to her now. Ferris put his hands around her throat, but suddenly he realized he didn't want to kill her, crazy-angry as he was. He had ripped the bodice of her dress straight down the front, and, tearing away the cloth, he kneaded the soft flesh of her breast with his harsh fingers, gloating to himself. He need not kill her to get revenge. There was a better way.

Neil heard Sarah's screams as he pulled up outside the house. He ran into the dining room, where he could make out the shape of Blunt's huge body bending over the prostrate girl on the far side of the room. With an angry cry he flung himself across the room, onto Ferris, grabbing him around the neck and yanking him back with such force that for an instant he thought he had broken the man's neck. That moment of surprise was enough for Neil to have an advantage over the other man, who was heavier and stronger. But Ferris, more the experienced fighter, quickly recovered. Crashing along the floor together, they rolled over and over, each trying to get a grip on the other's throat. When Darcy and Popham came running into the house, only the sound of their grunts and strains broke the crash of their bodies against the furniture.

Popham quickly ran into the hall and grabbed up a candle, which he lit, then hurried back into the room. In its dim light Darcy, who had recognized that it was Neil who was in trouble, stood there wringing her hands, unable to help him. But when the candle threw its illumination on the two men twisting on the floor, she could see Neil's pistol lying where it had fallen on the floor and grabbed it up. She was a poor shot, but she might be able to wound the other man and so give Neil an advantage. She saw Popham standing aside, watching and seemingly not interested in getting involved. This might be Neil's only chance.

Then Popham saw Sarah lying next to the highboy. Inching around the two fighting men, he knelt to hold the candle where he could see that she was not dead but badly hurt. Glancing up, he spied Darcy holding the pistol, moving closer to the two men tumbling on the floor.

"Put that thing down," he began, when a blast shook the room and a burst of flame spurted out.

One of the men wrestling on the floor slumped over. The second man, rising to his knees, breathed long, rasping gasps as he looked down at his opponent writhing and bleeding on the floor.

"I'm obliged," Ferris said between gasps.

With a wild, piercing shriek Darcy dropped the pistol and ran to stand over Neil. "What have I done! Neil! Oh my God!" she cried.

Falling to her knees, she bent over Neil, staunching with her hand the hole in his chest from which a dark stain spread outward.

His eye on the pistol, Popham started inching his hand toward it, but before his fingers reached it the room was suddenly full of men. Soldiers everywhere: pulling Ferris to his feet and wrenching his arms behind him, kneeling over Neil to pull open his military coat, lighting candles and dashing off into the rooms off the dining room.

Glancing at Sarah lying behind him, Popham swung off his cloak and draped it over her torn dress, covering her body. Darcy's wild sobs resounded in the room, punctuated by the rolling drone of thunder which still pealed over the river.

The soldier who had bent over Neil firmly removed Darcy's hands from the wound.

Neil turned his head, his eyes fluttered open, and he smiled as he recognized a friend. "The courier?" he muttered. "Did he get through?"

"Yes," Ian replied as he worked to fasten a makeshift bandage in place over the bleeding. "You did a splendid job."

"Neil!" Darcy sobbed, falling over his body. "Oh, Neil, I'm so sorry!"

"He can't hear you," Ian said quietly. "He's fainted." Then he added briskly, "This man is badly hurt. Come, mistress, get control of yourself. Is there a bed where we can lay him?"

"Yes, upstairs," Darcy cried. "In Papa's room."

"Show us the way. Here, Private, help me."

As they carried Neil out of the room, Popham knelt to raise Sarah up against his shoulder, gently turning her chin to inspect her face. She was going to have several nasty bruises, and one eye was already swollen. But her low moans showed she was alive.

"Neil?" Sarah groaned. "Is he all right?"

"My saints, but this Neil certainly has an uncommon lot of women concerned for his welfare," Popham said wryly. "What's his secret, I wonder."

As she began to remember where she was, Sarah gripped

Popham's coat in a sudden panic, looking wildly around the room.

"It's all right," Popham said more gently, stroking back the tangled hair from her face. "There's nothing to fear."

"Ferris . . ."

"He's gone. The soldier's took him away."

"Soldiers?"

"I don't know where they came from myself. Here, can you sit up? Let me get you some water, then perhaps we can find someone who will explain what's been happening around here."

"What's to be done with this lot, sir?" In the hallway one of the men who had a grip on the struggling Ferris spoke to Major Harron as they carried Neil up the stairs to a bedroom.

He gave Ferris one long, furious look. "Hang him."

"But sir . . ."

"Now, wait a minute," Ferris cried. "That's not justice."

"It's as much justice as you gave your victims these past five years. There's a fine tree down there near the river, Corporal. String him up to it, and make sure you do a proper job."

"You can't do this!" Ferris shouted, his concern mounting. He hadn't thought any of these men knew who he was. "I deserve a trial, at least. I didn't shoot that Whig soldier."

His protests grew in volume and intensity as he was dragged from the house and out toward the riverbank. Major Harron stood in the hall watching after him, then turned to run up the stairs to make sure Neil was safely put to bed. A few moments later he was back downstairs, where Popham heard him directing one of his men to ride to the Robinson house and bring back Dr. Timothy Dwight, as quickly as was possible. When he walked back into the

dining room, Popham had Sarah propped up on the floor,
her back against the highboy, and was trying to get a few
sips of claret down her throat.

"Who are you?" the officer said bruskly.

"William Popham, from Rensselaerwyck. A friend of
the Reed family," he added, to verify his reason for being
there. There was a pause while the two men looked each
other over. "I don't believe I've had the pleasure," Popham
added.

"Major Ian Harron. How did Lieutenant Partherton come
to be wounded?"

"Who? Oh, you mean the famous Neil. Why, I believe
it was Miss Darcy who shot him accidentally while trying
to wound that man you just so summarily dragged away to
be executed. A little sudden, don't you think?"

"Not at all. We've been after Ferris Blunt for years, and
I'm not one to let a heaven-sent opportunity escape me.
We can clear up the legalities later."

"But are you sure you've got the right man? You didn't
even ask his name."

"I didn't need to. We knew he was here. In fact, we
were expecting him." Kneeling beside Sarah, Ian ran his
fingers lightly over her face.

"She's not badly hurt, is she?"

"A little banged about, but not badly hurt, I don't think.
How unfortunate that since you knew the man was here
you could not have interrupted them before he got at her."

"We came as quickly as we could. We would have
saved Neil too but for that young girl's interference."

"Neil?" Sarah groaned again. "Where is he?"

"He's upstairs, Miss Reed," Ian answered. "He's been
shot, but I believe he'll be all right. I've sent for Dr.
Dwight."

"Shot! No. I must go to him."

"He's only up the stairs in your father's room. Stay

calm, Miss Reed. We'll help you up there as soon as you can get back on your feet.''

"I'm all right now, truly I am," she said, struggling to rise. "I want to go to him. Please help me.''

"Are you sure? Shouldn't you sit here a little while longer?''

"No, no. I'm fine. Please help me.''

."I'll get her upstairs," Popham said, gently helping Sarah to her feet, where she half stood and half leaned against him. "Take it very slowly now, Miss Reed. It's not far.''

"It's the first room at the top." Ian motioned to Popham. "Her sister is already there, I believe.''

"Fortunate Neil, with two lovely ladies hovering over his sickbed.''

Ian watched the tall man lead the girl from the room. "He's not so fortunate," he muttered, for the truth was he was not nearly as certain about the casual nature of Neil's wound as he had tried to make Sarah believe. That was why it was so important that Dr. Dwight get here as soon as possible. If Neil had any chance at all, it would be up to the surgeon.

He was standing at the window, trying to make out the indistinct shadows in the trees near the river, when Popham came back into the room. He made immediately for the sideboard, where he poured himself a glass of wine.

"Will you join me?" he asked Ian. "This has been an . . . 'interesting' evening, and I for one feel the need of something stimulating.''

"No, thank you." Ian turned to survey the man filling his glass. For all his talk of being unnerved, he looked very cool and composed. "Just what *are* you doing here?" he asked in clipped tones.

Popham raised his glass in Ian's direction, one eyebrow arched. "I might ask the same of you. I was accompanying Miss Darcy home from the Green Man when we walked into the scene you so providentially interrupted.''

"Do you have an interest in Darcy Reed?"

Popham sipped his wine, taking his time before replying. "Perhaps. You ask an uncommon lot of questions."

"An officer's prerogative," Ian said, smiling a little for the first time.

"Perhaps I might ask a few?"

"Such as?"

"For example, how you knew Ferris Blunt would be in this house this evening? What was going on here that was so important as to have both Reed girls in a state of anxiety and apprehension? Who was this courier Partherton mentioned?"

"Now *you* are asking an uncommon lot of questions. I really don't have to answer, you know."

Once again Popham lifted his glass in Ian's direction. "Your choice."

"However, now that it's all over, you might as well know. The entire plan was a trap to apprehend this Ferris Blunt, who has been a scourge of the area for several years. We also suspect he has been acting as a spy for the British, and, with things in the state they are now, it seemed an appropriate time to get him out of the way. We set up a false courier with a rumored cache of money arriving from Philadelphia in order to lure him here tonight, feeling certain that he would never allow an opportunity like that to go by. We were correct, it seems."

"But where are the rest of his men? He has a number of thieves who ride with him. Why didn't they try to rescue him?"

"Because we apprehended them on the river. There is a tunnel of some kind leading from this house to the river's edge. We found the rest of Ferris's men about half a mile north of the house, waiting obviously for some sort of signal from him to come tearing in. Unfortunately he never got a chance to give it to them."

Popham rested one hip on the corner on the table, turning his glass in his hand. "And was Lieutenant Partherton aware of all this?"

"No, unfortunately we had to dupe Neil into thinking an elaborate plan was being set in motion to move the army south, and the money that was arriving was crucial to that movement. He was our closest link to the Reeds and to Ferris Blunt, and we could not afford to let him know the truth."

Ian, beginning to relax a little now, took off his hat and wiped at his brow with the cuff of his sleeve. "I believe I might have a little of that wine after all," he said, reaching for the decanter. "Now that everything is over and re-solved I begin to feel a little weary." He took a long swallow. "I should hate for Neil to die and never know."

"Will he die?"

"I don't know. His wound is much worse than I wanted Sarah to know. He's been a good friend, and I would like the opportunity to explain."

"But you accomplished your main objective. Ferris Blunt is gone for good. Why should your conscience bother you over such a small deception? You only allowed your friend to think he was helping to expedite a large sum of money."

"No, it was not only that. It was all part of an elaborate lie. We had to do it. We had to convince Neil that an entire significant operation of the war rested upon his shoulders."

"You mean by making him think the army was about to move south."

"Yes," Ian answered reluctantly. "I lied to him. I even led him to think that we had received information from the French about a convoy being headed for the Chesapeake, when the truth is . . ."

He stopped, looking quickly at Popham.

"Indeed," Popham said laconically.

"Forgive me," Ian muttered. "In my relief and my concern for my friend's safety I am speaking out of turn. I really don't know you at all, sir, nor do I know anything of your sympathies. We all must be more careful in these times. I trust you will honor me with your descretion."

"You do right to be cautious, though I am as good a patriot as Mr. Nathanial Reed himself. As for the intentions of the military, the less I know of them the better. Then I would not by any casual word betray a cause I would gladly give my life for."

"Well said, sir." Ian downed the rest of his glass. "Now I had better go and see if my men have dispatched Blunt to his just rewards. You'll excuse me, sir?"

"Of course. I think I will just wait about a little longer. I have a fancy that Miss Darcy might be in need of some consolation once the doctor arrives and she can leave Neil's bedside."

Ian gave Popham a short bow and left the room.

The room kept blurring; the candle on its stand threw wavering, wraithlike shadows around the bed and the faces on the other side of it. Neil's still body was stretched the length of the bed, his face as white as alabaster and quiet as death, dark shadows creasing his cheeks. Now and then, with the wavering of the flame, the whole scene would fade out of focus and Sarah would run her hand across her eyes to clear them. Her head was pounding, and there was a searing pain in her cheek, but the heaviness of her heart hurt even worse. She struggled to remember how she had got in this upstairs bedroom, sitting beside Neil's wounded body, but even that memory refused to come. There was a grossness about it, a nightmare of repulsive features, violent hands, and a thick face leering into hers, but she could not remember to whom they belonged.

Someone had pulled away Neil's shirt and laid a pile of

clean bandages on her lap. Moving automatically, she pressed a clean cloth against the blood-soaked one on Neil's chest. Then she wrung out another clean one in the washbowl on the stand beside the bed and wiped his forehead.

On the other side of the bed Darcy sat sobbing, her hands over her face, keening and crying and weaving back and forth.

Why was she so upset? Sarah struggled to remember. How had Neil got like this, so cold and still?

"Darcy," she said, half moaning. "What happened? I can't remember."

Darcy looked over at her, her large eyes like black holes in her white face.

"Oh, Sarah. It's all my fault. Everything is my fault. I wanted to help, and instead I've killed him."

"No, no. He's not dead. Look, his chest is still moving ever so slightly. He's still breathing."

"But he might die. And it will all be because of me. How will I ever be able to live with myself?"

Leaning her arms on the bed, she broke into fresh sobs. "Oh, Neil. My poor, poor love."

Sarah stared at her sister. "Oh, Darcy! I knew you were fond of him, but I didn't realize you loved him too."

"I have for so long—and so hopelessly. I wanted him to love me back, but it was you he cared for, always. I hated you because of that Sarah. I wronged you and him, and now I've hurt you both so badly I'll never be able to forgive myself."

"Darcy, dear. Please calm yourself. Neil doesn't hate you for what happened. I'm sure you didn't intend to hurt him or me."

"But I did! Oh, I didn't mean to shoot him, but I did go to that witch, Maude Sackett."

Sarah's hand stilled over Neil's chest. "You went to see Maude Sackett because of Neil?"

"Yes. I wanted a potion that would make him love me instead of you."

"Oh, Darcy. Why couldn't you have told me?"

"How could I when it was you who were standing in the way of my happiness? Then when Ferris Blunt wanted to marry you, I thought the potion must have worked."

There was a clatter as Sarah dropped the rag she was wringing out into the bowl. Like someone in a trance she looked down, seeing the unfamiliar cloak around her shoulders and the torn bodice of her dress underneath.

With a cry she covered her face with her hands, fighting to keep from running from the room. It all came back, the dragging, hitting fists, the thick, slobbering lips. . . . Only Darcy's loud sobs kept her from breaking out into screams.

"That horrible man!" Darcy went on relentlessly. "When I see now what he did to you, how he treated you—and to think I was ready to trick you into marrying him so I could have what I wanted! Oh, Sarah, I hate myself! And then, trying to help Neil I've nearly killed him."

Calmness came with the knowledge of her sister's remorse. Now she remembered that officer ordering Ferris to be dragged out and hanged. Whatever had happened before, he was gone now and would bother her no more. Her sister's pain was more important. Reaching across Neil, she smoothed Darcy's hair back where her head lay on the sheet.

"Don't cry so, Darcy. Dr. Dwight is coming to take care of Neil, and with God's help we'll see him through this. I'm sure he won't hold what you did against you, and I certainly don't. It will be all right. You'll see."

Darcy lifted her swollen eyes, peering at her sister.

"Oh, Sarah, you're so good. If you had done to me what I've done to you, I'd never be so generous or forgiving."

"There's nothing to forgive, Darcy. You're my sister

and I love you. If Neil wanted you instead of me, I would simply accept it and wish you both joy.''

''Yes, I think you would.''

''But the important thing at the moment is to get him well. Then we'll face these other issues and try to resolve them as best we can. But please, don't blame yourself so.''

Darcy wiped at her eyes, calmed a little by her sister's generous words, even though not for a moment did she really believe them. With her crying stilled, she was all at once filled with a terrible weariness. The stifling room smelled of sickness and death and was abhorrent to her. It was as though the close and still air were too thin to support three people. Rising from her chair, she stood over Neil for a moment, longing to bend and kiss his brow, yet not daring to out of some kind of fear that he might rise up and accuse her. As Sarah reached out to wipe his face with the cloth, she glimpsed her sister's perfectly shaped features highlighted by the glow of the candle, beautiful even with the bruised and swollen flesh. Darcy turned and ran from the room.

She made her way slowly downstairs, almost without knowing where she was. She felt as though she could see herself with the clarity of a pristine moment of sunshine on a clear, sparkling day, and she did not like what she saw at all. She sensed that this moment would not last. It was like opening a shutter for a brief second, allowing a piercing glimpse into something beyond. The shutter would close again, very soon, and she would try to ignore or forget what had been so clearly seen. But oh, that terrible glimpse of truth.

What kind of person was she to have put her own obsession for Neil before the well-being of the sister who had always treated her with love? She was selfish, self-absorbed, stubborn, and determined to have her own way, whatever the cost to anyone else. She was not fit to live, not fit to be loved by anyone. She loathed and despised herself.

She was standing in the hall downstairs, not even knowing how she had gotten there. Leaning against the papered wall, she covered her face with her hands. Where could she go, loathsome as she was? There was the river outside. It would be dark and cold and choppy from the storm, but beneath its black depths a hopeless sinner might find justification and blessed rest. But did she have the courage? What was the alternative? If Neil should die, how could she face the long years of trying to live with the knowledge that she had killed him?

She felt a strong hand on her shoulder. Startled, she looked up to see William Popham standing beside her, his eyes smiling down into hers.

"Oh, Mr. Popham," Darcy moaned.

He did not answer. He simply put an arm around her shoulder and drew her into his embrace, resting his chin against the softness of her hair and closing her about with his comforting presence.

Thirteen

❧

IT WAS nearly dawn before Dr. Dwight rode into the stableyard of the Reed house. By then, though Sarah had managed to staunch the bleeding from Neil's wound, he had lost so much blood that his face in the candlelight looked as though it were cast in marble and his too-warm brow suggested the onset of a fever. It was with the greatest relief that she saw the surgeon stride into the room.

Without asking questions, Dwight went to work, probing and searching for the ball, calculating his chances of removing it safely. It had hit a rib but seemed to have escaped tearing into any vital organs. If Neil had a strong constitution and a will to survive, and if the wound did not putrefy, he would perhaps have a chance.

Laying out his surgical instruments, he took a moment before going to work on Neil to lift Sarah's chin and examine her face.

"You'd better put some tincture of marigold on those

bruises," he said gently. "And a little laudanum might help ease the soreness. I have some with me. Do you want it?"

"Thank you, no. I want to stay alert, at least until I know Neil is all right."

"My dear lady, you have already done an excellent job. The wound is clean, the bleeding has stopped, and your cool cloths helped to keep the fever down. You look exhausted. Why don't you go and rest, or else you'll be no good to anyone, least of all the lieutenant here."

"But will you try to remove the ball? You'll need some help."

"I promise I'll call you."

Her weariness was like a weight pushing her down. "Very well, if you promise." She stopped by the door, turning back to where the doctor bent over Neil's bed. "Do you think he'll be all right?"

Dwight looked up at her over the rim of his small round glasses. "I shouldn't like to say one way or the other quite yet. But we'll give it our best try."

Cold comfort, Sarah thought. And yet the surgeon was right. She did need to rest, if only to renew her strength to take up the vigil once again. As she made her way down the hall she thought of Darcy. Poor child, she was so upset earlier. She ought to go and find her and try to comfort her, reassure her that all this was not her fault.

But weariness won over good intentions. Entering her room, she fell across her bed, too tired even to remove the cloak that had covered her torn dress the whole night long.

When Sarah woke, the noon sun had already climbed high over the house. A large bluebottle fly buzzed noisily around her head, and from the stableyard outside she could hear Cato's familiar discordant singing above the sound of his hammer on the anvil. Though her body was one long ache, she forced herself to her feet, washing some of the grogginess in her head away with water from the bowl by the window. Quickly she changed to a clean, simple dress that had the blessed advantage of being whole. Her hair was tangled and unkempt, but she only took time to smooth it back and braid the long strands as best she could. Later she would brush and comb it properly.

Peering into Neil's bedroom, she saw that Dr. Dwight was sprawled in an upholstered chair near the window, snoring lightly. Sarah stepped to the bed quietly so as not to awaken him and bent over Neil, holding her breath out of anxiety. He too was asleep, though it was a fitful, tossing sleep without rest. She was relieved to see that his color was better than on the previous evening, and his forehead under her hand was cool. There were clean bandages across his chest and no sign of the bleeding that had been so apparent the night before.

"Bless my soul, I must have dozed off," Dwight said, stirring in his chair by the window. Pulling his glasses from the end of his nose, where they had slipped, he wiped them on the tail of his waist, set them back in place, and peered up at Sarah.

"I hope I didn't waken you," Sarah whispered. "I just wanted to have a look at our patient."

"You had quite a long rest yourself, and it has done you good. I can see the difference."

"Dr. Dwight, did you remove the ball while I was sleeping?"

"Well, yes, I did. Had to get it out, you know, or run the risk of infection."

"But you promised to call me."

"And I did. But you were sleeping so soundly, you never heard me at all. So I got one of the young fellows with Major Harron to assist. Worked out quite well."

"I suspect you did not call very loudly," Sarah said with a touch of irritation.

"No, probably I did not. It was better that you rested."

"I ought to be angry with you, but I'm not. I'm just grateful that Neil seems so much better. Do you think he's going to be all right now?"

Dwight walked over to the bed. "He has an excellent chance as long as no putrefaction sets in. There is always a risk of infection with a bullet wound. Only time will tell if he'll be spared. Right now, I think that both he and I could do with a little nourishment. You wouldn't be able to scare up some broth, would you?"

"I can do better than that. Jurie must be back by now, and she probably has a fire going in the kitchen. I'll only be a moment."

"Nothing too strong for the lieutenant here. A little soup or broth will do fine."

Sarah nodded and made her way downstairs, where she found Jurie working at the hearth. Ordering up a substantial meal for the doctor and some strong soup for Neil, she went in search of Darcy, hoping to make up for ignoring her the night before. To her surprise, Darcy was not to be found. Further, no one had seen her all that morning, neither the maids nor Cato.

"But I seen your pa, Miss Sarah," Cato told her when she went seeking him in the stable, "and he was in a rare takin'. Best you stay out'n his way for a while, seems to me."

"Where is he?" Sarah said grimly. She had forgotten about leaving Nat in Peekskill. He would be furious with her, but at least he had not been here the night before and could not be implicated.

Cato stared at her quizzically, trying to ignore the bruises on her face, his eyes full of questions. "He was sent for to go into the village to the Millers' ordinary. They come and asked him would he 'dentify the body of that outlaw, Ferris Blunt. They done hanged that man last night, Miss Sarah. From that tree over there by the water. Hanged him dead!"

Sarah looked quickly at the dark branches like splayed fingers on the black willow tree silhouetted at the river's edge. So she had not dreamed that. It was horrible, and yet at the same time it was a relief. Hateful man! He would never be a threat to her or her father again.

"Well, when he returns, Cato, would you tell him I'd like to speak with him? I'll be upstairs with Lieutenant Partherton."

"I'll do that, Miss Sarah."

"Oh, and Miss Darcy, too. When she comes in, ask her to step upstairs."

"Yes, ma'am."

Starting back to the house, she realized all at once how hungry she was. Perhaps she would take a little dinner with Dr. Dwight before Nat returned. She was not too surprised that her father had been called to identify Ferris's body, since he had known him for years. But where was Darcy? She would never be so macabre as to join the crowd from the village that was surely down at the Millers' now, gawking over the corpse of the infamous outlaw. Or would she? Smiling a little to herself, Sarah realized that right now she would not be surprised at anything anyone did, so badly had her own ordered world been turned topsy-turvy in the last twenty-four hours!

As the afternoon wore on toward evening, she was beginning to grow anxious about her sister when a brief note arrived from the Millers explaining that Darcy had asked them to let Sarah know that she had gone to Peekskill to stay with her Aunt Emerson for a few days. By nightfall Nat arrived home and Sarah got a blistering tongue-lashing, but more for taking off from Peekskill without his leave than for anything that had happened afterward. Sarah did not understand this until the next day, when she sat in Neil's room feeding her patient some of Jurie's good Brunswick stew and Ian Harron strode through the door.

Neil was sitting propped up in bed, his face shaven and washed, his hair smoothed back in a queue, with a clean linen shirt over his bandaged chest.

"You're looking very fit," Ian said, smiling at them both. "I think you should be up out of this bed and back to your duties by tomorrow morning at the latest."

Neil did not return the smile. "I've been hoping you'd come, you false friend." He glared at Ian. "I think I deserve some sort of explanation."

"Why, I don't know what you mean."

"Oh, yes you do. I don't understand what went on night before last, but I know it was not what I thought it was. Deceitful creature, explain yourself."

"Neil, are you certain you're strong enough for this?" Sarah asked, a little alarmed by the heightened color of her patient.

Ian pulled a chair up to the bed and straddled it. "He is. I checked with Dr. Dwight before he left. He thinks you are recovering nicely and agreed I might see you. I have to leave soon myself, but I wanted to talk with you before I went."

"Glad to know there's still some decency left in you."

"I was not merely anxious to explain things for your sake," Ian said, crossing his arms along the back of the chair. "It was for you as well, Miss Reed."

Sarah looked up from the spoon poised in midair. "Me? But why?"

"You'll understand why, I think, after I've finished with what I have to say. I never wanted to deceive you, Neil, but it was necessary. I couldn't risk having you know the truth and perhaps letting it slip to the wrong people."

"I deeply appreciate your confidence in me."

"Now, don't be annoyed. You were a very important element in the plan, albeit unknowingly, and you played your part perfectly."

"How nice. Now would you do me the honor of telling me just what it was I did so expertly?"

Ian sat waiting, drawing out the silence with a maddening deliberation.

"You see, we have suspected for some time that Ferris Blunt and—forgive me, Miss Reed—and Nathanial Reed were passing along information to the British garrison at New York. We also suspected there were others working with them around Cole's Landing, but we were not certain who they were. We wanted a plan that would catch Ferris and get him out of the way once and for all and that would also feed to the British the information that we wanted them to have."

Sarah's face had gone starkly white. "You knew about my father?"

"Well, let's say we suspected him. I don't think he would have been very effectual without Blunt, and now that he is out of the way, I think your father will mind his own business for a while and leave the spying to others better qualified for it. He's had a bad scare."

"Was there ever a letter from Admiral Barras?" Neil asked testily. "Was there really a shipment of money from Philadelphia? What was the point of it all—simply a trap to catch Ferris Blunt? It seems to me that might have been done without all this fuss."

"It would have, except that that was only part of it. And after all, we didn't expect to have Sarah here on the scene, or you wading in to her defense. Even your getting shot was due to her sister's rushing in to help. That was not part of it either."

"Go ahead and say it," Sarah said miserably. "We were interfering nuisances, and we nearly got Neil killed."

"It just goes to show that you cannot plan military maneuvers where love is involved—your love for your father and for Neil, even Ferris Blunt's feelings for you. None of that entered into our calculations."

He turned back to Neil. "But to answer your questions, yes, there was a letter from Admiral Barras informing us that a French convoy under Admiral de Grasse was setting sail for the Chesapeake. As for the money, His Excellency made an attempt last month to borrow thirty thousand dollars from Robert Morris in Philadelphia, but he was refused, as usual. He then turned to Comte de Rochambeau, who generously lent the Continental army ten thousand pounds. So, to answer your second question, no, there was no money in that courier's saddlebags."

"But why, then—"

"Because we wanted Ferris to believe there was money there, and a great deal of it, too. That was the lure to get him here. Our plan was to surprise him in this house, take him out, and hang him on the spot. That much, at least, we accomplished. And one other important thing as well."

"And what was that?"

Ian made a point of brushing away an imaginary speck of lint from the wide cuff of his sleeve. "It was imperative that we somehow convince General Clinton in New York that Washington and Rochambeau planned to attack the city. Then, while he was looking the other way, in one swift movement we would whisk the army off down south, where we wanted it to be. And that is exactly how it happened."

"And just how did you manage that?" Neil asked, still not willing to give up his irritation over being duped.

"Because I myself dropped the information to the proper source that very night. After you were brought up here, I stayed below long enough to convince William Popham that Admiral de Grasse's true destination was New York Harbor. By the time he got back to the city with the news, the American and French forces were already on their way across the Hudson, en route to Virginia. By now they must be nearing Philadelphia. The way our esteemed commander-in-chief was driving them, it would not surprise me if they faced Cornwallis in Yorktown by early next week.''

"So it *was* Virginia! Well, you might have let me know.''

"I told you as much as I could, Neil. Actually it was anyone's guess up until the very morning we began to ferry the army across the river. What was paramount, however, was that General Clinton be convinced that we never intended to go south.''

"William Popham," Sarah breathed. "Are you saying—''

"Exactly. Not 'William Popham' at all. His real name is David Lindsay, and he is a lieutenant colonel in Battalion Company, the Thirty-eighth Foot. He's been with the British army in New York the entire length of the war, and by now he knows Westchester and the city like the back of his elegant hand. Once he was convinced our real objective was New York, I began to breathe easier. He was gone on the morning tide, straight back to Clinton.''

Rising from her chair, Sarah turned her back on the two men and walked to the window. Below she could see the colorful gillyflowers and marigolds along the path gleaming brightly in the afternoon sun. The green stretch of lawn that sloped to the river looked as dreamily lazy as the day itself. Why, then, was there this sense of unease within her, so like the stirrings of a storm, so incongruous with the softness of the day?

"I don't know why, Major Harron," she said softly, "but I'm afraid that what you are telling me has something to do with my sister.''

Ian nodded and reached into the pocket of his tunic. "You're very perceptive, Miss Reed. Colonel Lindsay did not go back to New York alone. Your sister left with him—why, I don't know. However, she did leave you this. I didn't want to give it to you until I could explain the whole thing.''

He held out a folded letter toward Sarah. She stared at it, seeing the dark blob of sealed wax like a stain against the pale foolscap. Taking it in her hand, she looked briefly at the two men, then moved to the corner window where she could break the seal and open the paper without her face being visible to the others.

It was surely Darcy's careless scrawl, and there were tiny stains on the paper, the legacy of her tears.

> *Dearest Sarah,*
>
> *By the time you read this I shall be in New York town. I will never come back to Cole's Landing, and perhaps I may never see you again. Mr. Popham revealed to me that he is actually Colonel David Lindsay. He has convinced me that I should marry him and go to live in New York until the war is over. He is very rich, and who knows? Perhaps we will go to England and live on a fine estate. Heigh-ho! You are a good person and a dear sister, Sarah. I will not say that it breaks my heart to leave you, for I don't think I shall ever again love anyone enough to break my heart over them. William—or, rather, David—knows this and wants me anyway. I hope you have a happy life with Neil. You deserve it. I am not good, but I intend to get what I want in spite of that. Wish me good fortune.*
>
> Yr. sister,
Darcy
>
> *Please say goodbye to Papa for me and give my love to darling Neil. Ask him to forgive me.*

The stains were heavy around that last line, Sarah noticed. Poor Darcy! She had gone off in a fit of remorse, hating herself for hurting Neil. If only she had been able to see her first, talk to her, reassure her.

"Did you see Darcy before she left?" Sarah asked, turning to Ian.

"Briefly. I assure you she went quite willingly. Lindsay is not a bad sort for a lobster, and his offer seemed most genuine."

"I hope he doesn't intend to take advantage of a young girl," Neil said, reaching for Sarah's hand.

"Oh, somehow I got the impression that no one was going to take advantage of Mistress Darcy without her consent. She made it very clear that though she was greatly honored by his proposal, she was not in love with him, and he accepted that."

Folding the letter, Sarah slipped it in the bodice of her dress and walked back to the bed to take Neil's hand.

"She asks you to forgive her, Neil."

"For shooting me? I know she never intended to. It was Ferris she was trying to kill."

Ian swung his leg over the chair and stood up, straightening his waistcoat. The brass buttons and gold epaulets of his tunic caught the rays of the afternoon sun with gleaming brilliance.

"Well, now that all this is cleared up, I'd best be off. If I don't get down the road, I'm going to miss all the fun around Yorktown. And that would be too bad, because there is just a chance that this might be the most decisive battle of the entire war."

Neil, his anger mollified, gave his friend a half-envious smile.

"I wish you good fortune, Ian, in spite of the fact that you tricked me."

"Very magnanimous of you, sir. I would say take care of yourself, but I really don't need to," he said, winking at Sarah. "I can see that that will be done for you very capably indeed."

* * *

Sarah walked with Ian downstairs, seeing that his horse was brought and wishing him Godspeed. After he rode down the path and clattered across the bridge, she stood for a moment looking out over the calm river, trying not to focus on the black willow tree, trying not to imagine the body swinging from its dark limb. When she went back upstairs, Neil was lying propped against the pillows, his eyes closed. Quietly resuming her chair, she studied his calm face, then reached out to smooth back a long strand of hair that sloped over his forehead. His eyes shot open and he claimed her hand.

"I thought you were asleep," Sarah said, smiling at him.

"I very nearly was. Your touch brought me awake. Come, lie here next to me."

"Oh, Neil, do you think I should? I don't want to hurt your wound."

He scrunched gingerly over on the bed, making room for her. "You won't. And even if you did, it would be worth it to hold you."

Gently Sarah slid down beside him, lying back in the curve of his good arm, her head resting in the hollow of his neck. They lay without speaking, each savoring the delicious feel of the other.

"You seem so solemn, my love," Neil said finally. "Are you grieving over Darcy?"

For a moment Sarah did not answer. "Perhaps a little. In fact, quite a lot, but I realize that this might be the best thing for her. Cole's Landing is such a backwater, dull, provincial place. Darcy was always drawn to a livelier kind of life. She had ambition and energy; she wanted all the excitement that she would never find here. Perhaps she'll find it now."

"And what about you? Will you be satisfied to live

out your life in a dull, provincial place like Cole's Landing?''

Sarah raised her head and searched his face. "Me? Oh, yes. I love this house and the river and the mountains. I would be dreadfully unhappy if I had to live apart from them. It would be like losing part of myself. Most of all, I love you. If I can be with you, I'll be happy.''

He drew her back into his arms. "I think I can be happy here too. All the ambition I felt to rise in the ranks of the military seems to have faded with this bullet wound. I see myself now, raising a family, running a farm, sitting and puffing my pipe when I'm old, worrying about nothing so much as whether or not the weevils will get into the buckwheat. As long as you are there with me, it will be enough.''

"If only this war could be finished with," Sarah sighed. "Do you realize that if the British win in Virginia, that lovely picture will be only a fantasy. You might be punished or jailed, or even executed for treason. We could lose everything.''

"Oh, I don't think so. Even if the King has his way, we will never give up the struggle. The principle is too important. Independence will come sometime; it simply must. We are too far from England, and we have too rich and energetic a country to ever be satisfied with second-class citizenship. Besides, if Darcy's new husband really has all those highly placed connections that she thinks he does, she will take care of us.''

"What a thought!" Sarah laughed. "To be dependent on my little sister's benevolence!''

With his good arm, Neil pulled her close and hugged her fiercely. She lifted her chin, and he kissed her lips.

"Oh, Sarah. I do love you so.''

She frowned up at him.

"But Neil. They could win. It could happen.''

"Yes, my love, it could. And so we shall simply have to hope and pray that fortune will send us a great victory down there in Virginia."

And he kissed her again.

Historical romance with a twist of mystery...

MADELEINE BRENT